Space Marines

Edited by C.V. Walter

Raconteur Press

Contents

Marines

KELLY GRAYSON

On November 10, 1775 at Tun Tavern in Philadelphia, the first men signed up for a unit of naval infantry that would become the United States Marine Corps. Thirty minutes after that, a platoon of them were drinking rum liberated by a couple of corporals from the Naval officer's mess, bitching about their lieutenant, and plotting ways to get transferred out of this chickenshit outfit.

Thus has been the Marine Corps, and thus it shall always be.

Of all military units in the history of modern warfare, few are surrounded by the mythos of the United States Marine Corps. Enemies fear them, members of their fellow service branches respect them, are often jealous if annoyed by them, and call them many things; grunts, jarheads, leathernecks, Uncle Sam's Misguided Children and devil dogs, to name a few. Just don't call them *soldiers*. They're particular about that.

Through it all, Marines tolerate the good-natured jibes of inter-service rivalry because they know, with bedrock certainty, what their fellow service members know but are loathe to admit: *Marines are special*. If you ever doubt that, I offer to you as proof the third and least-known stanza of the Marine Corps Hymn, the last verse of which reads:

If the Army and the Navy
Ever look on Heaven's scenes;
They will find the streets are guarded
By United States Marines.

Only the United States Marine Corps would openly diss its country's other two service branches in its official hymn.

They have have fought with honor and distinction wherever we asked them. From the forest loam of Belleau Wood to the jungles of Nicaragua, from the mangrove swamps of Guadalcanal and volcanic ash of Tarawa and Iwo Jima to the triple canopy jungle of Vietnam, from the bitter cold of Korea to the hot and dusty streets of Fallujah, Marines have writ their legend and lore in their own blood across the globe. Their history is peppered with iconic places like Frozen Chosin, Mount Suribachi and Hué City, their icons men with hard names like "Chesty" Puller, "Manila John" Basilone and "Mad Dog" Mattox.

They are a warrior brotherhood of modern-day Spartans, their Agoge the sand of Parris Island or MCRD San Diego, the crucibles in which a few worthy men and women are forged into Marines. In the 2006 film *300,* King Leonidas asks several of the Arcadians they meet on the road to Thermoplyae, "What is your profession?" He is answered with replies varying from potter to blacksmith, but when he asks the same question of his 300 Spartans, he is answered with a thunderous reply of *"Xarous!"* which means "death."

Modern translation: *every Marine is a rifleman.*

Marines have a credo, *Semper Fidelis*. It means "always faithful," and Marines have honored that credo throughout our nation's history. They have remained faithful to their mission, to their country, and to each other. It is easy to admire such men, which I suppose is why we so love stories about Marines; they embody the faith, nobility and honor to which we all aspire.

America has another subject which captures our hearts and imaginations almost as much as the Marines: outer space. From the early days of NASA's Apollo and Mercury programs to the space shuttle program to our current fascination with SpaceX, Americans have always romanticized space travel. We are a people who, good or bad, have ever had their eyes on the horizon, and when we conquered our own horizons, we turned to the horizon of space. We have elevated intrepid astronauts like Armstrong, Aldrin, Glenn, Shepard and others to the status of American heroes, and as a nation we mourned the loss of the crews of *Apollo 1*, *Challenger* and *Columbia*. If you ever doubt America's pride and fascination with space travel, consider the old joke about the two types of countries on planet Earth: "There are two types of countries: those that use the metric system... *and the country that put a man on the moon.*"

That's us, America in all its arrogance, swagger and idealism, deserved or undeserved. It's who we are.

In this collection of stories, you're going to read about Marines in space. Whether it's a futuristic Chesty Puller and his men protecting colonists on a windswept terraformed planet light years away from Earth or it's Sergeant Hicks blasting wave after wave of xenomorphs in a bug hunt on LV-223, we love stories about space and we love stories about Marines.

In these pages, you're gonna get 'em both in one place.

Enjoy.

The Dance

J.L. CURTIS

TERRAN MARINE FIRST LIEUTENANT Ethan Fargo, twenty-nine, medium height and lithe, with brown hair, brown eyes, and a pained expression, stumped into Lieutenant Colonel Cronin's office in his undress greens, leaning heavily on his walker. He managed to straighten up and saluted. "Lieutenant Fargo reporting as ordered, sir."

Cronin, in his early sixties, looked forty. Black hair, with a sprinkling of gray, cut in a crewcut, wiry, but with the shoulders and arms of a weightlifter, he was the epitome of a Terran Marine commanding officer. Cronin looked up from his desk. He knew Fargo had been genied for athletics and hand/eye coordination as a child, and it showed, even with Fargo's current condition. "Welcome back, Lieutenant. You look like you're in pain, so take a seat." He pointed to the chair next to his desk and shut off his holoscreen as Ethan eased himself into the chair, painfully extending his left leg. Cronin looked at him critically, then said, "Well, looks like the regen took okay. Thirty days, correct?" He flipped two boxes across the desk. "Here's your 'I done good' medals."

"Yes, sir. Thirty days on the nose. Thankfully, they kept me under most of the time. Otherwise, I'd have gone stir-crazy in the tank." He reached out and pulled the two boxes to him, but didn't open them.

Cronin cracked a smile. "Well, it's better now than it used to be. Forty-five to sixty days used to be the norm. And with you being an empath, that had to suck to feel people's emotions." Fargo dipped his head in acknowledgement and Cronin said, "The medical paperwork got here three divs ago. Now I've got to figure out what to do with you. But first, I want to go over the Vega III operation from your perspective and your actions."

Fargo gulped. "Yes, sir."

The colonel pulled up a double-sided holoscreen and said, "Okay, intel was bad. That was on me and the command structure. Your platoon walked into an ambush. Why?"

Fargo flashed back to the patrol as he described the initial ambush. *Routine patrol, well out on the left flank of the battle lines. Nothing to see here, move along. Except they were halfway down the ridgeline, paralleling the military crest when the patrol column got hit. Gunny Garang was the first. "LT, taking fire from the left. Armor on the crest! Squad left, cover and fire!"*

My command net popped up with Gunny's targeting carats, just as more firing broke out up and down the column. There wasn't shit for cover, and they were targeting the leadership.

"Sir, I don't know why the intel was bad. I'm not in the S-Two loop. I think we were put out on the left flank by Captain Franks to get some patrol experience since I was the newbie platoon commander." Ethan looked up and said, "It was like they *knew* where the seniors were. I think the only reason I wasn't targeted initially was I was out of position, trying to catch up with the Gunny to ask him what he thought about moving up to check the other side of the ridge."

Cronin had been advancing the command shell replay from Fargo's HUD as he talked, and replied, "Yes, I believe you were right." He forwarded the replay to Fargo's targeting of the firing locations. "How did you do the targeting here?"

Command net. I can go platoon-wide. If I can...that one, that one, that one, they're all equally spaced. Extend the line, two Marines per target based on proximity— Send!

"Sir, I figured out they were equally spaced down the line of attack, and I just sent a platoon-wide targeting list."

"And then you went Leroy Jenkins, didn't you?"

"Sir?"

"Never mind. At that point, you jumped to get behind the Goons, correct?"

"Yes, sir. I had most of the squad leaders down, and somebody had to break the ambush."

"What the hell were you thinking? And what was that corkscrew jump?"

Ethan sniffed. "Um...sir, I thought maybe they wouldn't pay that much attention if they thought it was a random out-of-control suit."

Cronin stopped the replay and leaned back in his chair. "How did you come up with that?"

Ethan sighed. "Screwed up once at the MTC. Crossed my legs trying to scratch an itch during a jump."

"At the Moon Training Center? Who was the trainer and what did he say?"

"Gunner Lobsang. He...ripped me a new one when I told him what I did."

"You *admitted* it to him?"

Ethan shrugged. "I did wrong. Of course I admitted it, sir. Why wouldn't I?"

It was all Cronin could do not to smile at that, but he replied, "Most unusual for an officer to admit a mistake that stupid." He shook his head and then did smile at Ethan. "Okay, you simulated out-of-control, got behind the Goons along with Staff Sergeant Long and Private Murphy—"

Ethan interrupted the colonel. "Sir, I didn't order them to accompany me. They...did that on their own."

Cronin nodded. "I have their HUDS and statements. Continue."

Ethan blew out a breath. "I found what I thought was their command section, took that under fire with the laser, and then..." *Those three, right there. Target, penetrator, fire. Laser. Fire, fire, fire, dammit! Long, Murphy! Command carat all weapons projectile and laser. Move, move! Shoot and move!* "Well, Murphy took a penetrator in the right hip joint area and went yellow on my tracker. Long was sweeping up the ones I'd sent him, and I had a solid red on the laser and was almost out of projectile ammo."

Cronin forwarded the HUD vid of Ethan's micro-jump to Murphy. "And here you go after Murphy. He's flashing between yellow and red on your platoon tracker."

I gotta get Murphy out of here now! "Yes, sir. I grabbed his come-along and started toward the crest, sending a no-fire on my expected position at the ridge top."

"But you didn't make sure Murphy had gotten all his targets, did you?"

Ethan hung his head. "No, sir. I fucked that up."

"So you're dragging Murphy up the slope, a Goon gets up and takes you under fire. You try to turn to return projectile fire because your laser is red/hard down, but your arm won't articulate that far, so you put yourself in front of Murphy, square up, and go Winchester in less than a half-second. But the Goon lit you up first, hit you with a penetrator, and you're going down. You managed to pass command to Sergeant Long before your pharmacope put you out. Correct?"

Ethan looked up and met the colonel's eyes. "Sir, I don't honestly remember doing that. The last thing I remember is smelling long pork and the pain in my leg until I woke up in regen."

Cronin killed the holoscreen and leaned back. "Well, since you don't remember, do you know how many Marines you had down?"

Ethan bit his lip. "I remember four KIA. Abbott, Hurst, McKeon, and Bush. And eleven WIA, they were—"

Cronin waved him down. "We've got those numbers. Four KIA, fourteen WIA total. You lost damned near half of your platoon in less than ten minutes."

Ethan looked down and said glumly, "Yes, sir."

Cronin continued, "But your platoon accounted for either thirty-eight or forty-one Goon KIAs, depending on how they counted the bits and pieces. And you got a light colonel, two majors, and a scattering of JOs and senior troops. From the reconstructed material, you took out their S-two section. Long has been meritoriously promoted to Gunny, and he got a DSM for pulling your ass out of the fire, taking command, and extracting the platoon."

Ethan nodded. "He deserves that, sir."

Cronin shook his head as he looked at Ethan. "Now I gotta figure out what to do with you. I could send you to the sick, lame, and lazy, but since you *obviously* don't understand the working parameters of your armor, I think I'm going to send you to Gunner Cain, the armorer. Maybe spending your rehab with him will give you time to *learn* the limits of the armor and reflect on the correct utilization of lasers, especially since you managed to burn out the entire system, including the capacitors, which is supposedly *not* possible. Do you understand the duty cycle?"

Ethan straightened up. "Yes, sir! Our twenty-kilowatt laser is a Q-switched laser with ten-nanosecond pulse duration and one-kilohertz repetition rate, so they duty cycle of ten nanoseconds over one millisecond."

"That is correct. Now you want to tell me how you screwed around and burned the system out?"

Ethan thought for a second and said cautiously, "Um, sir, there is an override available through the command lace program and suit AI that allows a full second of fire, or continuous firing."

Cronin shook his head. "A first lieutenant has managed to do something that has *never* been done. Gunner will want to observe that." The lieutenant colonel stood. "Aren't you even curious about what's in the medal cases?"

Ethan got to his feet and picked up the cases, slipping them into his blouse pocket. "Sir, I figured if you wanted me to know, you'd tell me."

Cronin snorted. "You got a Silver Star and a Lifesaving Medal for Murphy. Now get out of here. I have work to do."

⁂

The armory was a cavernous building, and it took Fargo a while to hobble around to the main door on the far side of it. By the time he got there, he was sweating and his pharmacope had dumped a cocktail into his system to cut the pain down to a manageable level. *I've got to figure out how to walk again. I thought...well, I guess I didn't think about regen, meaning that I had to relearn how to do the simplest thing, like frigging walking!* He pulled the door open and managed to hobble through as the door pushed him into the outer office.

A young private sat at the desk, engrossed in whatever he was doing on his holoscreen. He finally looked up and jumped to his feet. "Sorry, sir! I didn't hear you come in. What can I do for you?"

Ethan leaned on his walker as he said, "I'm supposed to meet Gunner Cain." He nodded toward the closed door behind the private. "Is he in?"

"Ah, he's in, sir. He's back in the shop." The private pointed to a green door with a large, authorized personnel only sign on it. "Go through that door. You might have to look for him, since I don't know what he has on his schedule today."

"You can't escort me?"

"No, sir! The gunner said I'm to man the desk and not bother him unless the building is burning down around us."

Ethan bit his lip to keep from smiling as he nodded. "Roger all. If you would get the door for me, I'll go find the gunner." The private ran over and opened the door as Ethan hobbled through it. "Thank you, Private."

There was a large work area on one side, with a standard weapons cage running from the door to the far wall, the usual checkout counter behind the locked gate. As he hobbled forward, the smell of hydraulics, ozone, and the miasma of the armored suits grew stronger. Almost two hundred suits, enough for the entire battalion, crouched in their resting positions like Marines kneeling on one knee, row after row.

As he hobbled out into the main area, he heard a high-pitched screeching whine, punctuated by a gravelly voice cursing at high volume, off to his left. *That's got to be the gunner.* Hobbling down the aisle between the armor, he came to another larger work area, with cranes, chain falls, and a large open space. Five sets of mangled armor sat there, along with one pristine set that dangled a pair of legs out of the starboard ammunition bin. The legs moved as if the body was repositioning, the screeching whine started and sparks flew out of the hatch, bouncing off the legs and hitting the floor. "Come outta there, you useless sumbitch! I swear to Deity, I will rip your guts out and shit in your powerplant if you don't—"

A clang, followed by what had been a brace, came flying out of the bin, followed by grunting noises as the body worked itself back out of the bin, a grinder in hand. Ethan saw a white crew cut head topping a lean, muscular man about his size drop easily to the ground. As he turned, Ethan saw the scar that started at the hairline and ran to the right side of the mouth, puckering the right side of the gunner's face into a caricature of a smile. *Shit, I don't think he can regen. This...isn't going to go well.* "Well, well, well, a brand new shiny first looie. What can I do for you...sir?"

Ethan sighed. "Gunner Cain, Colonel Cronin sent me over to you for some *education* on the proper operation of the armor system. My name is Ethan Fargo, and I just got out of the tank after a regen."

The gunner walked around Ethan slowly, sizing him up and making him feel like he was back at The Basic School. "Left leg, mid-thigh down, correct?" Ethan nodded as Cain continued, "Can't walk, can't stand up straight. Walker is set wrong. L.T., you're about as fucked up as a wooden watch." He pointed to a stool next to a workbench. "Sit." Ethan sat with a sigh. "Extend your leg." He managed to extend the leg, but it trembled, and he had to put it back on the floor rather quickly. "Do you dance, Mr. Fargo?" Cain asked as he reset the walker.

Ethan blinked at the non sequitur and shook his head. "Um, no, not really."

Cain shook his head, then picked up the brace he'd removed. "Recognize this, Mr. Fargo?"

Ethan cocked his head and looked at it. "Uh, no I don't, Gunner. But I saw you throw it out of the ammo bin, so I'm assuming it came from there."

"Brilliant...deduction. Why was I cutting it out, then?"

"I don't have any idea."

Cain started pacing back and forth in front of him. "Because it's fucking useless! Without this piece of shit, I can get another hundred rounds of caseless ammo in the bin!"

Ethan goggled. "An extra hundred rounds! How?"

Cain motioned him to follow and rolled the autoloader around to the armor. "Watch!" The autoloader rumbled into life and spat rounds into the bin in the normal sequence. It stopped, and Cain asked, "How many rounds, Mr. Fargo?"

He looked at the counter and said, "Eight hundred fifty, Gunner—"

"Call me Cain. Now watch." Cain quickly reset the autoloader and punched the start button. It rumbled for a short time and beeped. "How many on the counter now, Mr. Fargo?"

"One hundred and one...Cain. But if the brace—"

"Deity damned engineers designed the bin to meet spec. Never talked to an armorer that knew shit. That brace is *not* critical to suit integrity or anything else. It's external to the actual armor plate and is nothing more than a manpurse hanging off the outside of the actual fucking armor that costs my Marines an extra hundred rounds they need in battle!" Cain turned and stomped off, threw the offending brace in a dumpster, and left Ethan staring at the armor.

I wonder if that's legal? Can he just cut up armor anytime he wants to? But he is a master gunner, so...not a question I'm gonna ask. He heard clanging further back in the armory and decided to go see what Cain was doing. He went around a corner and found him beating on a melted suit of armor with a large sledgehammer, and realized this was the armor morgue. Six suits laid face-up, and he trembled as he realized one of them was his unit, 112. He hobbled over and looked down at the damage, silently amazed that he'd survived at all. The left leg was almost totally destroyed, slagged through the ablative armor into the core armor. He could actually see the inner gel lining as he stood above it. It was obvious that the left arm had taken extensive damage, with the claw almost completely torn free and mangled.

Cain walked over. "Lucky you're alive, Mr. Fargo. I'm fixing to pop the other units, so you might want to leave. They don't smell so good, and you're looking pretty rocky. Be back here after therapy tomorrow and you can show me how you blew the shit out of the laser!" He didn't wait for an answer, walking over to the chain fall and hooking it onto one of the suits, then powering the unit over only its back.

Ethan blew out a breath and hobbled for the door in a hurry when Cain popped the back hatch and the odor of burnt body rolled out.

❧❧❧❧ ❧❧❧❧

Three days later, Ethan hobbled in after therapy, thankful his pharmacope was tamping the pain. He found Cain at the workbench, scanning something on a holoscreen. Cain turned and pointed to a room at the front of the armory. "In there. I'll be there in a minute." Ethan hobbled over, opened the door, and stopped cold. *A full sim? I didn't think any existed on the out worlds!* He eased over and sat next to the instructor station, looking at the racks of helmets off to one side. *Are they doing VR out here? Oh, there's the motion floor over there with the sensors on the walls and the straps. Damn...*

Cain walked in, picked up two helmets and dropped one in Ethan's lap, then sat at the instructor's console and said, "Gonna do this a bit different. You can stay there. Helmet is a full immersion with all the links, so your command lace will work. Gimme a minute to get geared up."

Cain picked up a gauzy-looking *something* and put it over his crew cut, then picked up the helmet and started seating it over the gauze. He turned and looked impatiently at Ethan, who quickly donned his helmet and gave Cain a thumbs-up.

There was a pop, and his headset came to life as Cain said, "Starting sequence now. I want you to hold off on integrating fully until I tell you."

"Roger." The HUD projector stayed greyed out, and Ethan dropped his shields a little. He sensed Cain and the turmoil and pain the man dealt with all the time. *How the hell does he put up with that?*

"Okay, L.T. Integrate."

Ethan felt for the connection with his mind and the frisson as his command lace meshed with the AI in the trainer. He jerked when he realized it was Amy, *his* AI. "How? I mean, that's my suit AI!"

Cain chuckled. "Easy. I just moved your AI over. Ain't no big thing, since one twelve is a strike. Just have to figure out which suit to give you next. I'm coming in." Ethan felt another frisson, and Cain was in his head, or so it seemed. "I'm now piggybacking on your command lace, so I'll see everything you do, and all your commands and interactions in real time. What I want you to show me is how you overrode the laser first."

"Um, you want me to talk through it?"

Exasperated, Cain replied, "No, just do it like you did on Vega. I'll watch everything."

"Okay. Here it goes." *<Amy, command control override. Menu. Laser. Carat bottom right. Execute. Menu. Control function. Override. Override lockouts. Accept warn. Override activate. Time sixty. Execute.>*

He heard Cain's sibilant hiss. "Damn! That ain't possible." He sensed Cain turning toward him in wonder. "Where did you get that second menu? That ain't in the system!"

"Yes, it is," Ethan snapped. "Go hard bottom right with the carat on any menu and there is a second buried menu that can be activated by doing an execute."

"You got to be shittin' me!" Suddenly, his HUD flipped from screen to screen as Cain took control, bouncing from menu to menu unbelievably fast, cursing the whole time. "Fucking engineers! They put their own fucking backdoors into the systems. I'm gonna ki...shit!"

Ethan reared back from the anger radiating from Cain, wondering what to do. *Is he losing control? What the hell do I do? And why is he always here by himself? I know he should have a dozen or so enlisted working here, not just a single private. I know this is our op base in this sector, but still...* He felt Cain locking down his emotions, and blew out a breath as Cain took off his helmet. Ethan dared to ask, "How did you, um, merge with me in the sim? I've never seen that."

Cain's gravelly chuckle amazed him. "Doc Hampson fixed me up with this." he dangled the gauzy net as he slipped it off. "I ain't supposed to have a command lace, but he built this, and I can put it on and have all the functions of a command lace. It also allows me to interface with the sims to review all kinds of things, like seeing the same thing you were doing real time."

Ethan nodded. "If felt like you were in my head with me! Kinda scary. Weird, too."

Cain got up. "Let's take a break. I noticed you're getting around a bit better." His face drew up in an approximation of a smile. "A month or so, and you can start ballroom dancing."

"You mentioned that before. Why ballroom dancing?"

"Balance. It's the quickest way to get your balance and control back." To Ethan's amazement, Cain suddenly struck the pose of a dancer with a lady in his arms and moved smoothly around the small space, spinning, dipping, and humming all the way. He dropped his arms and said, "Like that. I would recommend ballet, but that's too froufrou for a Marine to do."

Ethan's mouth hung open. He clamped his jaw shut and shook his head at the mental image of Cain in a tutu. *Not. Going. To. Laugh.* "Cain, can I ask where all your Marines are?" He waved his arm at the armory. "You should have some Marines helping you."

Cain's gravelly chuckle again startled Ethan. "Oh, I got Marines, but I got them doing things. Gunny Jin is TAD to MCCD at Quantico sitting on the armor board, Staff Lane is at MTC doing testing on new armor and systems, Staff Pickins is TAD to MIT at Lincoln Labs with the fuzzy-haired scientist working on new weapons, and getting his PhD. Staff Crane is the combat armorer for the Scout Snipers here. Rest of the Marines are out in the batt, checking armor, weapons, and conducting small unit training."

Ethan goggled. "You've got people TAD back to *Earth*! How? I mean, the amount of funds..." He shook his head. "But what are they doing? They're enlisted."

Cain bristled. "Yes, Jin, Lane, and Pickins...well, they can't regen. And all are coming up on their forty, and they're all combat vets, multiple campaigns. Who better to send back to give those idjits some real-world combat experience from the pointy end and rein in shit like that gahdamn brace? Eh, Mr. Occifer? You?" Cain shook his head. "Sorry, didn't mean it that way, Mr. Fargo. It's just we've lost way too many Marines to the fuckin' good idea fairies back home over the years that never saw combat," he said contritely.

Ethan asked timidly, "How long have you been in, Cain?"

Cain looked up at the overhead. "Well, I'm a hunnert and eight this year, so...eighty-four years."

Ethan mumbled, "Eighty-four years. My God."

Cain's laughter broke Ethan out of his thoughts. "Yep, eighty-four years. I was the colonel's gunny when he was a second looie." He tapped his legs and Ethan heard the 'thunk' of something other than flesh. "As you can see, I don't regen, either. Got these in the old Mark One suits. Laser took off the bottom third of the suit. Luckily, the laser also cauterized my legs. Otherwise, I'd have bled out right there. The colonel carried me a mile back to the aid station on his back. Took me three years to make it back on active duty." Cain looked off into the distance and continued softly, "That's when I learned about ballroom dancing as part of rehab. Met my first wife there." He blew out a breath. "Weren't for her and dancing, I'd have never made it back."

Ethan got up as Cain went silent and slipped out of the sim, leaving him with his memories, seemingly at peace with himself.

❦

Two weeks later, Ethan walked into the armory with just one cane. "Well, L.T., time to get you out on the ballroom floor!"

Ethan shook his head and laughed. "Cain, I can barely walk, much less dance. Shit, take away the cane and I'll probably fall over after the first step."

"Then you get up and try it again." Cain snorted. "But that's for later. Now I want you to get back in a suit." Ethan started to protest, and Cain overrode him. "No, you need to get in a suit. You ain't gonna have to go anywhere, but I need to do a good fitment for you, and I also want to show you how to maneuver a disabled suit."

As they walked back toward the back row, Cain snapped, "What is the load limit on the arm system, individually and together?"

"Fifteen hundred pounds per arm. Three thousand total."

"What is the weight of a full up combat suit?"

"Twenty-one hundred pounds, assuming complete we—"

"What is the safety margin built into the suits?"

"Uh, not sure, Cain. I've heard twenty-five, up to fifty percent."

"If that's true, why did you destroy the claw on the left arm?"

"I...don't know, Cain," Ethan said plaintively.

"Torque! Gahdamn torque. The claw is only designed for fifteen hundred pounds if locked in position within five degrees of parallel with the arm." He mimed cocking his hand down about twenty-five degrees, as if picking up something. "Guarantee this is what you did. Hell, you had to, to grab the come-along! That ain't parallel." He pointed to suit 252. "Welcome to your new suit. Your AI is already installed. Now climb your butt in."

Ethan again started to protest, but Cain was already hooking some kind of wiring harness to the access port on the back shoulder and slipping his gauzy head cover and helmet on. He cocked his head as he tried to figure out how to make the steps he needed to get up and in. He finally managed to get in the suit by stepping, swapping feet, stepping and finally sliding into the suit harness. He was panting when he got in, and Cain said, "Don't bother closing up. All I want you to do is power up and stand up. I'll be in the lace with you, just like in the sim."

Ethan started to say something about that being unsafe for Cain to be so close, and to be standing without the hatch sealed. Instead, he hit the master power button and simply said, "Amy, power up and BIT check, please."

Eight minutes later, Amy replied, "Built-In Test complete. Holding at aft hatch open."

Cain took over. "Amy, override aft hatch, execute."

"Aft hatch override complete."

"Stand up." The suit stood, and Ethan fought to keep his balance and not flail around as the harness tightened around him. "Lock," Cain said, and the suit stabilized.

Ethan breathed out in relief and asked, "Where is that command?"

Cain grumbled, "They didn't teach you that? That's a basic command for *any* armor, going back to the Mark One! That's getting the armor stable and upright. Now I'm wondering how much of the command override capability they taught you!" Cain climbed up behind him, leaning into the hatch. "Do you know how to command another suit remotely?"

Ethan said, "For targeting and massed fire, but that was really all they taught us. I take it I'm missing something?" He sensed Cain shaking his head behind him and his temper rising.

"Missed something? How about missing the most important commands! For fuck's sake. Watch this." There was a momentary silence, then Cain said, "Watch your HUD." A series of commands flashed across the HUD: *<Amy, command control override. Menu. Armor. Carat unit 225. Execute. Menu. Control function. Override. Execute.>* "Two twenty-five, stand up."

Ethan gasped as the unit across the aisle stood up. "How? I mean, I saw what you did, but—"

Another set of commands flashed. *<Amy, carat unit 225. Execute. Command override. Execute. Anti-Grav on. Execute. Plank. Execute. Three-foot clearance over floor. Execute.>* Two twenty-five slowly rotated horizontally to the deck and dropped to three feet above it. "That is what you should have done, L.T.," Cain said. "If you had, you wouldn't have screwed up your armor, and possibly wouldn't have gotten your ass half-blown away."

Ethan bit his lip in frustration. "I didn't know. Nobody ever showed us that."

Cain snarled, "It's in the bold face procedures. You should have had that—"

Ethan snapped back at him. "No, it's *not*! I have the emergency procedures memorized, and I'll guarantee you it is *not* in there." Cain watched the bold face start scrolling up the HUD and was startled to not see anything under the command override section of the bold face.

"What the hell?" he growled. "Power two two five down and shut down. Meet me in the sim."

Ethan felt him climb off the armor and heard a pop as Cain disconnected from the external port. And he wasn't in Ethan's head anymore. *How the hell do I get two twenty-five back in position and shut down? Frack!* "Uh. Two twenty-five stand up." Nothing happened. "Shit!" *<Amy, carat unit 225. Execute. Command override. Execute. Stand up.> Hah! That worked!* But 225 stood three feet in the air. *<Amy, carat unit 225. Execute. Command override. Execute. Anti-Grav off. Execute. Lock. Execute.>* The armor crashed back to the floor and Ethan winced at the noise it made when it hit. *Well, I guess Cain will know I fucked that up, but it's back on the ground and didn't hit anything else.* He looked for Cain, but didn't see him charging up, so he tried what he thought should be the shutdown commands. *<Amy, carat unit 225. Execute. Command override. Execute. Kneel. Execute. Open hatch. Execute. Shutdown. Execute.>* Unit 225 knelt, and it disappeared from his HUD. "Yes," he mumbled. He groaned as he started climbing out of the suit, almost fell twice, but managed to get back on the ground. He picked up his cane and walked slowly back to the simulator office. He expected to sense Cain in a bad mood, but he was actually cheerful.

Cain glanced up when he walked in. "Okay, L.T., I'll deal with the problem with the bold face procedures. That's well above your paygrade, anyway. Now what I want to do is get you started on the dance steps. First thing is, we'll start with a waltz. That will get your leg moving." Ethan opened his mouth to object, but Cain got up and stood beside him. "This is real simple. Six measly little steps. A set of three done in a forward direction and the same set in a rear direction. Now watch." He demonstrated the step, step, and slide going forward, then in reverse. "Now you try it."

Ethan got up, feeling slightly foolish, and more than a bit scared he was going to fall. Cain stepped up on his left. "Ready? Step." Ethan stepped out with his left foot and wobbled, but managed not to fall. "Step." He stepped up and over with his right foot. "Step." He managed to slide his left foot over to his right foot. "Good, now in reverse. Step."

Ethan stepped and flailed wildly as he tried to balance on his left leg. Cain grabbed him and held him up. "Step!" Fifteen minutes later, Ethan sagged into a chair, dripping sweat as his pharmacope pushed another round of pain meds and Cain looked down at him. "Get outta here. We'll do this again tomorrow. Go hit the whirlpool before you cramp up."

***

Two weeks later, Ethan walked into the armory without his cane and no pharmacope dump. The private was nowhere to be found as he stepped into the main work area. "Cain?"

"Back here, L.T."

He walked around the cage and found Cain in the work area with two kneeling units. One was 252, the other was 311. He was surprised to see Cain in an undersuit. "Go get in your suit. We're gonna work in the suits today." Ethan had learned not to ask stupid questions and quickly went to the fresher and got in his undersuit. By the time he got back, Cain was standing in 311. "Man up, L.T."

He climbed into 252, hit the master power button and simply said, "Amy, power up and BIT check, please."

Eight minutes later, Amy replied, "Built-In Test complete."

"Stand up." Unit 252 obediently stood, and Ethan looked out his HUD. "What are we doing, Cain?"

He heard a chuckle. "We gonna dance, L.T." Unit 311 turned, and Cain added, "Follow me." He moved lightly back to the cleared area at the back of the armory, stopped, and turned to face Ethan. "I'm going to show you how to do this, then I want to see you do it. Pay attention!"

Ethan was stunned to see Cain's unit waltzing softly, if two tons of armor could be said to be moving softly. "How?"

Cain laughed. "The same way you do it on the deck. Move your feet, sway your body, move your arms. Ain't rocket surgery there, L.T. Now you do it!" Ethan tried to do it, but being suspended in the harness confused him, and 252 was anything but graceful. "Gently, gahdammit, gently, L.T.! Small movements, remember you're dealing with latency in the response times!"

What seemed like an eternity later, he finally managed a relatively smooth set of moves, even as he sweated like a pig in the armor. "How's that?" he panted.

"Better." Cain moved 311 toward him. "Stop." Ethan obeyed, and Cain moved 311 right up against 252. "Now we're gonna try this as partners. You lead, I'll follow."

Ethan blurted, "Is this even safe? I mean we're not supposed to move suits closer than ten feet..."

"As long as you don't screw it up, we'll be fine, L.T. Now I'm gonna let you lead and I'll follow." As soon as he said that, Strauss's "Emperor's Waltz" came through his command lace. "And one, two, begin, L.T.!"

Startled, Ethan made the first step and banged loudly into 311. "Gently, L.T., gently," Cain said quietly.

"Tryin', Cain." Ethan took a deep breath and let the music flow over him as he got into the timing of the waltz, and realized the two suits were within inches of each other as they moved as one. Reaching out, Ethan sensed that Cain was as calm and at peace as he had ever been. *Damn, I guess music really does soothe the savage beast. It must take him back to a better time...*

A slow popping noise came over the external mics, and that pulled Ethan out of the music as he heard, "Cain, you finally found some fool to actually dance with you, didn't you!" Ethan scanned around with his cameras and saw Colonel Cronin slowly clapping his hands and grinning as he shook his head.

Cain laughed as he stepped quickly away from Ethan and said, "Told ya I would, John. Shut it down and take a break, L.T."

Ethan walked 252 back to its slot, shut it down, and climbed out, then headed for the door. Colonel Cronin said, "Not so fast, Fargo. Cain, let's go to your office." Scratching his eyebrow, he looked at Ethan again. "Never mind, Fargo. Go get cleaned up. Come see me at eighteen."

Ethan nodded. "Eighteen, aye, Colonel." He exited as quickly as he could, wondering how much trouble he was in.

Cain slipped behind his desk, reached down, and pulled a bottle of Old Bush and two glasses out of the bottom drawer. Pouring a shot in each glass, he pushed one across to the colonel. "Absent Comrades."

They touched glasses and Cronin muttered, "Absent Comrades." Throwing back the shot, he shuddered. "Don't see how you can stand that shit, Cain!" Blowing out a breath, he looked Cain in the eye. "What do you think of Fargo?"

Cain poured himself another shot and smacked his lips as he sipped it. "Well, he's sharp. He found shit I didn't know the damned engineers had hidden in the systems." He looked down at his glass as he rolled it in his hand. "He'll do, John, but he's a damned boy scout."

"Boy scout?"

"He's too gahdamn honest, but he stands up for what he believes. He came back at me a coupla times, don't think he even realized he was doin' it. And he uses his empath senses all the time. I could tell that just by the way he reacted to me."

"And you taught him to dance!" Cronin said with a smile.

Cain laughed. "Well, yeah. Them damned pukes over at PT don't know shit about getting people through the recovery process. He took it well, and I'd say he's probably back maybe ninety percent."

"Good enough to go back in the field?"

"Yeah, why?"

"I'm thinking about putting him in as a fill for the Scout Snipers. Moynahan picked up major early, and I won't have a backfill for him for a couple of months, if not longer."

Cain bit his lip. "That'd be throwing him off the deep end. Going from a platoon to a company of assholes like them! I've got Staff Crane over there as the armorer, he could...keep an eye on him."

Cronin laughed. "You never did like scout snipers, Cain."

"Well, them little shits are always modifying weapons. Shit ain't changed in eighty years. They think they're better than..."

"And you're not sitting here doing *exactly* the same thing, and using your troops to impact design and implementation for systems going forward?"

Cain leaned back and laughed. "Yeah, I am, John. But I *know* what I'm doing."

※※※※※ ※※※※※

Ethan strode into the scout sniper's billet at zero seven and saw the offices in the back corner. He made his way back to the sergeant manning the duty desk. He used his command lace to place the face and said, "Sergeant...Holmes, I've been sent over as the temporary commanding officer. Is Gunny Kerry in yet?"

Holmes popped to attention. "Sir, no, sir. He should be here in ten segs. Would you like coffee, sir?"

Ethan smiled. "I'd love some, Sergeant. Where is it?"

"Breakroom, sir. Last door. I'll be happy..."

Shaking his head, Ethan said, "No, I'll get it. I'm coming off rehab, but I can at least get my own coffee. When Gunny comes in, let him know I'd like a few segs of his time."

"Yes, sir!"

Ethan went in the break room, found the stash of styro cups, picked up the pot and gingerly sniffed it, surprised to find the coffee was fresh. He poured a cup and made his way to the CO's office, finding it very sparsely furnished, with a bookcase of rules and regs, a desk, a small conference table butted against the front of the desk, and four chairs around it. Stepping behind the desk, he sat gingerly and keyed on the holo screen.

He quickly typed in his access code and brought up the TO&E for the scout sniper company. *One officer and forty-six Marines. Breakdown is four scout sniper sections of nine Marines each.* He bounced that against the current manning level and saw that they were three people short. *Well, that's the first issue... Now, where are they? Section one and two are OPREADY, Section three is training, and section four...is short.* He sipped his coffee as he looked through the configuration of each section and weapons selections, and the relative ranks and strengths of each section.

A sharp rap on the doorframe caused him to look up. "Gunny Kerry? Please come in." Kerry started to come to attention and Ethan said, "Don't. I don't believe in standing on ceremony. Grab a cup of coffee if you want one. I need to pick your brain."

Gunny Kerry was built much like Ethan, wiry and compact, but his voice was a surprise, *much* deeper than expected, as he said, "Yes, sir. You need a refill?"

"Please. Black."

A div later, Ethan finally leaned back in his chair and sighed. "We're going to be at least two short on section four, even if Fox comes back from rehab, until we get two more qualified bodies."

"Yes, sir," Kerry grumbled. "We can plug and play and move folks around so section four doesn't get screwed with the duty all the time, and if it comes down to it, we've got *bodies* we can shove in to fill out that section. Holmes normally functions as our admin, but he's qualified, and Crane, our armorer, can shoot anything in the inventory. He's not sniper qualified, but I've seen him shoot, and I'd have no problems throwing him out there."

"What about Sergeant Mazdy?"

"Technically, he's our intel section head, and he's trained one person in each section as intel. He *could* go to section four, since Staff Sergeant Vincenti, who just ETS'ed, was the intel for section four." Kerry bit his lip, then asked, "You want to show four full sections on the morning report, sir?"

Ethan shook his head. "Hell, no! If we do that, we'll never get the bodies we need! Show us seventy-five percent capable, awaiting personnel."

Kerry smiled. "Yes, sir! Anything else?"

Ethan sniffed. "Uh, yeah. Where's the head? I drank too much coffee this morning."

⊱⊱⊱⊰⊰⊰

Three months later, the battalion was fully engaged on Davos. Ethan dismounted from 252 and sighed as he stretched for the first time in over twenty-four divs. Leaning back, his back popped, and he mumbled, "Oh, finally!" He looked at the TOC and at the billeting, then walked toward the TOC. *Screw it. I stink, but the colonel needs intel.*

Slipping in the hatch past the guard, he blinked in the bright lights, looked around and found the coffee pot. He poured a cup, not caring how old it was as he walked toward the holo screens and people hovering around the holo display at the front of the TOC. Sergeant Mazdy sidled up to him. "Anything new, LT?"

"Yeah, Mazdy, come on, you can hear it the same time the colonel does." The two of them walked over and stood to the side until Colonel Cronin noticed him.

"What do you have, Lieutenant Fargo?"

"A company tried to come through the rockpile again. Permission to link in?"

"Granted."

Ethan felt the frisson of his command lace connecting to the command computer. *<Command, carat 252, activate, execute.>* He felt Amy come alive in the link. *<Amy, dump data, execute.>* The data populated the holo in blue. *<Command, carat 252, deactivate, execute.>* Ethan quickly gave his report, ending with, "Any questions?"

Cronin glanced at him. "That attack on the Goon's command meeting. Who did that?"

Ethan sighed, hoping the colonel wouldn't ask that. "That was Sergeant Crane, sir. With a round from his Gustav."

Cronin highlighted Crane's location. "Interesting, considering he didn't have eyes on. Who did?"

Ethan sniffed. "I did sir. I was acting as his spotter because we're a couple of Marines short. I lased the target for him to shoot when we caught them in the open."

"You were behind them, weren't you?"

Ethan stiffened. "Yes, sir. We went ambient and used the photo chromatics to merge with the surroundings."

Cronin cocked an eyebrow and asked, "You went ambient? As in, matched ambient temperatures?"

"Yes, sir. We...ah...figured out a way to shut off the suit exhaust for up to thirty segs, which allows you to match ambient."

"So you distributed your section in the rockpile, made your armor look like rocks, and allowed the Goons to move over you. Is that what you're telling me?"

Ethan came to attention. "Yes, sir. I directed—"

Cronin shook his head and sighed. "Captain Baraofski, front and center!"

A veritable mountain of blond hair and muscular Marine popped tall. "Sir!"

"Lieutenant Fargo, Captain Baraofski is your replacement. I expect you to get eight divs of downtime and begin your turnover *after* those eight divs, which begin now! Do I make myself clear? I will see both of you back here in eight divs."

They chorused, "Yes, sir!"

When they got outside the TOC, Baraofski stopped and stuck out a massive paw. "Georg Baraofski. Call me Bear. I hate to do this to you."

Ethan's hand disappeared in Bear's grip, but he got his hand back in one piece. "Ethan Fargo. Just call me Fargo. I'm going down for a while. Been up over thirty divs and I need some downtime, and a shower."

Bear sniffed. "Yeah, you do," but he grinned when he said it.

Ethan found 252 back in the stack when he went hunting for it. Sergeant Crane was in the process of reloading the ammo bins when he walked up. "Sergeant, I *really* want one of those Gustavs. What you did yesterday was impressive!"

The ammo cart beeped, and Crane pulled it away. "I can probably get one when we get back to base. I only brought this one." He glanced up and added, "Here comes some captain. He's a big sumbitch!"

Ethan looked around and laughed. "Captain Baraofski, your new company commander. I've been relieved." He held up a hand. "Not for cause. I'm too junior to have had command. I told y'all I was a gap-fill."

Crane grumbled, "Yeah, but you kept us alive, sir! You done good!"

"Thanks." Turning to Captain Baraofski, he said, "Morning, Captain. Shall we get started?"

"Certainly, Lieutenant. Lead on." Crane decided being elsewhere was a good idea. Bear said, "They assigned me 302. It was apparently a spare suit. I got my AI installed last night."

Ethan thought for a minute. "Lemme see if I can transfer some data from my AI to yours..."

"How do you think we can do that?"

"If we both power up, I should be able to do a push from Amy to your AI. What do you call it, Bear?

Captain Baraofski kicked at the dirt. "Um...Bear."

A few segs later, Ethan said, "You ready, Bear?"

Bear replied tentatively, "I think so..."

"Here we go." *<Amy, carat 302, link, execute.>*

<Now linked, Ethan. What would you like?>

<Data push. All data on company personnel, all data from this detachment, including procedures, commands, and workarounds for systems.>

<I would caution on pushing workarounds, Ethan. Those are not authorized procedures.>

<Amy, if it keeps people alive, I don't care. Push. Execute.>

<Executing, and completed, Ethan.>

He leaned back in the harness and sighed. *<Amy, shutdown. Execute.>*

<Shutting down. Hatch opening now.>

Bear came over shaking his head. "That...is amazing! How did you figure out how to do that?"

"Well, we've got some time," Ethan said with a smile. "I need to teach you how to dance."

The End

One Time, One Night on Aldrin Station

BRENNEN HANKINS

"Morning, Sarge!"

Space Stargeant "Wild Bill" Grantham lifted his aching head from the side of his coffee mug and looked up at the young Spaceman First Class that had offered the greeting. It was *way* too damn early in the morning for that kind of enthusiasm.

"Morning, Padilla," he said, resting his head back against the steel of his mug, kept warm by the liquid nirvana inside. Stargeant Grantham didn't know if it was actually helping his hangover or if he was just experiencing a placebo effect, but it seemed to make him feel better.

"What are we working on today?" Padilla asked. The kid had just come to Aldrin Station from technical training school, and in the three weeks he had been assigned to the 497th Space Engineering Squadron's Electric Shop, his enthusiasm and cheeriness had not dampened once. At all. And he seemed to take a special liking to his crew lead.

By way of contrast, Stargeant Grantham had been stationed at Aldrin for the better part of eight years, the bulk of his military career. There had been a few deployments, to bases farther within the Milky Way, but other than that, he had remained within the confines of a base built on Titan. His grandfather had transferred to the then-new United States Space Force from the Air Force, also working as an electrician, and, some eighty years later, young William had followed.

There had been a time when he had shared Padilla's enthusiasm for the job, but that joy and pride had worn down over the years, just like his body had.

There had also been a time where he could spend a weekend drinking with the boys, and still manage to wake up bright-eyed and bushy-tailed for work the following Monday. Now, he was learning that may no longer be possible.

"We'll find out during the morning meeting," Stargeant Grantham said quietly, without looking up or taking his head off the mug. God, his head hurt.

The rest of the shop personnel had filed into the break room. A few of them greeted Stargeant Grantham, who merely waved. Shortly after everyone had got themselves settled, the NCOIC walked in.

"Morning, everybody," Technical Stargeant Watson said. "Hope everybody had a good weekend, but unfortunately, we're going to be a little busy today. Intel says that the Kalanuskanites are on the move, and that the Fleet is ramping up activity. We got a Task Force coming in within a few days, along with a few battalions of Space Marines, and we're going to have to make sure the spot the Star Marshall wants to stick them in is ready to go." He rifled through a large stack of work orders and passed them out to the various crew leaders. "Delgadillo, take Schmaltz and Bohling, and head over to Dorm Twenty-seven. Make sure the outlets and lights are all working. Rush, take Poujade and Jancewicz, and do the same. Deconinck, Bay Three of Hanger Ten has a bunch of lights out. Take Ironhart, Gershon, and the grav lift, and get them all fixed. I think Base Supply just got a new shipment of light ballasts in."

"You want me to head over there, too?" Grantham asked.

"No, I got a special job for you," Stargeant Watson replied. "They're finally getting around to installing a permanent power run on the plasma cannon in Zone Two. You have both a restricted area badge and you're the only other non-commissioned officer in the shop. I'm letting you take point on this one." Passing Grantham the work order, he said, "Spaceman Padilla's clearance paperwork finally dropped. Head over to the Security Manager's office, have him pick up his badge, and then take him over there with you."

"Cool!" Padilla said. Stargeant Grantham just groaned.   Stargeant Watson clapped his hands together. "Well, if nobody has any questions, let's get to work."

⟫⟫⟫⟫ ⟪⟪⟪⟪

"You alright, Sarge?"

Stargeant Grantham didn't bother looking up from the conduit he was screwing to the wall. They were having to run three-phase power from a mech room on the back of the plasma cannon's control tower underground to the massive turret on which the cannon sat. Fortunately, the heavy equipment operators had already trenched through the lunar rock, so they didn't have to. All they had to do was lay the conduit that the power conductors would rest in, then fish the wires through. He was having to straddle the end of the trench so he could screw in place the tubing that would bring the circuit out of the ground, and it wasn't doing his hip any favors.

"I'm fine," Grantham said, getting the final metal clamp screwed in place, securing the riser to the wall. "That's got it. Help me up." Working on the surface of Titan was always an experience. The moon of Saturn was dark, always dark, as the heavy atmosphere blocked out over ninety percent of the sun's rays. This made conditions at Aldrin Station incredibly frigid. On top of that, the atmosphere was a mostly nitrogen-methane mix, compared to the nitrogen-oxygen mix of Earth, so the atmosphere was completely unbreathable without a mask. Within the confines of the American space fort, a conversion plant simultaneously burned the methane for energy and heat, and converted the remaining waste into breathable air.

So far, though, that atmosphere only existed inside the massive dome, made up of sandwiching layers of pyroceram and Lexan glass, that covered the bulk of the station, which were divided into numerous compartmentalized sections within the dome for redundancy. Outside of that dome, though, existence was only possible with the aid of a conversion mask and a form-fitting heated power suit. Zone Two was a prime example of this. Working in ninety-two degrees Kelvin *sucked*.

On the other hand, it was possible to see the icy dunes and the massive Kalanuskan ice volcano beyond the station once one was outside of the dome, as well as the colorful auroras created by radiation from the sun reacting with Titan's atmosphere. The heaviness of the clouds, combined with the light output of the base within the dome, prevented its residents from seeing any farther than a quarter of a mile outside of it, and consequently, any of the scenery beyond. To Stargeant Grantham, the view reminded him heavily of the area around the little town in central Alaska he had grown up in, and thus, getting to see it was worth the hassle.

It was one of the few perks of his job he still appreciated.

Spaceman Padilla helped Grantham to his feet, and the NCO let out a grunt as he stood up. He leaned against the control tower, favoring his good leg.

"You all right, Sarge?" Padilla asked again.

"Yeah," Grantham groaned, rubbing his hip. "Old injury. Give me a minute." After a few moments, he puffed out a breath, then stood up straight. "I'm good. Round that stuff up for me, would you?"

"Sure thing, Sarge," Padilla said, putting the tool kit back together. Picking it up, he asked, "What do you mean, 'old injury?'"

"The Kalanuskan War," Grantham replied nonchalantly.

"You were here for that?" Padilla's eyes went wide.

"Happened a year after I got here," Grantham said. "Back then, this base was just a tiny outpost. Still is, compared to Armstrong Station, or any of the Space Ports back home, but back then, we didn't even have the dome built. We had to stay in suits twenty-four-seven."

"What happened? During the war, I mean," Padilla said.

Grantham let out a sigh. "Kalanuskanites didn't like us here," he began. "At the time, we had no idea there was life on this little rock, just that it was the closest thing to Earth, other than Mars, that was remotely close to habitable. We set out to build a base of operations for people looking to settle out here, and the folks trying to push out to points further in the solar system. The 'nuskies let us know we were invading their territory—the hard way."

"And that was when you hurt yourself?"

Grantham looked down at his right leg. "We sped off in a hovercraft to repair a breach in the security wall around the original camp." He raised his head, and Padilla watched him continue with a faraway look in his eyes. "'Nuskies had a grav gun. They fired it off, and when that round struck sand, it tripled the gravity in a fifty-foot radius, right in front of us." His eyes focused, and settled back on Padilla. "We'd just thought they missed. But then the nose of the hovercraft hit that gravity well, we hit dirt and flipped ass over tea kettle. Killed the driver and two passengers, and I was left pretty messed up afterward. I was on crutches for about five months after the fact. Lost some good people in that battle."

For a minute, Grantham's gaze developed a sheen as bright as the stars on the outside of Titan's fuming atmosphere. His reverie was interrupted by an errant question: "Think they'll come back, sir?"

Grantham looked hard at Padilla, and carefully replied, "I'm not sure. Anything's possible. Why do you ask?"

Padilla stammered, "Well, uh, if they come back, you could—"

"I could what?" Grantham asked. "Kill some 'nuskies? Exact some payback? Avenge my friends, maybe?" He shook his head. "I avenged my friends by outliving the ones that killed them. My continued existence—as well as that of this base—is just another giant middle finger to the Kalanuskanites. And I have no interest in killing any of them out of hand. Hell, I wasn't even issued a weapon in the last battle. They had our guys on damage control and left the actual fighting to the pilots and the Space Marines."

"Sir, I—"

"If your reasons for enlisting are to win glory in battle, then you signed up for the wrong specialty code." Grantham shook his head, then looked around. "Never mind that now. We got the conduit ran. I already know what comes next, but I want to hear it from you, make sure you know. How are we running the wire?"

Padilla pursed his lips, moving his thoughts back to the job at hand. "Dirtside, we'd normally use mule tape and be done, but out here, we only have fourteen percent gravity. Trying to pull on the mule tape would just pull us towards the building, rather than pull the wire through the pipe.

We have to grab the wire puller, stake it to the ground, and have it do the pulling."

"How are you going to stake the wire puller?"

"...Grav boots?" Padilla asked hesitantly.

"We could, if we had bothered to bring them," Grantham said. "Alas, there are twelve airlocks between us and those boots, and not near enough time in the duty day to retrieve them. But fear not! For there is another way."

"There is, sir?"

"Well, sure there is." Grantham smiled wide as he gestured towards the trench. "You see, we have this nice, solid run of rigid conduit below us to tie off to, and mule tape that can withstand 1,500 pounds of force..."

❧❧❧❧❧ ❧❧❧❧❧

"He tied your boots to the conduit?" Senior Spaceman Delgadillo asked.

After hours, there wasn't too much available to do on Aldrin Station. Sure, there was a little movie theater on base, as well as a gym and a gravball court, but beyond that, the only real place the spacemen stationed at the base could hang out was Ringo's, a small bar over in sector twelve. The tavern was divided into three sections—the club side, the "dive" side, for those that liked their drinks with a side of quiet, and the officer's lounge. Spaceman Padilla and several other spacemen from the shop had migrated over to the dive side for some fresh air. The club side was fun, but the electronica constantly blasting out of the speakers over there was best taken in small doses.

"He did." Padilla took a swig out of his mug. "Crazy, but it worked. Took forever to hammer the stakes into the ground, though."

"Man, Sarge is frickin' nuts," Deconinck laughed. The big spaceman had a beer in each hand, and was taking turns sipping from each one. "I remember once we were stringing lights in a drop ceiling in zero grav. Crazy son of a bitch would attach each light to the end of a roll of MC cable and float the damn things into place. Then he'd cut the other end of the cable after that and splice it into a J-box. It was like playing the dumbest game of frisbee golf ever devised, but damn if we didn't get the job done in half the time we thought it would take."

"Is Space Engineering always this crazy?" Padilla said.

"Not always," Gershon said. The Senior Spaceman somehow looked bored. Not much of a beer drinker, she was nursing a Long Island iced tea between her hands. "Most of the time, things are pretty routine. Most of what we do is maintenance. Every now and then, we'll get a project come down the pipe, but unless the 'nuskies get froggy, you gotta make your own fun." She took a sip. "I dunno why Sarge stays in, sometimes."

"Certainly not for the excitement," Delgadillo muttered.

"He actually did say that to me today," Padilla said, draining the rest of his beer. "Mentioned he was here during the Kalanuskan War."

"Yep," Deconinck said, matching Padilla's finish by downing both his beers and letting out a proud belch. "Sarge lost almost everyone he came up here with during that battle. Of the three that survived, two of them got medically discharged and sent dirtside, and the last one remaining is Sarge. For some reason, he just doesn't want to leave."

"Why?" Padilla leaned forward, curious.

Deconinck shrugged. "Who knows? Anyhoo, I got the next round. Waitress!" he called to the serving girl.

As she walked past, Padilla couldn't help but notice Stargeant Grantham sitting alone in the back, quietly drinking by himself.

"Attention all personnel! Attention all personnel! Ground attacking force inbound! Essential personnel, report to your duty stations immediately. Non-essential personnel, shelter in place! This is not a drill! Attention all personnel..."

Padilla woke up with a start at the message blaring from the wall intercom. He wasn't sure if he was essential or non-essential personnel and was unsure what to do. Then he figured that if he was essential, he'd know already, so acting on that thought, he grabbed the emergency kit off his barracks wall and hid under his bed.

A moment after he secured himself, his phone rang. It was Sarge.

"Hello?"

"Padilla, Stargeant Grantham. 'Nuskies are getting froggy again. Where you at?"

"Under my bed, sheltering in place, sir."

"Under your bed?" Grantham's voice sounded puzzled. "Why're you down there?"

"I wasn't sure if I was essential personnel or not, sir. I figured that if I was, I'd know about it. Since I didn't know, I figured I wasn't."

"Trust me, kid, you're essential. Get out from under there, get dressed and get to the shop, pronto. If you encounter anybody from the Defense Force or the Marines, tell them you're with Space Engineering and a member of the DART, and they'll let you through."

"Understood, sir."

"And leave your teddy bear in your barracks room."

"All right, gang." Stargeant Watson was standing in front of the assembled electricians in the shop break room. "No need to worry about our area. We have triple-redundant airlock systems in this sector, so we should be okay. That said, if shit really hits the fan and they make it through the dome *and* the airlocks, I'll remind you the emergency shelter kits are in the closet over there in the back.

"Rules are as follows: until we have to roll, we're all sheltering in here. Grab your toolbags and gear, and keep them in the break room for now, in case we need to roll in a hurry. Which, if we have to roll at all, will probably be the case. Nobody leaves alone, nobody leaves without a suit, nobody leaves without a radio. Beyond that, hunker down, and hopefully our services will not be needed. If there's any questions, come ask myself or Stargeant Grantham. He's been here before.

"Now," he said, picking a remote and turning on the break room TV, "who's picking the movie?"

"Stargeant Grantham," Stargeant Watson said.

"Hmm?" Grantham looked around blearily as Watson shook him awake.

Being on a Space Engineering Damage Assessment and Repair Team was far different from being a frontline fighter. While the Defense Force and the Space Marines were busy repelling the attackers, the DARTs were hanging back, taking shelter until they were needed. One could only sit in silence waiting in nervous anticipation for so long, and as such, bored, frightened spacemen would find ways to pass the time. Several of

Grantham's spacemen were watching the nintieth installment of *Fast &*
Furious on the break room TV. Others, led by Spaceman Deconinck, were
playing cards, alternating between hearts, spades, cribbage and euchre.
Grantham, expecting that he was going to be extremely busy in short order,
followed the time-honored axiom of "Rest When You Can, Work When
You Should," and had settled in for nap. Given that the NCOIC was now
waking him up, this seemed to be a good call.

"Grab Padilla and get back out to Zone Two," Watson said. "Errant
gravity round from the 'nuskies landed between the plasma cannon and
the control tower."

Grantham bolted upright. "They didn't..."

"Yep," Watson said. "That nice new power run you just installed and
buried? It's toast."

Grantham groaned. "Goddamn 'nuskies."

"'Goddamn 'nuskies' is right," Watson said, his voice tight. "That's the
only heavy weaponry we got on the west side of the base. Wing King wants
it back up, yesterday."

"On it," Grantham said, grabbing his tool bag.

๑๛๛๛ ๛๛๛๛

"Holy Toledo," Padilla said, observing the crater in shocked awe.

"Ain't nothing holy about it, kid," Grantham said, shaking his head.

The Kalanuskanites' gravity round had probably been aimed at the sentry control tower, yet despite missing the target completely, it had somehow by not-quite luck managed to hit another vital target. The missile
impacted the trench for the plasma cannon's power run almost dead-on,
and penetrated at least five feet down into the sandy soil. Grantham didn't

even have to completely uncover the conduit to know it was absolutely trashed.

What's more, there was still fighting carrying on in the distance. Padilla and Grantham were in their survival suits, which could protect against most of the light weaponry that the 'nuskies were firing, but if another gravity round hit near them, they were toast.

"How long do you think it'll take to repair?" The base tactical officer's voice was tense.

"Give me forty-five minutes, tops," Grantham said. "We'll trim the conduit back, splice the line, and turn it into a proper handhole later. Won't be pretty, but it'll work, sir."

"Copy," the TACO said. "Let me know as soon as you're done."

❧❧❧❧❧ ❦❦❦❦❦

"Hacksaw," Grantham said to Padilla, holding out his hand for the tool.

The pair had been working as quickly as they could to get the massive cannon back online. Being very careful not to nick the wire inside, Grantham had managed to trim a foot off the broken end of the conduit leading to the cannon, leaving just enough wire to strip back and splice to. After the battle, they'd have to re-pull all the wire, but at least they'd be able to get the cannon running for now. Grantham was just about the trim the other side, the side leading back to the panel, when the TACO came in over the radio.

"DART One, what's your status?"

"Almost halfway done," Grantham commed back, puzzled. They'd only been at work for ten minutes.

"Any chance you can speed up your timeline?"

"Negative," Grantham said. "Why?"

"Look out to the west."

Grantham and Padilla poked their heads out of the crater. Beyond where there were isolated pockets of fighting just outside of the station's security perimeter, both men could make out a sizable force, maybe two, three hundred Kalanuskanites, cresting the hills on the horizon.

"Oh, fu...foxtrot," Grantham said over the radio.

"'Foxtrot' is right," the TACO said. "We need that cannon up, yesterday."

"Uhh, give me one mike." Grantham started looking out frantically. Finally, his eyes fixated on something on the side of the control tower, and he grinned. "Padilla, I got a solution, but I want to make sure you're tracking. What do you see on the wall over there?"

"A convenience outlet, Sarge?"

"Exactly," Grantham said. "We don't have time to strip back the other conduit and splice new wire in. But fear not, for there is another way!" He commed back to Stargeant Watson. "Electric One, DART One. We're going to need a bunch of extension cords..."

***

When Delgadillo and Deconinck showed up, they didn't bring just a few extension cords. They'd brought every single one they could find in the shop. Delgadillo passed the cart off to Padilla before splitting off to go repair damage elsewhere on the perimeter. Meanwhile, Grantham was frantically checking outlet circuits inside the control tower.

Padilla pushed the cart into the mech room. "Whatcha doing, Sarge?"

"Trying to find outlet circuits I can tie into," Grantham said. "I need each one to be on a separate phase to get the three-phase power that cannon needs, but I only can find two." He looked around. "Pick three extension cords. Lop off the female ends, strip them back, and cap off the neutral and ground wires. Quick."

Padilla pulled out his wire strippers and immediately got to work, though his hands were shaking. "Sarge, how long until the 'nuskies get here?"

Just then, there was a loud sound of impact from outside. The control tower rattled, and the lights flickered.

"If they're close enough to make the lights flicker, I'd say they're pretty close," Grantham said, then he paused. "Wait, that's it! Lights!"

He quickly pulled out an eleven-in-one screwdriver and tore open the light switch to the mech room, then checked it with his meter. "Ha! Found our C phase!" He turned the light switch off, then lopped the male end off an extension cord and began stripping it back with his own set of wire strippers. He jammed the end of one wire into the bottom end of the switch. Screwing a wire nut onto the remaining unused wires of the cord, he commed the tactical officer. "TACO, DART One."

"Go."

"Got a solution, we're going to have you up in a couple of minutes. However, this is the field expedient repair to beat all field expedient repairs, so you're probably only going to have the one shot. Once we get you up, make it count."

"Copy. Standing by."

"Padilla, give me the cords you cut," Grantham said. "Then start plugging extension cords together. I'm going to wire these guys in."

"On it, Sarge," Padilla said.

Grantham took the cut cords and ran over to the crater. A grav round hit about a hundred meters outward from him, and the strike was powerful enough to suck in any debris, some as close as arm's reach, towards the center of the round's impact. He cursed to himself as he dove for the safety of the original crater, then began splicing the cut cords into the power feed for the cannon. Once that was done, he ran back, still cursing all the way, and helped Padilla get all the cords plugged together. Their effort was rewarded with a loud, audible hum coming from the plasma cannon.

"Yes!" Grantham said, pumping a fist. "Padilla, get back inside the mech room!"

As the pair began to run for cover, Grantham commed the TACO. "Cannon is live! I repeat, cannon is—"

Before he could finish his transmission, the world suddenly turned white, and Grantham saw stars that had nothing to do with the universe. He came to a moment later, where Padilla, who apparently hadn't been harmed by the strike, dragged him into the mech room, right as the plasma cannon turned toward its assailants and fired a fourteen-thousand-degree Fahrenheit reply.

A blinding white light erupted forth and tore into the amassed ranks of Kalanuskanites. Padilla couldn't really make out what they looked like from where he was standing, but the wailing and screaming of the mortally wounded was vaguely humanlike in nature. Roughly two-thirds of the attacking force were simply *gone*. The rest simply scattered.

Almost immediately after the cannon fired, the main breaker for the electric panel in the control tower blew out, knocking out power to not only the tower, but a good portion of Zone Two. The mechanical room went dark, just as Stargeant Grantham's vision was beginning to.

"Electric One, DART One, we need medical assistance to the Zone Two Sentry Control Tower!" Padilla frantically commed as he tried to reset power. "Don't worry, Sarge, we got 'em..."

⁂

"I still can't believe this shit," Padilla said, obviously annoyed.

The battle hadn't lasted long after the medical teams arrived to haul Stargeant Grantham to the infirmary. The base defensive forces, initially caught off-guard by the attack, had managed to rally and repel the Kalanuskanites after the cannon shot. The regional commander had come down a day later, and several medals for heroism had been handed out that day. Unfortunately, after having suffered five broken bones and a concussion, the only thing Grantham had received for his trouble was another Purple Heart, and a pending transfer back dirtside.

"You win one Purple Heart, kid, you've won them all." Grantham shrugged in his hospital bed, trying not to wince. "After all, 'Shoot me once, shame on you; shoot me twice, shame on me...'"

"Seriously, not even Commendation Medals? We at least warrant *those*." Padilla folded his arms.

"Stargeant Watson got the Commendation Medal," Grantham said drily. "After all, he was the lead for the Electrical DARTs."

"I don't get it," Padilla said. "Is this really all there is to Space Engineering? Sacrifice yourself for the mission and get sent back to Earth unceremoniously once you have nothing more they can take from you?" The young spaceman was growing increasingly angry.

For a moment, Stargeant Grantham looked at Padilla, a sudden weight on his chest. He flashed back to the days where he wasn't a grouchy old

Space Stargeant, when he'd been as happy-go-lucky as Padilla normally was, and remembered how that young spaceman eventually became the jaded, cynical NCO he was now. He could see Padilla slipping onto the same path, and the thought of that happening left Grantham with an awful feeling in his stomach.

Taking a deep breath, Grantham looked at the younger spaceman. "Padilla, I'm going to tell you something. All that stuff you're talking about is incidental. You did good work out there, but if all you're focused on is medals and recognition, your career is going to be a long and lonely one."

"Then why do this? Why do *any* of this?" the young airmen asked, exasperated.

Grantham thought for a second. "Did you get a chance to look around outside, when we were working?"

"Yeah?"

"What'd you think of it?"

Padilla frowned. "Working outside of the dome?"

"Yeah," Grantham said. "Specifically, the environment. Pretty cool, huh?"

"I suppose," Padilla said, skeptical. "I mean, the light show in the clouds was kind of cool—"

"And the sand dunes?" Grantham asked. "The ice volcanoes?"

"Yeah, that's something you don't get see back home," Padilla said.

"Exactly," Grantham said. "Most of Earth's population will never get to come to Aldrin Station. They won't get to see any of the crazy terrain or weather out here. What's more, most of those folks will never get to know that their efforts are going towards making these places safe for eventual human exploration, or colonization.

"Meanwhile, I've spent eight years of my life out here. Made it through two battles, and my efforts were partially responsible for victory on both fronts. When my grandkids are sitting on my knee, having been able to safely travel and explore worlds without fear of being attacked by the likes of the Kalanuskanites, I'll be able to tell them, 'Yeah, I was out there. I helped pave the way.' And so will you."

Padilla frowned in thought. "And that's why you were content to stay out here? That's really enough?"

For the first time, Stargeant Grantham gave Spaceman First Class Padilla a smile of encouragement. "Trust me, bud, it's enough."

Station Search

JORDAN CAMPBELL

MY NAME IS GALLO. Just Gallo. Never had a surname, at least not that I could remember. Foundlings like me tend not to get them. Some things never change, regardless of what epoch it is. The master I worked for in the colony before I was recruited…let's just say I wouldn't be taking his name anytime soon. People started calling me "Gallo" back in basic training and I got used to it.

I could see the station even at this distance. It was hard to miss—eleven hundred feet long and twenty stories high, it would have been about the same size as an old Earth aircraft carrier from a powerful nation's naval forces. I ran my fingers over my helmet; the visor didn't impede my vision in the slightest. Criminals had boarded on the space stations—hijackers who would see fit to risk a sovereign planet's ruin and throw the whole of the Galactic Confederation into chaos. We'd destroy them…all of them. We don't negotiate with terrorists.

"How many of them are there?"

"At least eighteen, but the total number is indeterminate because the transmission cut off," Asino answered. "The broadcaster wasn't sure who was boarding them. Said she could see placards from a dozen different planets. Interplanetary crews never run that many different squads, but that tells us exactly who we're dealing with: Ulvosairs."

Asino's jaw tightened. He wasn't a handsome man in the best of times: staggeringly tall, even by Space Confederaton Marine standards, narrow-faced with a harsh voice, combined with a tendency to clear his throat too often, but he showed absolute resolve. His eyes narrowed and I held my breath. I'd seen what happened when Asino lost his temper before. It wasn't pretty. The man had a memory sharper than crystal and more eternal than the diamond star of Centaurus.

"Those devils," Asino said. "They'll doom us all if they've killed the diplomats."

"Not if we kill them first," I replied. I pulled my sidearm and walked over to a bench to clean it. A Halley-Orson pistol, loaded with armor-piercing rounds: the right tool for the right job. Small enough to be maneuverable in close quarters with as light felt recoil as possible. I reloaded the pistol, set the safety, and holstered it. I double-checked the rest of my gear. Six extra magazines for the Halley-Orson, each with seventeen rounds. A Hyaku-take plasma rifle for longer shots, with twelve thirty-round magazines in my pockets. Three knives, plus a smaller ballistic blade in each boot. My armor was titanium, alloyed with carbonized metals from four other planets, and it was specifically designed to fit me alone. Nanotechnology would enable my suit to fly for short bursts. If I got pushed out of an airlock somehow, I'd have up to five minutes to re-embark onto the station or return to our own ship. It'd be perfect if I needed to escape or evacuate an injured civilian.

If there are any civilians left to evacuate. I shook my head. Thinking like that would certainly guarantee failure. The mission came first...

Our squadron had gotten the distress call less than an hour ago, an emergency broadcast from someone—she hadn't identified herself—on Versailles Vista, a small station used especially for diplomatic meetings. Ambassador Olivia Ophelia Ortega had been hosting a meeting there between a half-dozen planets from the Galactic Confederation and the

Independent Systems...and they'd been taken over by Ulvosairs. The transmission had cut off not long after, but it wasn't as if we had nothing to go on entirely. Our ship had been closest, so we were the ones who were going to engage.

"We're outnumbered, at least four-to-one," Asino said. "Maybe more, but there should be reinforcements coming within three hours. In the meantime, it's you and me, Cane and Gatto."

As if he'd been waiting for his cue, Gatto leapt down from a rafter. He was slightly built, though taller than me by a head. His golden eyes, a telltale sign of genetic augmentation undergone when he'd first been drafted into the Confederation's military, shone bright. I grinned despite myself; Gatto had always had a bit of a flair for the dramatic. Said it lowered the guard of his enemies and allowed him to pounce. If it worked, it worked, and Asino didn't seem to mind.

"This is our first mission together," Gatto said. "The four of us, a united front. We shall endure. Come the hellfire of K2-141b to the icy canyons of Ningen, we shall endure, we shall survive, and we shall complete the mission."

The mission: board the space station, rescue the diplomats and kill or capture every single pirate. I pressed my hand to my helmet. I'd trained for this...I'd seen the havoc those bastard Ulvosairs were capable of. The station loomed over us, a mass of metal, urethane, and glass.

There was a shuffling from the corner and Cane, Asino's right-hand man, rose. He was taller than Gatto, but not as tall as Asino and had a commanding voice, deeper and richer.

"May the Creator see us through," Cane said. He turned towards the station, fixing his eyes on his target. Not just his eyes–his face, his shoulders, his whole body hardened with conviction. Unnerving and yet reassuring, it was as if his entire being was tied into the station's presence. "Let's roll."

Cane disabled the autopilot on our cruiser and steered towards the hangar on the starboard sector of the station. It was wide and spacious, ideal for landings, whether from marauding pirates or a rescue mission from the Galactic Confederation's Space Confederaton Marines. Our cruiser was small, barely larger than a trailer tram from the countries in the Earth continent Europe, but it was more maneuverable than most ships in the Confederation's fleets. Most notably, it had a very friendly ejection system. While Cane stayed in the cockpit, gripping the controls tightly, Gatto and I braced ourselves.

"Closing in...on my mark," Cane said. "Almost there...now!"

He pressed his finger against the button and the hatch above our heads opened. I launched myself upwards, with Gatto at my heels. We soared through the hangar and landed ahead of our cruiser. Gatto and I broke into a run as Cane pulled the ship to a halt.

Ahead of us, there were two large Ulvosairs, standing guard. They were wearing little in the way of armor. They were as tall as Asino, broad-shoul-dered, and their faces were hard, ending in snouts instead of mouths. Sharp teeth flashed and glowed against the light from the poles they wielded, crackling with power. One of them aimed his pole at us and blasted off a bolt of electricity.

I went low and Gatto went high, and the bolt missed, but some of the static still flowed through my armor. They engaged us first—there would be no quarter. I pulled my rifle and started shooting. The Ulvosair fired his pole again and the blast intercepted the plasma rounds. The impact sent out a shockwave, and the round of concentrated plasma fell to the floor, burning a hole as it melted and hardened. The Ulvosair snarled and bared his teeth, blasting another bolt of electricity at me. I dodged but was a touch too slow, and it grazed my arm. One of those bolts was enough to cripple a human, but even without my armor, I wasn't an ordinary human anymore.

I rolled to the side and fired three more shots. The first round of concentrated plasma caught the Ulvosair in the shoulder and he howled in agony, dropping to the ground...which saved his life, since the second shot only grazed his cheek, and the third missed entirely.

The Ulvosair raised his electric pole again and blasted just as I fired two more shots. This time, the plasma round pressed against the bulb that connected the electric current to the pole, shattering it. Glass and wire burst everywhere and the Ulvosair snarled in fury, tiny pieces of glass shredding his flesh and fur. Blue blood began to seep out from a dozen cuts and the Ulvosair lunged at me, knocking me to the ground.

The Ulvosair was bigger than I was, swearing in a language I didn't speak, and trying to claw at my eyes through my helmet's visor. His hands were large, but his fingers were shorter and stubbier than a human's fingers would have been. He was strong, but not strong enough to break through the alloy of my visor, and he had neglected to try to pin me properly. My arms were free. I raised my Hyakutake and fired again; at this range, it was impossible to miss. Flesh burned and fur singed as the plasma round burrowed through my enemy. The Ulvosair roared and continued the attack, but he didn't get out of the way, and I fired again and again and again. The Ulvosair slumped against me, and I pressed myself to the side to move out from under him. I pulled my rifle up and aimed down the sights, but it wasn't necessary. The Ulvosair was twitching in its death throes.

I am a Space Confederaton Marine of the Galactic Confederation. As such, I am honor-bound to protect the powerless, serve the starbound, guard the galaxies...Ulvosairs are thieves at best, but usually far worse. I did not regret killing him.

I turned to look at Gatto. Ever the dramatic, he had foregone his firearms to engage the second Ulvosair in hand-to-hand combat. The Ulvosair was much bigger than Gatto, but much less heavily armored and his arms were lined with cuts where Gatto had sliced at him. The Ulvosair had put his electric pole to the side and had unsheathed a long, curved sword. Gatto was matching him step for step with two smaller knives, one in each hand. He swiped and slashed and parried. Despite the Ulvosair's advantage in size and reach, there wasn't so much as a chip in Gatto's armor. With each blow, Gatto managed to strike at the Ulvosair, but the pirate was stubborn and pressed on. The Ulvosair slashed at Gatto again, but Gatto caught its blade between his two knives and stepped forward. There was a flash of light and the Ulvosair's sword clattered out of his hand. The pirate lunged for it, making to stab Gatto in the belly to disembowel him, but Gatto dodged, driving his own knife through the pirate's heart.

He backed away faster than I realized; he was by my side before I even saw him move. Gatto nodded at me, his golden eyes gleaming. His opponent laid completely motionless. Hell of a thing—it would have been nice to have one of the Ulvosairs captured so we could interrogate him, but neither Gatto nor I had much of a choice.

"Gallo!"

I turned around. Cane had gotten our cruiser docked in the back of the hangar, and he and Asino were rushing towards us. Our cruiser was one of the only ships that wasn't ruined. Along the hangar's opening, there were a dozen banged up tri-finned fighters, which might have been the ships that the Ulvosairs had flown in on. They were damaged but seemed operational. There were other ships, most of them in varying stages of destruction.

Cockpits had been blown up, wings torn off, boosters crushed...there were several small fires still smoldering.

"Are you two ready to push on?" Asino asked. "Let's roll."

We walked in tandem towards the first set of doors. None of us had a clue where the diplomats were being held captive, but it was a better place to start than anything else. The station itself had to be more than a hundred times the size of the hangar, but a hefty percentage of that would be the chambers housing the powering systems and heaters.

We hadn't gone more than a hundred yards and weren't even through the gate when Cane stopped short and turned his attention towards a short, stout spaceship: a Halifax-Hubble tugging vessel. It would have been used to help ferry larger, less maneuverable ships into and out of the hangar. Cane's shoulders set and then he charged at the felled vessel.

"Somebody's trapped inside!" Cane barked. I wasn't exactly surprised; Cane's hearing was by far the most precise out of any of us. He launched himself at the door and seized it with both hands. There was a terrible grinding as metal and plastic tore against one another, and then he ripped the door off its hinges.

A figure tumbled out of the ruined ship and leapt up to their feet. He was smaller than I was, even without my armor. He wore an ill-fitting uniform, covered in stains, some blue and some red and some black and greasy.

"Thank you," the man gasped, quivering as he looked around. His eyes lingered on the bodies of the dead Ulvosairs and the ruined ships and then on us in our armor. "I...I...everyone else is dead, aren't they? You're with the Galactic Confederation..."

A nametag reading Seppio had been stitched onto the breast pocket of the man's shirt, and judging from the color, a crisp, pale blue, he was most likely a hireling who served one of the ambassadors personally rather than a military pilot. Galactic Confederation pilots, when they weren't wearing their armor, wore silver suits. Gatto placed a hand on Seppio's shoulder.

"You're safe now," Gatto said. "We've got reinforcements coming in. One of them can extract you. Are you injured?"

"I don't think so. Most of this blood isn't mine...my brothers are gone." the pilot's blue eyes darkened, becoming sapphires. "I will avenge them, if it's the last thing I do."

"Good man," Asino said. "Now, tell me, how well do you know the bowels of this station?"

"Quite well," Seppio answered. "I've been serving Ambassador Ortega for several years, and there's only so many times I can stay in the hangar for hours on end. I know my way around—all the nooks and crannies."

"Then you'll lead..."

Seppio led us down a corridor wide enough for us to spread out, a labyrinth in all but name. The hallways broke off at forks and intersections every minute or two. I counted two lefts, then a right, then two more lefts, then two rights, and then we came to what was almost a clearing. An enormously empty room—was this some sort of air shaft? The pathway had narrowed down to a bridge that was barely wide enough for two.

"You're all larger than I am," Seppio said. "Perhaps you should go first to test it."

There were scorch marks on our end of the bridge and more spent casings and bits of shrapnel, mingled with stains of blood and ash. Gatto nodded at us all, saluted, and then ran across the bridge. He leapt up, balancing on the handrail. He leapt up again, somersaulted in midair and then landed on the other side. He crouched down and pulled both knives from their sheaths, ready to ambush any Ulvosair who might investigate the commotion.

Cane and I went next. Cane ran as fast as his legs would carry him, and the bridge creaked and moaned beneath him. I slapped a button on my armor, just above my hip, and a surge of power traveled down my spine and centered in my boots. I leapt up, and rather than be drawn down by artificial gravity, I hovered. Booster flames crackled from the soles of my boots. It wasn't truly flight, but the power was enough to carry me across the way easily. I turned back. Asino nodded and walked steadily. He was larger than any of us and more heavily armed, in weapon and armor. The bridge moaned and groaned under his weight, louder than before, as if it were crying out in agony. Right before Asino reached us, there was a terrible roar that was half-thunder, half-gunshot, and the bridge began cracking.

The cracks spread and Asino tore into a run. He stumbled under the shattering platform just in time for Cane to seize him by the arms and pull him to safety. Asino straightened up and nodded.

"Seppio, hold on," I called. "I'll hover back and bring you over."

"No need for that. Stand back a bit."

The pilot crouched down and leapt up, and for a moment, I thought he was flying himself. He landed in front of us, a single bead of sweat dripping down his forehead. He raised himself up slowly.

"You can jump...what powerful legs..."

"All the better to get across crevices," Seppio said. He rubbed at his eyes. For a moment, it was as if they flickered from blue to green and then back again. "My planet is very rugged and mountainous, and where there aren't mountains, there are skyscrapers a mile high. You need to learn how to jump, or you die. A little gap like that is nothing to me."

He clapped me on the shoulder, and we continued into the next corridor. While the last few corridors and hallways had been barren, this one was crowded. There were bodies...bodies everywhere. A half-dozen corpses were lined up in a row and standing over them were three Ulvosairs, stripping off valuables.

"Fine crystal-core watch, we can strip that for parts. I know a buyer in Leo who never asks questions. Uses the core to power the lamps for his crops."

I raised my rifle and opened fire. The first Ulvosair dropped like a stone, roaring in pain. The other two leapt to their feet, diving to the side. One was obsidian, the other marble white. Both were armed, one with a shotgun, the other with one of the electric poles. The obsidian Ulvosair pulled a small sphere from his belt. He tossed it at once, and yellowish smoke broke out.

Yellow smoke grenade...probably sulfuric acid. There was no shortage of planets where it could be harvested. I leapt up and slammed down on the button on my armor again. The boosters in my boots erupted and I hovered over the gas. It probably wouldn't have done much to me, anyway—my armor was strong enough for that—but it made fighting that much more difficult. I couldn't fire my rifle here–if the sulfuric smoke caught fire, it'd ignite the entire room. The Ulvosairs had clear shots at me, though, and they both opened fire.

I dodged their shots. I couldn't chance something hitting my armor and dropping me back into the sulfur. The Ulvosairs bellowed in rage, roaring obscenities.

"Raaah!"

The first Ulvosair was back on his feet, covered in burns from my rifle and the sulfuric smoke alike, but still very much alive. He raised his gun–not a rifle, but what looked more like a Wierzchos shotgun–and fired. I was knocked back before I could retaliate. The force hit me hard, but I heard howling...the next moment, Cane darted forward and slammed the Ulvosair down. The Wierzchos went flying, and Gatto caught it in midair. He leapt backwards, clinging to the back wall, and opened fire.

These three Ulvosairs were far more formidable than the first two we'd fought. The obsidian Ulvosair drew a small bar from his pocket and threw it down. The moment it hit the floor, he drew his electric pole and fired a bolt. The bar exploded and, in its place, a translucent barrier emerged...a forcefield. Bullets from our rifles were deflected, but cracks began to form. It wasn't enough, though, and I didn't have an angle to get at them from above.

"Stand back!"

Asino charged forward, slamming against the forcefield. He was knocked back, but he ricocheted off the wall and landed behind the Ulvosairs. All three of them turned on him and that made the forcefield break off, and it gave Cane, Gatto and I three easy targets.

Our guns rang out in near-perfect unison and the three Ulvosairs dropped. Their faces were all frozen in painful grimaces. The sulfuric gas had dissipated, by this point. I landed firmly and looked around.

"Any survivors?"

There weren't any...two pilots, two guardsmen, what appeared to be a chef and a sixth victim dressed sharply. A secretary perhaps? I bowed my head and Cane made a small sign with his fingers over the bodies. An apology, for not being quicker...for not being better.

"What about our pilot?"

There was shuffling from near the front of the room, and I realized that Seppio had fallen behind some crates at some point during the fight. He rose to his full height and walked over to us. His eyes were watering—now they looked faint, almost pale—and his cheeks bulged. After a moment, he exhaled harshly.

"Were you holding your breath all this time?" Asino demanded. "The battle wasn't particularly brief. That should have done you severe harm."

"My race doesn't suffer oxygen deprivation when we hold our breath." Seppio shrugged. "All the better to survive...and with as foul as some of those cities can get, it's a necessity."

"Did you know them?" I asked, gesturing down at the bodies. "Any of them?"

Anything valuable—buttons, badges, emblems, watches, jewelry—had been stripped away and the pilots' bodies in particular were battered beyond anything I could recognize.

"No," Seppio said, shaking his head. "I don't know who these people are...we should keep moving."

We walked on, clearing three more rooms and hallways. There were more scorch marks and broken apparatuses. We passed two dead Ulvosairs on the way. The raiders had met some resistance; there weren't any bodies of the station's crew or any diplomats.

"Any idea where we are?"

I looked around the chamber; an elevator chute stood to the side. Right, this station was twenty stories high. The door chimed as it opened; there were several large boxes stacked neatly inside. That made sense. An elevator, even if it were only for freight, would be a necessity on a station this size.

"Look out!"

I turned around. Two more Ulvosairs were charging towards us. One of them slammed into me and I wrapped my arms around him, reaching for his throat. We rolled into the elevator shaft with such force, the guardrails cracked underneath his back. He kicked me against the wall, and I raised my rifle and fired. The bolt of plasma burst against the Ulvosair's chest. He roared in pain. I turned my head just in time to see Seppio pull his blaster from his hip holster.

"Brace yourself!"

Seppio fired his blaster, but the shot was off: it hit the cables of the freight elevator and the cables broke free. I caught a glimpse of one of the cables whipping out and catching the second Ulvosair in the throat but then it was nothing but black as we plummeted.

Trapped in the elevator, the Ulvosair and I fell into the darkness.

⁓⁓⁓⁓ ⁓⁓⁓⁓

I groaned and lifted myself up slowly. I had landed on my rifle. The Hyaku-take was durable, but hardly indestructible. I wouldn't be getting much use out of it now. I shifted around to get my bearings.

The elevator laid behind me, broken and smashed. The Ulvosair I had been stuck with was dead. He had fallen out and hadn't had anything to brace himself with, or protect himself from the crushing weight of the elevator. There were broken boxes and crates that formed a labyrinth, but I still had my trackers. It would be difficult to find my way out of here, but not impossible.

Creeeeek...

The noise was subtle enough that I might not have heard it if it weren't for the echoing of the chambers. My rifle was ruined, but I still had my pistol. I pulled my sidearm and raised it up. I had killed the Ulvosair in the elevator, somewhat by accident, but there could be another down here waiting to spring an ambush or looking for a way to sabotage the station's integrity.

Creeeeeeeeekkk...

There! Behind a shattered podium, leaning against a wall, something or someone was hiding. I walked over to the podium and ducked down, ready to fire. My heart stopped.

Pressed up against the wall, tucked into the fetal position, was a young girl no older than thirteen. Deep brown eyes peeked out from behind darker hair that fell to her shoulders. She as dressed in a pink tunic, with a scarlet cloak warped around her shoulders, crimson trousers, and black boots with red shoelaces. Somebody liked the color red.

I bit back a curse. There hadn't been anything about a kid being part of the crew, and this girl was dressed way too nicely to be a maid or serving girl. Darn it, not a stowaway. Why a stowaway? And why was I, out of any of us, the one who got stuck finding her? I wished Cane was here; he'd taught Sunday School back on his planet, and he had a way with kids. The girl began to tremble. Her dark eyes blinked back tears, and guilt kicked me in the stomach.

"Hi," I said, crouching down. I was still in full armor, but I kept my voice low. "My name is Gallo. What's your name?"

"My name? No." the girl shook her head. "I'm not telling you my name. I won't. I'm not supposed to talk to strangers."

"Kid, the station is crawling with Ulvosairs," I said. "This isn't the time or place for you to be choosy."

"It's the perfect time to be choosy," the girl retorted. "Ulvosairs can shapeshift. How do I know you're not just one of them in disguise?"

That wasn't an unfair question. I had forgotten that little nugget about Ulvosairs, but that didn't mean the kid was thinking clearly.

"I understand," I said. "But look at what I'm wearing. This is genuine Galactic Confederation Space Confederaton Marine Mach-4 Armor. It's fitted to me down to the DNA. I can't be an imposter."

"That doesn't mean that I'm telling you my name," the girl said, backing up further. Her voice trembled. "I'm not...I...I just want to go home."

"I understand," I said. "And I want to help you get home. Please..."

"Red," the girl said. "My friends call me Red."

Given everything she was wearing—good grief, even her nail polish was red—that seemed quite the appropriate nickname. But that didn't explain what she was doing here.

"I wasn't supposed to be here," Red said, as if she read my mind. "But I snuck on board the shuttle my grandmother flew in on. I just wanted to spend time with her. She's always so busy."

I winced. There were a lot worse things in the universe than some kid who just wanted to spend time with her grandma.

"Chin up," I said. "There's a squad here and reinforcements coming. Let's get you out of here and I'll find them."

I held out my hand and the girl slowly reached for me. Her fingers curled around my hand, and I pulled her to her feet. She was a tiny bit of a thing.

We walked back the way I'd come. I wasn't sure how long Red had been down here and I wasn't sure I wanted to know the answer. We didn't stop at the crushed elevator shaft I'd come down. Red insisted that it was too dangerous, and given that there were jagged pieces of glass and metal crackling with electricity sticking out all through the shaft, she was right to worry. We walked on until we came to a second freight elevator. It was humming with power, and we shuffled into it. Red pressed the button and the doors closed on us.

"Red," I sighed. This was going to be difficult. "There's been...there's been a lot of fighting up there. There's a pretty good chance that...I hope I'm wrong, but the thing is..."

"I'm not a little girl," Red said, although the tremble in her voice betrayed her lack of confidence. "The Ulvosairs are vicious, but they wouldn't have killed my grandmother. They wouldn't..."

She chewed her lip and shut her eyes for the remainder of the elevator ride. As we got closer to the upper levels, Cane's deep, reassuring tone was discernible even through the doors. Finally, the elevator stopped and the doors flew open.

Ding!

"Gallo!"

Gatto and Cane grabbed me by the arms and yanked me back onto solid floor. Red scampered behind me. The elevator continued to hum behind us, and it continued upward, growing fainter and fainter. Asino and Seppio were a few steps behind and closed the distance between us. Seppio glanced from me to Red and then back again.

"Good to see you're doing well," Asino said. "But...who is this? A stow-away? Child, state your name."

"She calls herself Red," I said. "Says she tagged along to spend time with her grandmother. But she didn't want to tell me anything else, so I don't even know who she's related to. Are the reinforcements here yet? She needs to be evacuated."

"Not yet," Cane said. "One of us will have to act as an escort."

"Oh, I don't think that would be necessary," Seppio said. "I'll take her myself."

"Seppio." Asino shook his head. "You're the only one who knows the layout of the station. We need you. And it's against our protocols to leave a child unattended...we don't even know her real name."

"Her name?" Seppio chuckled. He took a few steps forward. "This is Rosalina Elizabeth Dominga Hermosa Olivia Ortega-Delgado. The ambassador's granddaughter..."

If Seppio had served Ambassador Ortega for even a few years, he would be the one to know that. Red took a step backwards. Seppio took a step closer and smiled, wider than his face should have been able to allow.

"What...what big teeth you have..."

"The better to eat you with!"

Seppio whipped his arms out, slamming Asino to the ground. He lunged for Red, his gold eyes gleaming...gold eyes? The little girl screamed and ran to the side. Gatto swept his knife at Seppio. Seppio chuckled and grabbed the blade. Blue blood poured from his fingertips, but he betrayed no pain as he kicked Gatto backwards. Gatto practically flew from the force of the hit, but he landed on his feet. That was normal for him.

I pulled my pistol from its holster and aimed it at Seppio, but he threw down a small sphere from his belt. He slammed it down and gray smoke bellowed out. A smoke grenade, but a simpler one than the sulfuric gas grenade. I gritted my teeth. The first thing I had learned in the Academy was to treat every weapon as if it were loaded. The second thing I had learned was to never shoot at something I couldn't see. Cane barked an oath and clicked something on his armor. The smoke dissipated at once and I raised my pistol.

"Stop, or she dies, here and now!"

Through the smoke, Seppio had wrapped an arm around Red's chest, pressing her against his body. In his other hand, he held a thin knife to her throat. Red grimaced and squirmed, trying to kick at her captor's legs, but Seppio was tall enough that Red's feet dangled a few inches off the floor. She didn't have the leverage she needed. And none of us had a clear shot that wouldn't risk getting her in the crossfire.

"Let her go."

"I don't think so," Seppio said. "I think I'll keep this little cub for myself. She's young, yes, but with enough meat to make quite the meal."

He lightly ran his knife across Red's cheek. She cried out, in pain and fear and frustration, and blood dripped from the gash onto Seppio's fingers. His eyes flickered and his smile grew wider.

"Oh, I should be thanking you, my friend," Seppio said. "You delivered me just what I wanted. How I've waited for this day…"

Seppio's body began to shift. His face widened, the back of his head growing longer and his nose and mouth stretching down. His fingertips were darkening and sharpening. His clothing burst at the seams as it stretched out. His uniform fell away, leaving behind no shirt and a pair of trousers. Seppio's chest was transparent–his organs were moving about by themselves. Even the flow of his blood was visible. His arms were covered in thick black fur. He bared his teeth into a twisted grin.

"Like it?" Seppio asked. "This is my true body. My brothers and I tend to stick to a more hominid shape in quarters such as these, but sometimes, well…there's only so long I can keep a secret."

Seppio was an Ulvosair, a shapeshifter…and he had played us.

"And now…" Seppio said, dragging Red towards the elevator. The lift was coming back down. The doors opened and four Ulvosairs rushed out, armed to the teeth. Guns, blasters, swords, grenades…four of them against four of us.

"Take them," Seppio said. "They've killed our brothers! Avenge the fallen. Do your duty to our clan!"

He stepped backwards, tightening his grip on Red. The girl gasped and she locked eyes with me just as the doors closed. Wide, terrified, tearful…my stomach churned. The Ulvosairs converged on us. An Ulvosair wielding a sword charged at me. I fired my pistol, over and over and over. A few rounds ricocheted off the sword and a few missed, but the rest struck true. The Ulvosair wasn't slowed, though. I discarded my pistol's magazine and fitted a new one in, just in time for the Ulvosair to crash into me.

I was knocked backwards, and the Ulvosair began punching me in the helmet, trying to break my visor. I kicked out a boot, catching the Ulvosair in the thigh, but he continued his assault. He had one hand around my throat. I couldn't see anything, couldn't reach for my fallen pistol...but I wasn't completely unarmed. I pressed the button to engage my boosters. The propelling flames erupted from my boots, igniting the Ulvosair.

If you know what to listen for, there are slight differences in the way someone screams when they're hurt. Ulvosairs, Earthlings, Martians, Centurians, Sirians, just about everyone has the same screams. A scream is a scream...but no one scream matches any others. A scream of rage is more guttural than a scream of pain or fear. And fire...

Screams from fire are different. Just about every being fears fire. We say we don't, but we do. Fire is a force in its own right. It doesn't think or feel, but it's alive in its own way. And fire is always looking for a way to grow. Fire needs to burn...and right now the Ulvosair was burning as the flames from my boosters consumed it, fur and flesh and what little it wore for armor. I rolled to the side as the Ulvosair screamed, trying to bat away the flames spreading up his chest and arms.

My pistol had fallen to the side. I grabbed it and jumped to my feet, and I pulled the trigger until the magazine ran empty. The Ulvosair laid dead in front of me, still smoldering. I turned my head, just in time to see Gatto stab an Ulvosair through the temple with both of his knives. Cane fired his rifle, catching his opponent in the gut. Asino was fighting hand-to-hand and kicked his opponent squarely in the neck. The Ulvosair flew back and fell to the ground, twitching, his head at an unnatural angle.

"Everyone all right?" Asino asked, looking at each of us in turn. "Let's get moving. We need to catch up with the others."

"Seppio was one of them the whole time." Cane shook his head. "This is my fault. If I hadn't gotten him out of the downed ship..."

"That was a set-up." Asino stomped on a dead Ulvosair's arm for leverage as he pried a sword free from the pirate's grip. "He set us up...he was trying to sabotage us the whole time."

"The metal bridge," Gatto nodded as we walked towards the elevator. "Hmm, this is too obvious, we should try a different path...but Seppio knew the metal bridge was faulty. And firing that blaster to make Gallo fall in the elevator, that was a way to knock us down to three."

"The reinforcements are still on their way, though," I said. "Killing me means one less fighter against him now, but it would only draw more force from the Confederation down the line."

"But take us out and he gets to keep up the facade," Asino said. "And he has the girl as a human shield."

Red. I grit my teeth together so hard, the grinding echoed through my helmet. Children should be off-limits. I'd kill Seppio with my bare hands if that's what it took to get the kid back, and save whoever else was still alive.

"All this from a band of pirates?"

"Is it that surprising? Ambassador Ortega brought down the wrath of God on that band of marauders that stormed her ship over the Pasar-Panex System. And that was before she got into politics. I bet you anything Seppio—if that's even his real name—has been planning this for a long time."

"Enough talk," Cane said. "We fight."

***

It took us less than twenty minutes to find Seppio and Red's trail; the girl had taken to tearing pieces of her cloak off and dropping them along. It could be a trap, but it was also our best option. Sure enough, less than ten minutes later, we found them one level below us. We had the vantage point, but our targets were standing right in front of a smaller hangar, where several escape pods hummed with power.

There were a dozen Ulvosairs left, not counting Seppio. They lined the walls, in a mocking imitation of soldiers standing at attention, while also giving them leverage over their prisoners. Ambassadors, diplomats, aides, secretaries, crew, about twenty-five or thirty people in all. I didn't recognize most of them, but all politicians blend together after a while. Seppio stood over Red. She looked smaller than ever: her cloak was nearly gone, her face was so pale it was gray, bruised and bloodied. Most of her clothing was torn and ripped in places, but she was alive...for now.

"Let my granddaughter go!"

Ambassador Ortega was instantly recognizable: the same snow-white hair, the same square jaw, her eyes were identical to Red's, dressed in a five-piece suit and scarlet shawl.

"I don't think so," Seppio said. "You Confederation types never listen. I have no intention of letting her go. She'll make a fine meal...but I'll make sure she gets to say good-bye to you first, Grandmother Ortega."

Seppio began to laugh, and the other Ulvosairs laughed, as well. Higher pitched than I expected, but every bit as cruel as I would have thought. But it was just the distraction that Asino, Cane, Gatto and I needed.

The four of us fired at once, and four of Seppio's men instantly dropped, the bullets striking them in the heads before the gunshots were even audible. I kicked forward, pressing the button powering my boosters so hard, it cracked. The flames protruding from my boots shot out, pressing me forward. Red screamed and tried to roll out of the way, but Seppio grabbed her by the scruff of her neck. Out of the corner of my eye, I saw Gatto pinned down by two Ulvosair. Cane and Asino were shepherding the prisoners out of the line of fire. One Ulvosair raised an electric pole towards me, but his aim was off and the blast scorched a wall. I tossed a grenade down at the pirate's feet—it exploded before he could get away.

"Seppio!" I roared. "Let the child go!"

"Show me what you've got!"

I charged forward, slamming into Seppio. Red fell to the floor, feebly stirring. We rolled into an open escape pod and my foot caught against a level. With a great lurch, the pod jettisoned outwards, down the attached tunnel. In less than a minute, we would be hurtled into space. I slammed my fist into Seppio's jaw.

This isn't going to work," Seppio growled. "You've lost this one, boy. Your little crew is outnumbered, and even if your precious reinforcements get here, the alliance will fall apart. Too many bodies, too many dead diplomats. My brothers and I have won!"

"You led them to their deaths!" I punched Seppio hard enough to break three of his teeth, but he just began to laugh. "You're a terrorist, a warmonger, a child killer, and all of this for greed and pride?"

"Isn't everything?" Seppio chuckled, blue blood dripping from his torn lips. "You're going to try to kill me for an alliance that doesn't know you from any other sapient. You're a pawn, a serf, a slave, working for overlords who will forget your name. You're nothing to them. You pretend you're better than us, but you aren't. Confederation, Free System, us—we all steal to survive. It's the natural state of things! And I got my pound of flesh. Ortega breeds like a rabbit, but I got her brat."

"You got your own men killed! You tried to kill an innocent child!"

"We all die, sooner or later," Seppio said. "And today's your day to die!"

The escape pod flew out of the exit tunnel, and the hatch that would have sealed the pod broke off entirely. Seppio and I were in outer space. I could see two small ships converging on the shuttle, most of which was on fire. Seppio wore no armor, had no oxygen supply, nothing that could help him survive in the vacuum of space. I watched his eyes dull and grow glassy, but his face was still twisted into a defiant smirk. I wasn't going to give him the satisfaction. I aimed my pistol and pulled the trigger.

There's no sound in space, but I still felt the recoil travel up my arm. A perfectly round hole appeared in the center of his chest, tearing through what might have been his liver. It was hard to tell with the way that his organs still shifted around, but the defiant smirk was gone. Seppio's eyes widened and then grew completely still. He was dead or would be so in another second or two. I kicked away. His body could be recovered by the reinforcements.

I turned around. We were far from the station now. The button controlling my boosters had cracked and now it was sticking. Flames shot out and propelled me forward. I had less than five minutes to get back to some semblance of safety before my suit's survival systems were completely compromised.

One one-thousand, two one-thousand...

A larger ship had emerged during my fight with Seppio. Foam was being sprayed onto some of the fires, smothering them. The station would be salvageable, though maybe the Confederation would take care to have an advance guard going forward. The flame-suppressant foam had a sheen to it, like stars.

Three one-thousand, four one-thousand...five one-thousand, six one-thousand...seven one-thousand.

I crashed through the opening left by the jettisoned pod and landed hard. Something cracked—armor or bone, I couldn't be sure—and I skidded across the floor. So many fires were burning.

Asino, Cane, Gatto...they had to still be alive. We'd fought enough Ulvosairs, even a dozen at once couldn't be too much for those three. They were the best men I'd ever known.

Had Red and her grandmother and the others been shepherded to safety? That had been the mission. Save the diplomats, secure the station, save the day... The mission came before all...

Something very heavy fell from the ceiling and landed on my legs. More hurt, more breaking. I couldn't move. This was the end of my story, but if the day was saved, that was enough...

❧❧❧❧❧ ❧❧❧❧❧

I opened my eyes slowly. It took a long time. It was as if my eyes were still asleep, but eventually, I managed and I got my bearings. I was in a small room, lying on a bed. White walls with light blue trim. There was a framed flag of the Galactic Confederation on one wall. Sitting in a chair, resting his eyes, was Gatto. He awoke in a flash, and a thin, wide smile spread across his face.

"Gallo, you're awake! Well, you've been waking up and falling back asleep over and over the last three days, and that after a month in a coma...I guess I should ask whether you're lucid."

"Gatto?" I groaned and leaned my head back. It wasn't easy. Both my legs were in casts and my arm was splinted. An IV was set up next to my bed and pouring...something into my bloodstream. Whatever it was, it was green. I decided I didn't want to know. "What...what happened?"

"You got crushed by one of those support beams," Gatto said. "Scared Ortega Junior to death, but Asino and Cane pulled you out of there. But you were in rough shape—your emergency systems were damaged, so you were almost dead from exposure before the crash landing. Got you in traction and then got you stabilized and then got you moved out of intensive quarantine into here. We've been taking it in shifts to keep an eye on you."

I wasn't sure how to reply. It had been a very long time since I've had someone looking out for me like that. Before I could even try to say anything, the door at the end of the room opened and Cane and Asino were there. Cane was holding a thick book in one hand, but he tucked it under his arm as he walked towards me and grasped my unbandaged hand with both of his.

"Thank the Creator," Cane said. "Red will be most pleased to hear that you're awake."

"No visits just yet," Asino said, holding up a hand. "We've got...we've got some things to discuss."

"How many casualties?"

"The Ulvosairs killed nine," Cane said. "But we killed every single one of them. We rescued thirty-two, plus a dozen escape pods filled with people. You're a hero, Gallo."

"I don't really feel like a hero."

"Good," Asino said. "Duty is heavier than mountains and humility will keep you up at night, but it's better than the alternative where you stop caring for the fallen and realize you no longer save anyone. Enough about that for now. We'll move forward, together...just remember to keep living."

It was bizarre seeing Asino dressed in even casual fatigues, and part of me wondered whether it was the medicine coursing through my veins. It was even stranger to hear him put our duties on the backburner. It was lunacy when he pulled out a small harmonica from his pocket.

"How are you at music?" Asino smiled, handing me the harmonica. "As it happens, Cane, Gatto and I are musicians, and we need a fourth man."

I stared at him for the longest minute of my life and then I took the harmonica.

My name is Gallo. I am a Space Confederaton Marine of the Galactic Confederation, out of the Bremen Division.

If you're in trouble, rest assured, I'll be there.

THE END

One Way Out

EVAN DESHAIS

THERE IS BUT ONE way out of the Force Recon (FR) teams. I know that, and so does every FR trooper. We remote pilots are so rare and precious that we cannot let go of the obligations we hold. We stay in the fight too long. I am that man in the mirror. Yet, here I am, planning to break that tradition.

I am older and I've new scars on my face and many more on my body. The mottled pink lines are souvenirs from my life in the teams. Some are old scars, healed and barely discernible from my normal skin tone. These new scars, though, are terrifying. I look at them and know paralyzing fear. This war is over, and I make up my mind: I'm done with war in general. It is time for me to make a new life, one outside of the teams.

I inspect my scars, as shaving them is a pain in the ass. My collar and jacket are perfect, and I settle my cover on my head. I turn to the open FEED display and close out the message from my mother. I shift in my small cabin aboard the *Cataphract*. I am not special enough to rate private accommodations; I am the last of my roommates alive. The other FR team members who shared this cabin took the one way out. If not for me, then for them, I must make a new life. We made Titan station a week ago, and before I muster out of the teams, I've one last task.

I pick up the folder at the communal desk and tap it against my thigh. I have the whole file memorized. My FEED system beeps, and I exit into my cabin's airlock. Twenty minutes later, I am sitting in a vestibule of a conference room. I've skimmed the file twice since arriving.

There is a crackle-pop from one of the Compact Space Merchant Service (CSMS) MKVI SkipJacks guarding the hatch into the main conference space. I get the nod from the SkipJack and stand. I straighten and nod back to the SkipJack and the pilot who commands it from some pod deep within the *Cataphract's* hull.

"CMS Mateo, the admiralty board is ready," a pod head trooper says through his MKVI.

The airlock hatch hisses open, and I step inside. Two minutes later, its opposite hatch opens. I step into a longer than wide room. At the opposite end of the space stands one Admiral and four Commodores. I hold my salute while they finish conferring. With a flash from the Admiral's hand, I am released.

"Take a seat, CSM Mateo," the *Cataphract's* acting Commodore says.

I do not remember this man's name, as we had lost the first and second commanders of the *Cataphract* in the war with the Thraxyian Alliance. I remember acting Commodore Ruel, but I have no clue who this man is. I nod, remove my cover, and pull out my chair. I place the folder squarely in front of me.

"You've put in a Sargent Bronsky," Admiral Preston Woody says, "for a campaign star cluster." The Admiral's eyes look from his FEED to me. "I've got dozens of candidates for a campaign star cluster."

The idea of a pod head sargent being recommended for a medal by an FR team CSM is laughable. Yet somehow, my request warrants an Admiralty oral board. I know Sgt Bronsky now; while he wasn't my instructor when I went through FR selection, he trained those who trained me. Moreover,

I'm the only FR team member alive who experienced the action on the Einarin homeworld.

"Why?" Admiral Woody says. "He isn't even a remote pilot."

"Sir, I have several reasons," I explain. "If not the action I list, then certainly he deserves a medal for his actions during the retaking of the Cruiser *LeMat*. Aside from my own experience with Sgt. Bronsky during the recovery mission on the Einarin homeworld, I've seen him lead pod head troopers and FR team members. Second, he trained almost all the remaining FR team members. Lastly, he was personally picked by the Lion of the Compact to train the FR teams in remote piloting."

"He's over a hundred," the second Commodore on the right says. "Well into his fifth term of service. How is he even fit for combat as a pod head, let alone well enough to participate in these combat drops?"

"He passed all his physical and psyche stress tests," I say. "FR team Blue was hard-pressed when Able squad landed."

The Admiral holds his finger off the table, and the conference room stills. The *Cataphract's* Commodore closes his mouth, and I let my answer fall from my mind.

"I won't lie, CMS Mateo," Admiral Woody says, drumming his fingers. "I had hoped you would take the offered Officer Candidate School slot. The FR teams will need competent leadership in the years to come. Colonel War told me you wouldn't, but I want to ask: is that still your answer?"

The non sequitur question throws me. Is this inquiry a way to leverage me to reenlist in the teams? A quid pro quo? If I take the OCS slot, does Sgt Bronsky get his medal? Obviously, they don't know Bronsky; he'd pawn the medal to pay for a lap dance. I nod, not trusting my voice to betray me. This horrific war is over. I've fought and bled for twenty-five years; I'm done with war, and I will not go out feet first.

"Very well," Admiral Woody says. "Can you detail the action that took place on the Einarin homeworld to recover our prisoners of war?"

※※※※ ※※※※

I looked up and down the FR team's dropship hold; there were eleven other men and their MKVI SkipJacks. As I pilot a Chicken Walker MKII (CW), I'm the lone man out. Major Blue turned to me and nodded. The light in the bay flashed orange.

"Secure your SkipJack," I said into my helmet's pick-up. "Charge weapons; see yourselves secured in your drop spikes."

The men bustled about the drop bay, securing their gear. This mission was a Hail Mary pass. Fleet intel said several of our captured dropships made it down to the surface. There was a possibility that some of the crews were alive and were captive.

Humanity could not allow ourselves to be prisoners of the combined alien races known as the People of the Thraxyian Alliance. If the People managed to get a breeding pair of humans, our efforts in this war were lost. Therefore, our mission was clear: rescue or sterilize the captured CSMS personnel.

I stepped up to the first drop tube to check the trooper's MKVI, then the trooper in his drop spike. My eyes visually checked as my hands physically confirmed everything was secure. My hammer fist slammed the red button between the two compartments. The two doors sealed shut, and I watched the visor of his helmet go opaque. One by one, I checked all the men, Major Blue following behind me, stabbing the second button with his thumb.

"All the men are clear for drop, CSM," Major Blue said.

"Don't worry, sir," I quipped. "I'll tuck you in nice and tight. Let me get El Diablo tucked in first."

Blue's hand patted my shoulder as he stepped to his MKVI Command Variant SkipJack. I made my way back to my Chicken Walker. I've remotely piloted SkipJacks since I was a kid, first in the factory brawls that helped to feed my family, and then for the New North Americas Compact. It wasn't until I was asked to help upgrade the CWs to the new MKII that I came into my own. I locked El Diablo into its much larger drop spike. I manually charged its weapons and triple-checked its attachment points.

I looked down the bay to Major Blue; he gave me a thumbs-up as he charged his personal carbine (PC) and stowed it in his drop spike. I wished we could have dropped with a complete sixteen-trooper team, but there weren't many of us left. Hell, I was one of five CW pilots remaining in the FR teams. I didn't like being down four troopers, working on a team I've never worked with, or dropping onto a hostile planet for a smash-and-grab of our people held hostage by who-knew-what forces.

I closed the hatch to El Diablo's drop spike and stepped down to Major Blue.

"Think we can do it?" Blue asked.

"If anyone can, it's us, sir," I said.

"We can't leave our people there," Blue said. "Not with how they use us for their blood magics."

I checked my visor's HUD. Major Blue's vitals showed an increased heartrate, and even his temperature was a bit high. Was it pre-drop excitement or jitters? Unfortunately, I didn't have a way of knowing, and it was too late now to do anything about an illness. We were three days into this ballistic run and two days past our point of no return.

"We got this," I said. "We've been over the intel. It looks good; all we have to do is secure the area where they're holding our dropships. When we've secured the beachhead, the pod heads will come behind us with their dropship and start a systematic sweep for our people."

"Bring hell from the ground," Major Blue said.

"And spread it around," I said, completing the shortened FR motto.

We bumped helmets and slapped backs.

The Major stepped into his drop spike, and I triple-checked his gear. With a double-tap on his buttons, I sealed him in. I made my way over to my drop spike and prepped my gear. Once ready, I stepped inside. I cleared for the drop with a command from my FEED unit.

⁕⁕⁕

The new Commodore of the *Cataphract* breaks the flow of my recounting of the battle. "The mission was clear to FR Team Blue?"

"Yes, sir," I respond. "We knew our responsibilities. Secure the landing area, ping for CSMS ship-suit transponders and provide location data to the incoming pod heads."

"You had other," Admiral Woody begins, and after a long, thoughtful pause, "less dignified orders."

"We did, sir," I say. "If humans could be found but not retrieved, we were to sterilize the prisoners."

The panel of four Commodores turn to the Admiral, their faces tight with shock. Admiral Woody's face remains stoic as he looks at each of them. Commodore Brigitteson from Battlevessel *Jomsviking* turns to me.

"Would you explain what you mean by sterilize?" Commodore Brigitteson asks.

"Humanity is the Thraxyian Alliance's best food source for their combined peoples," I explain. "We breed fast and require little effort to sustain. Moreover, we are their most potent source of blood for their magics." Then, I turn to look at each of the four. "The Einar, the Murinn, the Dumnin, the Oni, the Muki and their warrior thralls, the Thrax, only need a few breeding pairs to restore their empire. Therefore, our orders were to deny them that option at all costs."

"The preference was on the recovery of our people?" The *Cataphract's* Commodore asks with wide eyes.

"It was," I say.

❧❧❧❧ ❧❧❧❧

Major Blue said, "I want suppressing fire on that cluster of Oni."

I dashed from one of our downed dropships to another even as El Diablo started shucking railgun darts at the Oni priestesses. The first few layers of shields these ugly ladies put up buckled under its fire. I peeked around the corner and turned back, waving my squad forward. My two remaining men dash ahead, using their MKVI's to provide covering fire from the Einarin slingers of magics.

"Baker is gone," Sargent Beets said. "Ice lance through the neck."

"That's four dead," Major Blue said on our private comms.

"They were waiting for us," Beets said.

"I've got no CSMS ID pings," our comms tech Algron said. "If they're here, they aren't wearing their ship-suits."

"None?" I groused. "Check for FEED system links; I doubt the People figured out how to remove those."

I lost track of the conversation between Beets and our comms tech. Instead, I focused on using El Diablo to put down this batch of Oni priestesses. These bitches were hard to kill, especially when they had a ready supply of enslaved sacrifices to fuel their blood magics.

Through El Diablo, I let loose another half-dozen railgun rounds into their wall of magical shields. I watched the trio of hags as they buckled under the strain of keeping their magic shield barriers up.

"Alley-oop," I said over comms. "Mortars inbound on the Oni from Diablo."

Pwoomp, pwoomp, pwoomp resounded through the courtyard where our dropships were parked. The trio of 120mm mortars arced high into the sky. A dozen blasts of fire and galvanic lightning streaked upwards to meet them. It was too late, as modern mortars were gauss-driven. If you reacted to them, you were already behind them—in other words, dead. Three loud pops echoed as the mortars separate, and their intelligent munitions dropped toward the beleaguered priestesses.

"Comms," I said, "ETA on the pod heads?"

The smart munitions started striking the Oni's redeployed shields. El Diablo fired six rounds of railgun darts. The priestesses had a choice: they could defend against my railguns darts or defend against the intelligent munitions.

I honestly don't know what killed them first. I peeked around the dropship and saw the whole southeast corner of our beachhead had turned to rubble from the mortars. The line of collared Einarin sacrifices was a red-brown smudge of dead and broken pointy-eared bodies.

"Comms?" I repeated.

"Comms is down," Sgt Beets said. his strangled gurgle lets me know the northwest side is still under heavy pressure.

I turned to the north and saw Major Blue's squad advancing to support the remainder of Beets's men.

⁂

"The point of that speech, CSM Mateo?" The *Cataphract's* Commodore asks.

"To illustrate how the Thraxyian Alliance changed its tactics. This mission was a trap, a chance to bring more humans within their grasp. They did not expect an FR team. The Thraxyian Alliance knows how to deceive, how to plan. They may not have long-range weapons as we do, but in those last months of the war, we had taught them how to understand Humanity well enough to lure us into a trap," I explain.

"Is that commentary on the mission, CSM Mateo?" the Commodore of the *Hessian* battlevessel asks.

"No, sir," I reply. "The intel was solid. We landed amid seven of our pod head dropships. Each one of those contains 144 pods, nine heavy lift trams (HLT), seven crew, and slots for 144 MKVI SkipJacks. They landed safely, somehow. The chances of the Thraxyian Alliance having live human prisoners was substantial. Moreover, the chances of them having multiple breeding pairs across all the pods and crew were also considerable."

"You didn't think the mission a folly then?" Admiral Woody asks, his steepled hands flexing together.

"The missions on the elder Masters in space were suicide runs for the teams and pod heads," I say. "We lost millions of men on those drops, and I know them to be worth the effort. The possibility that some of our people made it to the surface as prisoners is not something I would discount. No, sir, I do not consider this effort to save a few dozen prisoners a folly."

My two squadmates traded fire with a group of Einarin spell casters. I targeted the buildings the Einarin spell weavers were concealed in and fired El Diablo's guns. The railgun darts easily pierced the Einarin glossy stone building.

"We are good, Top," said Pastole.

"Major Blue," Said a thick, raspy voice. "This is Sargent Bronsky of Able squad. Our drop spikes are free and inbound as support. Spikes, landing in seven, six, five..."

I shifted my PC to my shoulder and fired a three-round burst into a Murinn skulking up out of a nearby waterway. The trio of 6.5mm rounds put the frog man down. In my mindspace, El Diablo shifted its sensors to cover the water channels and my men to the right of me. A group of the short Dumnin people exited a building, dragging what was left of our comm tech's body.

I knew he was dead, as half his leg and a section of his lower abdomen were missing. The quartet of Dumnin dragged the corpse with its entrails spilling across the ground. A lone Oni gestured from inside a doorway to them as the first of Able squad's drop spikes hit the ground. A staccato of explosions resounded in the courtyard as the drop spikes expeled the piloted MKVI SkipJacks.

"What's your latency, Sgt Bronsky?" I asked over comms.

"Not as good as yours," Bronsky answered. "We're here, ain' we? Charlie squad is dropping in sixty seconds."

"I need ten men split between the Northeast and West, Sgt. Bronsky," Major Blue said. "Mateo, you get the six remaining."

I knew of Bronsky; I'd reviewed the after-action of the retaking of the *LeMat*. "Sgt. Bronsky," I said on a private comms channel. "Stay on Blue actual."

Two clicks from his mic hit my ears. In moments, his MKVIs were at my men's side. The ping was atrocious; they were walking targets for the magics of the People. Thankfully, it took a lot of magic to directly hurt a 250-kilo steel war machine.

There was a significant difference between pod head pilots and the FR teams. The pod heads had a container that took the mental computing power off their brains and extrapolated that into actions. The pilots were separated from most conflicts by that pod. They piloted their SkipJacks from that pod inside an HLT, and the further away they were from their SkipJacks, the slower their MKVIs' reaction time.

Those of us in the FR teams were remote pilots. We carried the mental mass of piloting in a separate mind space. We fought and piloted as two separate entities, human and SkipJack, not one. We in the FR teams had double our firepower, often at the cost of our lives.

El Diablo fired a staccato of rounds, pinning the Oni priestess down long enough for my reinforced squad to put down her Dumnin thralls.

"Incoming Thrax," Major Blue said. "It's the Canton's border guard. Maybe two score of them."

"Well, ain't they some ugly sons of bitches," Bronsky said into comms. "Able squad, partner up with an FR trooper. Stay calm; Charlie squad has a docking collar delay and their HLT can't separate from the dropship yet."

Thrax are the warrior class of the People, living carbon-silica beings. They looked like a cross between a silver-blue wasp and a mantis. They lived to feed. I'd fought my fair share of Thrax on Earth Prime, and on the elder Masters in space. The Thrax could live for extended periods in space with minimal survival gear. Putting down Thrax was why El Diablo was designed. I started to shift El Diablo to the north.

"Mateo, keep our rear clear," Major Blue said.

❧❧❧❧❧ ❧❧❧❧❧

"Were you in disagreement with the order to protect the rear?" the Commodore of the *Hessian* asks.

"I understood Major Blue's reasoning," I say. "It turned out I was initially needed to guard the rear."

"Can you elaborate?" the same Commodore asks.

"The Frigate that launched our dropships was attacked in orbit by a newly awoken elder Master," I explain. "It was a moderate-sized Master, not one the hundred appendaged moon-sized monstrosities that we faced early in the war. It had more maneuverability than we initially expected. The pod head dropship that Able squad detached their HLT from was recalled. Able squad knew we were in a pickle. Able squad's HLT fell from orbit." I shift my hand to my FEED system and thumb over the sensor packets I compiled. "Sgt Bronsky's decision saved Able squad along with our mission. Moments later, the elder Master turned several of its lenses on the pod head dropship. The other eight squads never made it back to their berth."

"How many of you are there on the surface at this point?" the Commodore of the *Cataphract* asks.

"Roughly four other FR troopers, with their MKVIs, myself with El Diablo, and Able squad's sixteen active MKVIs operating off his squad's HLT," I explain.

"HLTs are not rated for planetary insertion," *Cataphract's* Commodore says, his disapproval clear.

"They are not," I agree. "Sgt. Bronsky's pilots landed it with vigor."

"Carry on, CSM Mateo," Admiral Woody interjects, stopping the flow of questions from the acting *Cataphract* Commodore.

A pair of creases grace the corners of his eyes. I get the distinct impression he's smiling, even if the rest of his face doesn't show it.

❦

I heard the fighting kick off to the north through my helmet's pick-ups. The thrum of the Thrax disruptor weapons was only discernible over the sounds of battle because of its unearthly sound. I keyed up my two FR squad members.

"Start moving the alpacas with their ammo and power cells to Blue," I said.

Mic clicks returned. The alpacas were an FR team's legs. They carried our mesh uplinks for remote piloting, extra power cells for the MKVIs, and, most importantly, a crap-ton of ammo. I watched the pair disengage from a firefight with a group of mixed Einarin and Dumnin spell weavers. I leveled El Diablo's rail guns at the mixed batch of magic casters while putting a couple of bursts from my 6.5mm carbine their way.

"ETA on Charlie Squad?" I asked Sgt. Bronsky.

I turned my head to the sky so my HUD could pick up the pod head's dropship. The screen filled with plots, dots, and vectors. There were too many. One dot was headed straight for us, and another angled back towards the Frigate it launched from.

"Small change of plans," Bronsky said. "The dropship was recalled, Able squad's entering atmo, and we're coming in hard and fast."

I locked my eyes on the quickly approaching dot and its vector from the planetary North Pole.

"Sgt. Bronsky," Major Blue said. "Where is Lt. Wang?"

"Didn't make it off the last drop," Sgt. Bronsky said. "My pilot wants to know where to park?"

There was a short few seconds' pause before Major Blue responded, "South end. It puts you under CSM Mateo's cover and close to an actual dropship. Get us a new ride off this rock."

Bronsky wasn't slow on the uptake.

"Roger that. The HLT is spent, or will be. Able squad will cover my pilots and cycle my men to new pods in a new dropship," Bronsky said.

At this point, the flaming vapor trail of Able squad's HLT was evident when I looked up. Some would say that the CSMS contracts often went to the lowest bidder, but sometimes the CSMS overbuilt things. The dropships and the HLTs nestled within them were far more durable than bean counters wanted. Who would have anticipated an HLT riding the air currents from orbit flaming like a comet?

"The Thrax are thinning," one of my FR teammates said over comms.

"Get back on that FEED system sweep," Major Blue barked.

I shifted around a dropship while piloting El Diablo onto a ruined building. I started tagging hostiles in my HUD and dispensing hypersonic justice via El Diablo's railguns.

I turned my head upwards as the roar of Bronsky's HLT picks up. I watched the smoking nacelles and its nose pitch upward as they tried to halt their forward momentum. The HLT was nearly vertical now as it screamed over the courtyard my team had secured.

El Diablo lashed out at several new Einarin and Dumnin that stepped forward to take their shot at downing a damaged vessel. A message popped up in my HUD.

"I'm going to need a reload evolution," I said.

The HLT leveled out horizontally and fell the remaining thirty feet to the ground, crushing its landing skids. Able squad's ride was blackened and smoking, but it was down.

"I have a couple of men who can do that evolution," Sargent Bronsky said. "Prentice, Warnum, reload evolution on the CW. The rest of you apes cycle out of your pods as ordered."

Maybe half a minute later, a pair of MKVIs dragged over my ammo spike. Inside were four quick-change canisters of railgun darts. The CW MKII took four, one for each of its railguns. With 200 rounds per canister, it gave me much to say about what happened during this mission. While the men were cycling out the empty dart cans of El Diablo, a quartet of their peers were guarding the three pilots as they ran from the flaming HLT to a dropship.

The pilots shifted from the first dropship to a second and finally a third.

"Sgt. Bronsky," a female voice said. "I've got our ride. Three full HLTs. Putting up marker now."

"Start cycling out of the pods, apes," Sgt Bronsky bellowed.

"Major Blue," Corporal Dillon, one of my FR team members, said. "I've got FEED pings."

The world and comms turned surreally quiet for a fleeting moment with that statement. I could hear my heartbeat as I waited for more info.

"Eighty," Dillon remarked offhandedly. "Half a click to the north. It looks like that large building one block up."

"Roger that," Major Blue said. "Sgt. Bronsky, get your men swapped over to the new pods. CSM Mateo, get that evolution done, but keep El Diablo on overwatch there."

A series of double mic clicks passed up the line as we acknowledged the shift in our orders.

"I've got four FR troopers up here with me," Major Blue said. "The Thrax advance was crushed; we've got a window to advance. Mateo, you bring up the rear while keeping El Diablo on overwatch. Bronsky, soon as your guys boot into their new MKVIs, get us a defended path back to that dropship."

"Seventy-nine," Corporal Dillon said. "Seventy-eight. Fuuuuck!" he growled into coms. "We are down to seventy-four."

"Sacrifices," Major Blue said. "Hustle it, boys."

"Apes," Sgt Bronsky barked, "you heard the Major. Do we want to live forever?"

I swapped out my PC mag on the run. I was half a kilometer behind the remainder of my FR Team.

❧❧❧❧❧ ❧❧❧❧❧

"Were there casualties in the HLT's vigorous landing?" the lone female Commodore asks.

"If I remember correctly, the pod heads had some bumps and bruises," I say. "One pilot suffered a hairline fracture in their left wrist, but it is unclear when that happened."

"You left the pod heads without your personal supervision for cover?" the *Cataphract's* Commodore asks.

"CSM Mateo is an FR trooper," Admiral Woody interjects. "He pilots his SkipJack without the aid of a pod."

"Doctrine says," the *Cataphract's* acting Commodore begins.

"I have it on good authority," the Admiral says, his hand and frown stopping the acting Commodore from interjecting further, "that CSM Mateo is the finest CW pilot in the CSMS."

There are a pair of people Admiral Woody would consider an authority. I shift my gaze from Admiral Woody to the acting Commodore. His eyes harden, but he relents on trying to pin the limited success of this debacle on me. I suppose being personally recruited by the Empress of Earth and her former FR team member husband as a young man buys me a little respect.

I am not one to trade on my friendships; I am a man who lets his deeds speak for themselves. I have as many combat drops in my twenty-five years as any in the FR teams.

"There's generally but one way out of the teams," Admiral Woody says in a mild voice to the *Cataphract's* frustrated Commodore. "CSM Mateo has beaten all the odds and buried nearly everyone he knew and worked with. So leave it be, John."

The Commodore's head turns from me to the Admiral, and his jaw sets, his lips pale as he tries not to wear his emotions on his face.

I don't know what I could have done to piss in the Commodore's breakfast, but I am glad for the change in his demeanor as he nods to the Admiral and turns back to me.

"My apologies, CSM Mateo," the *Cataphract's* acting Commodore says. "I knew Ruel. We...well, we grew up together. We've been friends for decades, or were friends. Commodore Ruel was my best man at my wedding and my children's godfather. To have him die of an aneurysm months after those forced disconnects...well."

I nod in sympathy. So that is how Commodore Ruel died.

"I did what medical I could when I helped General Janks pull him from the pod," I say. "The Captain of the *Cataphract* didn't recover quickly from the initial focused attack from the elder Master's lens. Commander Ruel and his staff booted in right after, but the damn Master hit the *Cataphract* with a second gaze from its lens," I explain.

"I kept Commodore Ruel stable while the emergency medical team was still working on the original forced disconnected crew. Commander Ruel came around and was up in just over three minutes. Yes, that's a bit longer than recommended, but he wouldn't let the medical teams look him over.

"When the *Cataphract's* fight with the elder Master was losing steam," I say with a sudden tightness in my throat, "Commander Ruel and his team stepped in to help shoulder the burden."

The Commodore stares down at his hands. He closes his eyes and breathes deeply.

"Thank you, again," the Commodore says quietly. "My sincerest apologies, CSM Mateo. I didn't know that he refused medical. That is something he would do."

I give a curt nod. It is a rare day a senior officer apologizes, let alone twice. I let the issue drop and shift a half-dozen FEED files to the board assembled here.

"What happened when Major Blue made it to the building?" the Admiral asks, while looking at the *Cataphract's* Commodore.

⧼⧼⧼⧼ ⧽⧽⧽⧽

"Corporal Dillon," Major Blue said. "Are the charges placed?"

"Yes, sir," Dillon responded. "Sixteen, we'll have four entrance points."

"Sgt. Bronsky," Major Blue said. "How long until our path back to the dropship is secure?"

"The last of us are reaching our positions now," Bronsky replied.

"Mateo," Blue said. "Anything headed our way?"

"No," I replied as I piloted El Diablo in a circle. I used its enhanced sensors to pick out targets and stragglers. "It's as if they're holding back or maybe pulling back. Nothing is closer than 1,600 meters. I can reach out and hit them, but doing so might spur them to attack."

"No, if they move in, open up at 1,200 meters," Blue said. "How does our way back look?" Major Blue asked on a private comms.

"Sgt. Bronsky knows his stuff," I said. "He's got the high point covered for us, and I hear the dropship's grav drives spooling up."

"Dillon," Blue said, "Blow us some doors in five."

After two mic clicks and five long heartbeats, a rapid succession of thrums resounded through the neighborhood. The pressure wave hit my chest 500 meters away, but I felt little of it through my armor and gear. That was another area where the CSMS didn't skimp on resources. Our protective gear was the best humanity could create. This gear had saved my life on more than one drop in the last six months of fighting.

"Go, go, go," Dillon said.

I watched my HUD as my four FR teammates dashed into the complex behind their piloted MKVIs. I couldn't see through the dust and haze hanging in the air, but I heard muted screams and the weapons fire of our MKVIs' 20mm and 25mm guns. The shorter bark-like sounds of my team members' 6.5mm personal carbine rounds echoed in three-round bursts.

"Dillon is sending them out, CSM Mateo. push them back to the drop-ship," Major Blue ordered.

The weapons fire inside the building increased. I watched the tally of active FEED units on my HUD plummet from sixty-five to thirty-one instantly. Finally, a spiraling tornado of galvanic fire blasted through the roof of the building as the first hostages exited our improvised doorways. I pointed, yelled and gestured for the naked hostages to head down the cleared path to the dropships.

"Contact," Sgt. Bronsky said. "They need to get a move on."

El Diablo began firing as a wave of hidden Einarin spell weavers appeared near the corridor to our dropships.

"Thrax inbound," said one of Bronsky's men. "At least fifty of the damn insects."

El Diablo shifted as Bronsky's team marked the incoming Thrax for my HUD.

I growled. "Fuckers, let me show you why they call me El Diablo." I toggled my CW's fire control systems and swapped from single shot to triple round bursts. There was little recoil with the railguns; I could drop three rounds on the same 40mm spot within one-tenth of a second of each other. My chicken-walking devil began laying out hate and discontent to the Thrax. I delivered multiple rounds stitched through their unique central nervous systems to end their lives swiftly. I'd fought Thrax many times before, and this was kind of work that I loved doing.

I pushed the freed prisoners past me, turning them in the right direction down our cleared causeway to the dropship. It was an easy path to follow, but I had yell at them to run. With the noise of battle, and the explosives now rebounding in the main building, it took the shambling CSMS personnel a moment to start rushing.

"Something is here," Major Blue said. "The Oni priestesses are down, but something is moving and pulling the sacrificed blood into the center."

"Keep moving," I bellowed through my helmet's speaker. "Follow the SkipJacks."

A second firefight broke out inside the worked-stone building. I watched as the number of FEED connections on my HUD dipped even further. We dropped from thirty-one to twenty in a matter of two heartbeats.

"There're more Oni on the south side," Corporal Dillon said.

"Frag them," Major Blue ordered.

I watched Major Blue and his MKVI SkipJack shove people out of one of the four entrance points.

"Frag out," Dillon said.

My sensors detected the blip of the MKVI's 40mm high explosive grenade, followed by three more. The resulting explosions sent ripples of cracks through the finely worked alabaster stone building.

"That's it," Major Blue said, "Dillon, Fagen, cover our pull back."

There were double mic clicks in the affirmative as Major Blue and our fourth man, Private Saren, exited their improvised doorways. Our fourth stooped to help up one of the freed prisoners that stumbled over some rubble. The last three naked prisoners shambled past my location while I encouraged the stragglers of the fifteen recovered CSMS personnel onward.

I turned back to watch the exit as Fagen popped through his opening, followed by Dillon. Moments later, their MKVIs backed out, letting loose a pair of frag tube rounds near the wall they had entered through. It didn't take much to bring that side of the building down.

"CSM Mateo," Major Blue said. "Let them bring up the rear. "It seems like Sgt. Bronsky has things in hand, but I would feel better if an FR man is there at the dropship to smooth things over."

I tapped my mic twice and conducted a final sweep before falling back toward our dropship.

❊❊❊❊❊ ❊❊❊❊❊

"CSM Mateo," the *Cataphract's* Commodore says, "we recovered a dozen prisoners, yet you just told us fifteen." He looks up from his FEED screen, and the stare sticks me firmly in my seat. "We went from eighty active FEED connections to less than fifteen in under six minutes." His hand scrolls through his FEED screen. "By the official timeline, Major Blue's team spent less than two minutes inside the building where they were held. Is it possible other prisoners remained alive?"

I swallow hard, anger, frustration, and bile boiling in my gut. I had thought his apologies were genuine, but clearly they were not, and I am more the fool for believing him. This man has an axe to grind, and as such, he has no business being in command. I highly doubt he has faced a Master of the Thraxyian alliance during this entire campaign.

"No, Commodore," I say. "The rite used by the Oni is their most sacred. They bind the blood and flesh of the slaughtered and give it a new life. The Oni priestesses were slaughtering their collared Murinn and Muki slaves for weeks, but the rite kicked into overdrive when they got their hands on humans. Those remaining sixty-five human prisoners allowed them to succeed in bringing a new Master into life."

I thumb a FEED image of the moment the newly-born Master exited the building's rubble to the seated panel.

"The Empress and Colonel War confirmed that this is a young Master in their review of the action," I explain. "The young Masters only have the central lens when born; as they age, they gain other appendages with more specialized lenses." I pause and thumb forward a short video to the Admiral. "This is a video of Private Fagen's last moments."

Admiral Woody forwards my FEED vid to the conference table's central display.

"As you can see, we were falling back in good order," I explain, pausing the short vid. "At this point, the dozen prisoners that lived are less than 400 meters from the reclaimed dropship. I am roughly 600 meters from the same dropship. Private Fagen, Corporal Dillon, Major Blue, Private Saren, and the last three humans are about seventy-five meters from me. This puts them within 400 meters of the Master."

I resume the video. The prisoners run and shamble through the Einarin causeway, the pod heads' MKVIs urging them along. Major Blue and Private Saren are just behind them. They and their remotely piloted MKVIs pause and turned around to provide cover for Private Fagen and Corporal Dillon.

This leapfrogging pattern continues until the rubble moves. Private Fagen and Corporal Dillon spin at the sound, their MKVIs locking on the moving debris as the young Master lifts from the ground to hover about seven meters above the rubble.

The Master lacks the telltale appendages of its elder brethren in space, but the central lens and its hide marks it as one of the space-faring Masters that rules the People who make up The Thraxyian Alliance. Moments after it clears the rubble, rounds of 20mm and 25mm fire from Private Fagen and Corporal Dillon echo through the streets. The Master rocks under the impacts and shifts, and the chitinous lens focuses on their SkipJacks.

I pause the video again. "Here is where things go disastrously wrong," I say. "The Masters, even as young as this one, can use their central lens to hold debris in midair or feed themselves food. As you are about to see, once it focused on our MKVIs, and the rounds from it weapons stopped long before they could harm the Master. The central lens is the only lens the Masters have that could forcefully disconnect an FR trooper, pod head, or pilot on a CSMS vessel in space. The older they get, the further they can focus their various lenses."

The five-member panel watches as the central lens turns upon Fagen, hidden behind the cover. Private Fagen is dragged up from behind cover by forces unseen and lifted high into the air. His arms and legs are flailing for purchase on anything.

One moment he is alive and struggling for freedom, and the next, his body is ripped apart into constituent components. Meat separated from bone, skin from the meat, and his blood from everything. His blood forms a whirling ball that makes its way to the new Master.

The Master's lens roll upward as it slurps the blood with its chitinous beak. The few wounds we have managed to give it begin to heal even as El Diablo begins laying triple taps into it from each of its four railguns.

The central lens rotates to El Diablo, and my railgun rounds are diverted in midflight, even as the Master's beak continues to slurp Private Fagen's lifeblood.

The panel is silent as my FEED vid ends. The central display closes, and the four Commodores turn to Admiral Woody. Three of them display the grim looks of people who have seen this horror firsthand when fighting the elder Masters in space. The last and newest Commodore from the

Cataphract is ashen and turning greener by the moment. My opinion of him drops even further.

"Continue with the narrative of events, CSM Mateo," Admiral Woody says while looking at the *Cataphract's* Commodore.

When Fagen started screaming into the comms, Major Blue began pushing everyone at top speed. I was ahead of my FR team members, guiding the first group of prisoners to the dropship. I watched as the Master turned its lens on El Diablo's incoming fire. My rounds diverted wildly into harmless space. I sent up my last three mortars, hoping they would either damage it or distract it long enough for me to land a devastating blow.

Unlike the behemoths in space, this new Master was fast; with little effort, it lifted high into the air, diverting my mortar rounds harmlessly away. It hung above us, shifting its central lens about our space. I had the distinct impression it tracked every living thing in the area we controlled. I knew our control of where the dropships where landed was about to be contested by this new Master. I shoved a freed prisoner past me as I turned to follow.

Through El Diablo's optics, I watched the Master drain the last of Fagen. The cuttlefish-like beast throbbed and its color shifted rapidly into an aggressive palpitating, pattern. There was a pressure and a presence that built in my mind, and in my mindspace. I began to see the black halos work their way in from the edges of my vision, and I realized the Master was attempting to force-disconnect me. I did my best to fight back its mental will.

I woke as a SkipJack dragged me by my armor's haul strap.

"I've got him, Sargent," the young voice said. "I didn't see any others."

"Keep moving, Private," Sargent Bronsky's grizzly voice said. "I'm booting into this toy of his."

"I've found Major Blue," said a thick voice. "What's left of him."

"I've got the Master lifting up another blood ball," said a fourth voice.

"Return to the dropship," Bronsky commanded. "We're getting off this rock."

I faded back out as my head bumped against something, and the pain forced blackness to retake me.

Sgt. Bronsky's voice woke me up.

"I need eight of you to yank every power core and power cell you can find," Bronsky said. "Preference on the cores, power cells if you can't find cores."

"Power cores," I whispered into comms weakly.

"The CSM is awake," squeaked a young man's voice.

"I'm going to give the Master a surprise," Bronsky said distractedly. "The medic says you'll live. Sit down and don't make trouble for my men while they're working."

"Where's...Major Blue?" I asked.

"No one further than you lived," Bronsky said. "It force-disco'd the life right from them. You were far enough away not to be ripped completely apart. As it is, you're leaking heavily from dozens of lacerations. Listen to my medics, or they'll sedate you."

Something pushed my head to the side, and it took me a second to realize my helmet was still on. I turned the visor from opaque to clear and let the HUD display fade into oblivion with its disastrous news. Twelve team members' names were grayed out. Those missing names marked the near-complete death of my ninth team in almost as many drops. I had made eighteen drops on this campaign.

In front of me knelt two pod heads. Each of their forearms had the red and white stripe of a CSMS medic.

"Lie still, CSM Mateo," the female one said. "Your armor kept the brunt of the lens's disruption blast from ripping you apart."

"It's the exposed areas," the second younger male voice said. "You'll be the only man I know who survives death by a thousand cuts."

"Check his head, Sterling," the female one said.

The man looked up from my lower leg and grimaced. "Keep the helmet on, and don't worry," he said. "Chicks dig scars."

I tried to smile and felt the nearly-set lacerations around my face split back open.

Over private comms, I asked, "What's the plan, Sargent?"

It took a moment on our open channel for Bronsky to respond. But I knew he was there, as the comms link was open, and I heard his labored breaths.

"I'm self-destructing your toy's fusion core," Bronsky said. "Now, shush. I need to concentrate as the dropship climbs."

A moment later, we reached the high-altitude turbulence that most alien worlds seemed to have.

***

"He self-destructed the fusion core?" the *Cataphract's* new Commodore asks. "Impossible. Without fuel, they starve themselves out."

Commodore Brigitte raises an eyebrow at me and responds before I can. "No, John, it isn't impossible. You've not been in command of a vessel very long. It…" She pauses, turning back to me. "Maybe you'd better explain it, CSM Mateo."

I nod. "As CW MKII pilots, we have fusion cores instead of a MKVI's power packs. There are certain procedures to shut the power cores down. There is one procedure to deprive the enemy of our material." I turn from Commodore Brigitte to the *Cataphract's* Commodore. "As far as I know, it hasn't been done before." I grimace at the thought of having to do it.

"Why is that?"

"The time it takes, mostly, and the control the pilot has to exude," I explain. At his perplexed look, I shift my explanation tactics. "A ship like this one has a massive fusion power core. When you enter the self-destruct command and are required to revert to manual piloting, this includes the magnetic dampeners that contain the fusion. Instead of piloting a ship in a pod, you pilot the magnetic field that sets the boundaries of the fusion containment area. You hold back the literal fires of hell with your will alone. You have to ride the lightning, so to speak, until the containment reaches critical mass and is breached."

The *Cataphract's* new man looks to the rest of the panel and returns to me, frowning at their nod.

"I was told it would take a pilot of unique skill and will to bind themselves to a birth of a new star," I say. "Bronsky's mind should have been shattered. However, my layman's guess is that the pod handled much of the feedback load as the fusion containment finally hit that magical 175-percent operational capacity. Additionally, the distance the dropship had gained towards orbit provided enough lag for his mind to shut down before the backlash killed him."

"That hardly seems exceptional," the new Commodore says coolly.

"It is exceptional," Admiral Woody says. "I've consulted with Colonel War about the type of mind it would take to hold back the birth of a star." The room goes silent at the mention of the living avatar of his name.

Admiral Woody gives us each a glance and turns back to me. "There is more, isn't there?"

"Yes, sir," I say. "Sgt Bronsky had the foresight to acquire every power cell and power core he could. The dropship cores couldn't be removed, but he ramped their output up to 105 percent. As a result, six dropships and hundreds of power cells encircled my MKII Chicken Walker. These provided the necessary fuel to sustain the brief growth of the new sun on the planet's surface." I forward the last FEED video we have of the Master.

"The new Master made a slow journey under constant fire from our MKVIs piloted by Able squad. When the Master forced them to disconnect, new team members cycled into the fight, and others accepted the power cell collection duties. His squad rotated efficiently, giving each member time to recover from the forced disconnects," I explain.

"How many disconnects?" Admiral Woody asks.

"As best I can tell, everyone force-disco'd at least three times, some four," I say.

A gasp comes from one of the Commodores, and all of us here know why. So many discos in a short timeframe leaves permanent brain-scarring. This fight might have ended Able squad's careers. It is the very same kind of injury that eventually killed Commodore Ruel, if what I was told a while ago is true.

The Admiral forwards the FEED vid to the conference table's center display. We watch Able squad dance a virtuoso under Bronsky's leadership. The CW MKII, El Diablo, is on top of their burned hulk of an HLT, doing its best to lay down railgun fire into the Master. Minute by minute, Sgt. Bronsky lured the Master closer to my CW MKII, even after our dropship climbed high into the atmosphere. Eventually, the Master rose to the height of El Diablo and turned its central lens towards it.

"That's when the fusion power core hit 175 percent," I say. "A new sun was briefly formed on the surface of the Einarin homeworld. It was fueled by six other cores and hundreds of MKVI power cells." I smile grimly. "The atmosphere on the Einar homeworld shrank by seven percent in the aftermath of that blast. Sgt. Bronsky turned 150 square kilometers to glass."

I close my folder. "There are but two people to have ever taken a Master down single-handedly," I say, looking each of the panel members in the eye. "We all know the first." I let that slight grim smile fade from my face as I hold the *Cataphract's* new Commodore's gaze. "Sgt. Bronsky is the second human ever to do it. Yes, it was an infant. It doesn't matter. It is still one more than any of us has been able to achieve."

I pause and look at each of the members of the admiralty board. "We've lost so many. We will never know all the heroic deeds done in this war. Whole teams and companies wiped from existence in the blink of an eye. We do know this one feat, this one moment where a man stood defiant against desperate odds to save even a few of his own. If we can't tell every story, at least tell this one. We Humans no longer fear the deep darkness of space and the terrors that try to come for us."

Leave the Humans Alone

ANDREW MILBOURNE

Gy'Vyrk, The One Without Fear, senior Ni'Gorb to the Vra'Khil Gorb'ak known as Khov'la, The One That Cheats Death, lowered his eyestalks and crossed his pincers in deference as he approached his leader. The Gorb'ak acknowledged his underling with a perfunctory dip of his carapace.

"Speak, Gy'Vyrk," the seasoned leader of a Khat'ahzt of nearly one thousand of the most dreaded marauders in the known galaxy commanded. "You have identified a suitable target for our Khat'ahzt to take?"

"Indeed, my Gorb'ak," Gy'Vyrk replied, "A ripe world, ready for the plundering." Kh'ovla gestured with one chela to a pair of his subordinates, who quickly activated the holoprojector in the center of the Gorb'ak's War Dome. The image of a lush world of red seas and gold continents appeared before the assembled raiders, who excitedly clicked their chela in anticipation. "A small Class-M planet in the Esk'hay system, my Gorb'ak. Its occupants refer to it as 'Taikius.' The Taikai, as they call themselves, are bipedal mammals, of a technological level similar to ours, though they have foolishly devoted themselves to the cause of peace." This brought forth a roar of laughter from the assembled Khat'ahzt that echoed through the vast chamber. Xu'ul allowed the merriment for a moment before raising one chela. The room instantly fell silent.

"Continue, Gy'Vyrk," The One That Cheats Death ordered.

"Yes, my Gorb'ak. As a result, their army is a pathetic shadow of ours, and their world is busting at its carapace with resources. Their seas are filled with nutrients with which we might sustain ourselves for centuries, while their planetary crust is full of rare elements needed for the construction of weapons and starships." As Gy'Vyrk spoke, lists of the specific resources appeared over the planet. "And," Gy'Vyrk finished, "their females are considered quite beautiful and, therefore, desirable by many other species." That remark, and the accompanying image of a rather attractive female Taikai, garnered more excited chattering. Slaves were an especially valued prize among the Vra'Khil and were a source of enormous wealth for the Khat'ahzt. The Taikai were attractive enough to interest more than a few of the hexapodal crustaceans. Perhaps their Gorb'ak would allow them to keep a few prizes for themselves—after he had taken his pick, of course.

"A most excellent choice of target, my trusted Ni'Gorb!" Khov'la exclaimed. "And you say this world is completely without defense."

"Effectively so, my Gorb'ak. They have entered into a defensive alliance with another race of bipedal mammals: humans. And less than five thousand of them."

Many of the assembled Khat'ahzt clacked their pincers in excitement, for they knew that even the tallest Humans stood a full meter shorter than the average Vra'Kril, and they lacked a carapace of their own and were exceedingly fragile and easy to kill. Five thousand Humans would surely not be enough to defend a single city against the terrible onslaught of a Vra'Kril Khat'ahzt, let alone defend an entire world.

To Gy'Vyrk's surprise, his Gorb'ak was not among them. Instead, Khov'la seemed to stiffen in fear at Gy'Vyrk's declaration.

"What sort of Humans?" the Gorb'ak demanded of his underling.

"An aquatic-based subspecies," Gy'Vyrk replied, voice strong with certainty. "The Humans refer to this subspecies as 'Marines.'"

"*Marines?* You say that this world is defended by five thousand members of the Terran Space Marine Corps?"

"Indeed, my Gorb'ak. This...concerns you?"

"It does indeed. As it should the entirety of my Khat'ahzt." Khov'la stilled himself, raising his voice so it echoed through the War Dome. "We shall not move against the world Taikius! Such an attempt would be naught but folly! This is the word of your Gorb'ak!"

The assembled Vra'Khil glanced amongst themselves in nervous disbelief. What could have possessed their Gorb'ak to make such an abrupt and radical change of heart?

"You would deny us such a ripe prize?" Gy'Vyrk demanded, voicing the opinion that many in the Khat'azht shared but only one dared voice.

"No prize, no matter how ripe and plump it may be, is worth facing the demons that fill the ranks of the Terran Space Marine Corps! Or perhaps you have forgotten The Rout on Serilia?"

"Serilia?" Gy'Vyrk scoffed. "Serilia is naught but a legend! A myth perpetuated by *weak* Gorb'ak as a means to conceal their *cowar—*"

Khov'la leapt from his dias, landing atop the unsuspecting Gy'Vyrk and driving his diamondite-tipped pincers through his disrespectful underling's carapace. The Khat'azht watched in muted horror as their leader sawed the Ni'Gorb apart, filling the dome with the putrid stench of spilled entrails and the awful irregular clattering of a Vra'Khil's death rattle.

When Gy'Vyrk's corpse had finally stilled, Khov'la looked over his Khat'azht. The Vra'Khil averted their eyestalks in fearful submission.

"Hear my words, Khat'azht of Khov'la, The One That Cheats Death! The Rout on Serilia is no myth! I know: I was *there*! I witnessed the destruction with my own eyestalks! I tasted the death and destruction those demons wrought upon our kind! You believe that Humans are naught but weak, pathetic bipeds that will be easily swept away by our might? Then heed my words as I tell you the truth of what these Humans, these Terran Space Marines, are truly made of!"

A half-dozen Vra'Khil raiding vessels blinked into existence over Serilia with no warning.

Aboard the lead raider, the navigator Khov'la turned to his Gorb'ak.

"Reversion successful, oh Gorb'ak. All ships accounted for and in position."

"Good. Very good." Xu'ul was Gorb'ak over a Khat'ahzt nearly six hundred Vra'Khil in strength, and clacked his pincers in anticipation. The inhabitants of the world below had surely noticed their arrival and were no doubt in the grip of rising terror. Foolish bipedals, devoting their lives and their world's extensive resources to the pursuit of peace, leaving their planet—and their females—ripe for the plunder.

"Broadcast our arrival to the planet," Xu'ul commanded. "Inform them of the consequences of resistance and order them to prepare a suitable tribute for our arrival. Then begin atmospheric entry and charge weapons. We shall give these fleshy weaklings an example of what awaits them, should they defy us."

The five Vra'Khil on the bridge quickly moved to carry out their Gorb'ak's commands. Any sign of laziness was sure to bring about the most humiliating and gruesome fate of Xu'ul personally sawing their carapace open with his diamondite-encrusted claws.

An alert suddenly sounded from the panel of Xu'Hynt, the communications specialist.

"My Gorb'ak, we are being hailed. The signal comes from the planet's largest continent."

Ah. Pleas for mercy. Xu'ul was fond of these. Like all Vra'Khil, he reveled in the fear of his impending victims, and in the utter terror and humiliations they showed when he revealed that their requests for mercy would be in vain.

"Put it on the central holo."

Xu'Hynt did as his Gorb'ak ordered, and the holographic display came to life. Xu'ul stiffened in surprise: the creature before him was a fleshy biped. Not a willowy blue-skinned Serilian, but a dark-colored creature with a broad torso that Xu'ul quickly recognized as a human. This human was clad in a strange multi-colored fabric with icons pinned to its collar, and wore a strange headpiece with a different icon sewn into its center.

"This is Major Williams, Terran Space Marine Corps," the human said, not waiting for the superior species to address him first. "To whom am I speaking?"

"Impudent biped!" Xu'ul snarled, "I am Xu'ul, The One Which Knows No Mercy! Gorb'ak over the six hundred Vra'Khil that are, as we speak, preparing to descend upon this world and put its pathetic inhabitants to our claws! You are not of this world, Major Williams! Flee before it is too late, and I may show you and your kind leniency."

The human pulled its lips back into an expression the Vra'Khil recognized as a "smile."

"You mean 'retreat?'" Williams asked, then let out a noise that humans called "laughter." "Hell, we just got here! And I guess your people missed the memo: Serilia has signed a treaty with the Terran System and, as a result, is under Human protection. So if you want to plunder and pillage your giant space crab guts out, you're going to have to go through me and my Marines."

"Then you and your Marines shall be slaughtered like shnee-shnee!" Xu'ul declared. "We shall crush your pathetic attempts at resisting our might, and then we shall break you, brain and body! We shall remove your genitals and rend the flesh from your bones while you watch us defile your own females and those of the pathetic bipeds you have sworn to protect, and then we shall take you with us to your pathetic Terran system and watch as we butcher your progeny and your ancestors until your genetic line is eradicated from existence! And then, only then, shall we allow you the sweet mercies of death!"

All others who had heard that declaration had cowered and despaired before the great and terrible Xu'ul. This human did not: he pulled his lips back further, showing the Vra'Khil his teeth. It was an unsettling expression.

"I don't think so," Williams said, his voice as hard as the purest diamon-dite. "All that bullshit you just spouted? None of that is going to happen. What *is* going to happen is one of two things. Option one: you turn your ships around, go back to Khil, tell your High Gorb'ak that the Serilian System is off-limits to him and all of his underlings, and then you *never* come back here ever again. Option two: you land here and try to carry out those threats of yours, and me and my Marines figure out how good you and your minions taste steamed and buttered. One of my mortarmen's from Baltimore, and he's got a container of Old Bay in his rucksack that he's just itching to break out."

"What!" Xu'ul snarled, aghast. "You *dare* defy a Gorb'ak of the Vra'Khil?"

"Yes, sir. I do."

"Then I shall ensure that you and your progeny suffer the longest!" He gestured to his underlings. "Trace this impudent human's broadcast signal to its source, then instruct our fleet to set down at that precise location! These humans shall be the first to fall before us!"

"Gorb'ak, I'm not going to lie: my Marines and I were hoping you'd say that. We'll see you soon." Williams turned to someone outside of the holocam's viewing area. "Gunny, prepare to repel landers, and somebody tell Kazlowski to unpack his Old Bay." The Major made a gesture with his hands, and the communication ended.

Xu'ul's carapace rattled as he quivered with rage. How dare that human treat him with such contempt? Did he not hear the truth in Xu'ul's words? Did he not grasp the terrible fate that now assuredly awaited him and his ilk? Well, that Major Williams would learn. Within a few short hours, all Humans would learn what such arrogance and impudence would bring. And they would quiver with fear at that knowledge.

The Human transmission had come not from the Serilian capital city, but from a small settlement at the base of a mountain some three hundred kilometers west of the capital. From the air, the settlement appeared to have been fortified. Surprising, but no real matter: Xu'ul and his Khat'ahzt would effortlessly crush it as they had done to countless others. The six Vra'Khil ships set course for this settlement, as their Gorb'ak had commanded. The raiders landed line-abreast on the open plain to the south of the settlement, over a kilometer away, as was their custom. The better to terrify their prey: the sight of hundreds of three-meter-tall hexapods racing towards them had never failed to strike fear into even the strongest of their prey.

The ground shook as six hundred Vra'Khil raiders poured down a half-dozen landing ramps, pounding the thick lavender grass into dust beneath their spiked feet. The raiders formed into ranks fifty across and twelve deep, then stood motionless and in perfect silence as Xu'ul slowly marched to their head. He inspected his Khat'ahzt and found it to be a truly terrifying sight indeed. The pathetic Humans would quickly wilt and fall before them.

Xu'ul took his place at the head of the Khat'ahzt. For a long moment, all was silent. No animals moved or sang in the grass. They could sense the horror and destruction that was about to be unleashed upon this place.

Without warning, Xu'ul abruptly began to stomp his feet and clack his pincers in the slow, bone-chilling rhythm of a Vra'Khil war dance. The entire Khat'ahzt joined in after the first repetition, the noise thundering across the plain to the settlement. A cloud of dust sprang up and enveloped the raiding party as the dance grew faster and faster. Those humans in the settlement surely knew their doom was imminent; that when the war dance reached its zenith, the Khat'ahzt would charge and effortlessly over-run their pathetic fortress.

As the Khat'ahzt began to enter into a frenzy, a high-pitched whistle pierced the air over the plain. The Vra'Khil barely noticed the sound over the thunder of their war dance even as it grew louder and lower in pitch. They *did* notice the sudden *BOOM!* that rattled their carapaces and brought the war dance to an abrupt, ragged stop. A gust of wind scattered the churned dust and debris, revealing a greasy grey cloud ascending to the sky above a deep crater gouged into the soil less than ten meters in front of Xu'ul. A crater that most certainly had *not* been there when the Vra'Khil had disembarked.

A second whistling sound, this one clearly audible, came echoing over the plain moments later. The assembled Vra'Khil glanced about, unsure of what the sound was or where it was coming from, but unwilling to betray confusion in the presence of their Gorb'ak. As the noise became almost frighteningly loud, at least one Vra'Khil towards the left edge of the Khat'ahzt glanced skywards. The raider began to shout a warning.

Too late. He barely managed to get a single syllable out before the object struck the top of Vra'Khil in front of him and exploded, shattering the unlucky raider's carapace like cheap plastiglass, showering the Khat'ahzt with innards and ichor, and sending shrapnel and bits of carapace ripping through the Vra'Khil formation.

Legs and claws were severed, carapaces were cracked. Pained wails filled the air. But this was all wrong: these wounds should have been inflicted *by* the Vra'Khil, not inflicted *upon* them!

Another explosive projectile—for what else could it be?—came whistling towards the Khat'ahzt, then another, then a third. Then a fourth. Then more, still. The Vra'Khil knew that death was imminent, and to maintain their position and continue their war dance would surely result in their utter annihilation. Fortunately, their Gorb'ak realized this, pointed towards the settlement with one great claw, and roared a single command.

"CRUSH THEM!"

The Khat'ahzt surged forward at Xu'ul's order, racing towards the fortified settlement as the explosives began to rain down. The order to charge had come late for the Khat'ahzt's rearmost lines, which were devastated by the half-dozen explosives that struck atop them and between them, reducing their number by dozens in mere seconds. But the danger had surely passed now: as unexpectedly effective as the Human weapon had been, the raiders had quickly moved out of its killing zone, and the Humans would not be able to set the proper range and fire until the Vra'Khil were upon them.

Small yellow lights began streaking from atop the settlement wall towards the charging horde. Some struck the ground before them, some streaked overhead, and all were accompanied by a strange buzzing-hiss or snapping sound. A few Vra'Khil noted that there seemed to be more of the strange sounds than the lights.

Xu'ul and his lead ranks laughed at the sight, for what could such a puny thing do against the armored carapace of a mighty and terrible Vra'Khil? They could not hear the booming *chug-chug-chug* sound of the Humans' ancient guns over the echoing rhythm of their own footfalls. Had they heard, and had they known of the legendary service of that weapon, perhaps they would not have felt such arrogance. But the Humans found their range within seconds, and then the heavy projectiles began to impact the Vra'Khil, cracking and piercing their vaunted armored carapaces and blowing off limbs. Those in the lead ranks that fell were trampled beneath those behind them, crushing those that were not already dead. Then a rocket streaked down from the tower at the corner of the settlement and blasted a quartet of raiders to chunky bits.

The Khat'ahzt's collective arrogance and bloodlust began to vanish under the relentless onslaught. In its place emerged a sensation that no Vra'Khil had felt in many centuries: fear.

The charging ranks began to falter, slowing and spreading apart as the certainty of victory began to vanish before them. Xu'ul ordered them forward even as he began to fade back towards the center of the group. He saw now that the tactic meant to terrify the humans into submission had inadvertently played to their great advantage, but despite his Khat'ahzt's steadily shrinking numbers, victory was still all but assured...*if* they could reach the settlement. No matter how advanced and devastating the bipeds' weapons might have been, their range and destructive power would be nullified in the fortress's close quarters, and one mighty Vra'Khil was surely worth at least one hundred Humans when the fight became mandible to mandible. The Humans would suffer for the grave insult they had inflicted upon his Khat'ahzt, as would the Serilians under their supposed "protection." He would make sure of it.

After a seeming eternity under the nonstop onslaught of heavy projectiles and explosive rockets, the Khat'ahzt at last reached the settlement's outer wall. The lead rank crashed into the metal structure, causing the wall to shake violently, but the forty-meter-tall structure did not give way. Not that it mattered, for the Vra'Khil were skilled in overcoming such puny obstacles, even under the withering fire of the Humans' terrible weapons. As the forward ranks reached the base of the wall, the Vra'Khil clambered onto their backs, their intact carapaces easily supporting the weight, until they formed an organic ramp. Other Vra'Khil leaped atop the wall and scattered the Humans from their posts, knocking some from atop the wall and splitting others in two with their powerful claws.

The Humans quickly withdrew from the wall as the Vra'Khil overran their positions, retreating down to ground level and deeper into the settlement. But they did not flee in blind terror as their Serilian allies now did or as so many others had before this Khat'ahzt: they were methodical and organized. Disciplined, even. And they continuously poured fire from their projectile weapons into the oncoming marauders. Such puny things should not have been able to harm a Vra'Khil, except perhaps an incredibly lucky shot to a weak or vital spot. But these Humans seemed to be making a shockingly high number of those incredibly lucky shots. Joints were immobilized or destroyed. Eyestalks were put out or blown off. Already damaged sections of carapace were punctured and cracked, exposing vital innards to the Humans' withering counterassault.

The last of the Humans vanished into the lanes between the outermost structures just as the Vra'Khil managed to open the fortress's main gate, and leading waves of the Vra'Khil followed—only to die as hidden explosives detonated and drove clouds of tiny spherical projectiles into the

Vra'Khil, cracking and splintering carapaces and tearing away limbs. The air was now thick with the foul stench of spilled entrails and the horrible irregular clacking of Vra'Khil death rattles. The Khat'ahzt slowed, and some even dared halt, but Xu'ul ordered them onwards. These Humans may be ferocious, but they were still only Humans. Tiny, fleshy, weak, pathetic, inferior bipeds. They would not be allowed to use the narrow confines of these streets and alleys to their advantage. The Vra'Khil, at their Gorb'ak's command, threw themselves against the sides of the settlement's buildings. These structures were far weaker than the fortress's outer wall and easily gave to the mass and momentum of charging Vra'Khil, collapsing atop any Humans or Serilians unfortunate enough to be taking shelter within and forcing their compatriots to remain in the open, where they became easy prey for their advancing doom.

Yet while the Humans and Serilians continued to fall back and die, the Humans sold their lives dearly. For every Human that fell, two more took its place. Every meter into the settlement the Khat'ahzt advanced was paid for with dozens of damaged limbs and carapaces and eyestalks, and in too many cases, lives. But Human ferocity and stubbornness could only count for so much, and their weapons only do so much damage. The outcome was inevitable: the Vra'Khil eventually managed to drive the surviving Humans and Serilians back into to the large three-story structure in the center of the settlement.

This building was of far stronger construction than the others within the walls, and Xu'ul knew at a glance that it would not collapse when rammed. He ordered the Khat'ahzt to form a perimeter around the building while he moved before the large double doors that were certainly the main entrance. As the Khat'ahzt moved into position, Xu'ul could not help but notice how drastically their numbers had been depleted. By his count, at least one third of the Vra'Khil under his command were dead or dying. Oh well.

The fewer Vra'Khil, the greater share of plunder and glory, and a testament to his strength and skill as Gorb'ak. Surely their legend would spread across the stars, making him the most infamous and feared VraKhil in the known galaxy. Infamous enough to challenge for the Great Throne, perhaps. No, such dreams must wait until his victory here was complete.

"Humans! I will speak with your Major Williams of your puny Terran Space Marine Corps!" the Gorb'ak roared.

"Oh yeah?" a voice bellowed back from a first-story window. "Who's asking for him?"

"Know, Human, that you cower before the presence of Xu'ul, The One Which Knows No Mercy! Gorb'ak of the six hundred mighty Vra'Khil that have just now crushed your pathetic attempt of resistance!"

"We ain't cowerin' before shit!" a second voice responded.

A third voice bellowed, "GAAAAAWWWWDAMMIT PRIVATE! YOU SHUT YOUR GAWDAM JAWBONE 'FORE I RIP IT OFF YOUR THICK SKULL AN' BEAT YOUR ASS WITH IT!"

The second voice squeaked out a meek, "Yes, Gunny," before the original voice gave its reply.

"Well, Mister Xu'ul who knows no mercy, the Major is no longer with us."

"Hah! Your leader has fled in terror before our might! Surely now you realize that all is lost!"

"The Major didn't run nowhere. He died up on the wall. You can meet him soon enough, if you want. For now, if you want to negotiate surrender, you'll have to do it with me. Captain Jerome, Second Battalion Fifth Marines, at your service."

"Surrender? We do not accept your surrender!"

"Sorry, Gorb'ak, but I didn't mean our surrendering to you: I was offering you the chance to surrender to me. Right here, right now."

"Your continued impudence aggravates me, Human!" Xu'ul snarled. "Know that while I indeed know no mercy, I do in fact know some small kindness. Lay down your pathetic weapons and exit that structure, and I give my word that my Khat'ahzt shall gift you with a swift death and spare you the ravages that we shall inflict upon this world!"

"I see. And the Serilians under our protection?"

"They shall pay for allying with a race that dares defy me!"

There was no hesitation in Captain Jerome's response.

"Nuts to that!"

A mighty cry of "*OORAH!*" echoed from the building at Jerome's proclamation.

Xu'ul's eyestalks swiveled in confusion. So perplexed was he by the Humans' utterly nonsensical response that he actually looked to his underlings for guidance, but the Human's words were just as mysterious to them as to their Gorb'ak.

"What does this mean, 'Nuts to that?'" Xu'ul was forced to ask. "Is that a positive response or a negative response?"

"Negative, Sir!" Jerome called, his voice sounding strangely jovial. "Most assuredly and emphatically negative!"

"Then you shall suffer tortures so horrific that your pathetic biped minds will warp and break at the mere thought of such agony!"

"Maybe, Gorb'ak Xu'ul. But not today. Gunnery Sergeant Daly, if you would, please?"

"BATTALIIOOOOOOOOON!" the third voice roared, "FIIIIIIIIII-IIIIIIIX! BAYONETS!"

A ragged clack of metal on metal echoed from inside the building, followed immediately by another roar of "*OOHRAH!*" that seemed to shake the very walls within which the Humans and their allies had taken refuge.

"POWER OOOOOON! BAYONETS!"

"*OOHRAH!*"

That third battle cry—for as alien as the chant may have been, its purpose was unmistakable—was quickly followed by the high-pitched, carapace-rattling whine of vibroblades powering up. The Vra'Khil began to shift uneasily. A few began to slowly creep backwards, away from the building.

There was no warning before the rockets streaked down from atop the roof into the Khat'ahzt. The perimeter buckled as a full score of Vra'Khil were either grievously wounded or outright blown to bits.

"COME ON, YOU SONS OF BITCHES! DO YOU WANT TO LIVE FOREVER? CHAAAAAAAAARGE!"

The Gunnery Sergeant's order was drowned out by a mighty, ground-shaking, "*OOOOOOOORRRRRRR-RRAAAAAAAAAAAAAAAAAAAAAAAAAHHHHHHH!*" as the Humans poured from the building and charged into the ring of Vra'Khil.

It was unimaginable. Unbelievable. Unthinkable. No creature, especially none as small and puny as these Humans, had ever attacked a Vra'Khil Khat'ahzt, save in moments of terrified desperation, and certainly never in defense of a race not their own. Yet these Humans—these *Marines*—showed not the faintest sign of desperation or terror: their eyes were instead full of determination and rage. So taken aback were the Vra'Khil by this impossible action that many remained frozen in place as the Marines fell upon them, stabbing and hacking and slashing at foes three times their size with their wicked vibayonets. The blades, vibrating at a rate of hundreds of times per second, carved through Vra'Khil limbs and carapaces like diamondite shards through Gossamary Lace-Moth wings.

The pained screams of their brethren and the sick crunching sound of carapaces rent apart galvanized the Vra'Khil to action. They kicked at the Humans, spearing them with their sharpened footstalks, but still the

Humans attacked. They bashed them with their heavy claws, flattening their skulls and crushing their bones, but still the Humans attacked. They grabbed them in their pincers and sheared them in two, showering their compatriots with their gore, and *still* the Humans attacked. Rather than break their spirits, the sight of their comrades meeting such horrific fates seemed to strengthen their will and fuel their bloodlust.

What manner of creature—of demon—were these Marines? What terrible thing had the Khat'ahzt unwittingly provoked to such a fury?

Then, the truly unthinkable occurred.

"The Gorb'ak!" one of the Vra'Khil—Khov'la, in fact, the navigator of the Khat'ahzt's flagship—wailed, "*THEY HAVE SLAIN THE GORB'AK!*"

It was impossible, but true. A pair of Humans had managed to slip past Xu'ul's pincers and chop off three of his left legs with their vibayonets. The mighty Gorb'ak pitched over onto his side, his balance ruined. The two Marines swept behind him, avoiding his swinging mandibles and thrashing leg-stumps, and drove their awful blades into the Vra'Khil's exposed soft underbelly, somehow using their strength and the falling Xu'ul's momentum to flip the mortally wounded Gorb'ak onto his back. Four more humans joined their compatriots, leaping atop Xu'ul's underside and slicing their blades through the soft, vulnerable flesh.

The bone-chilling screech of the dying Gorb'ak brought the melee to a momentary halt. And in that horrible moment, something that had not taken place in many centuries, perhaps not in the entire recorded history of the known galaxy, occurred.

A Vra'Khil Khat'ahzt broke.

Those Vra'Khil that were still able turned and fled, sheer terror gripping firmly at their hearts. Those that still lived but found themselves crippled or immobilized were quickly set upon by the Marines and their terrible weapons.

The survivors fled over the debris of the structures they had destroyed such a short time before. Eyestalks swiveled to the rear revealed a horrifying sight: the Marines were giving pursuit. The few Vra'Khil that turned to fight in a vain attempt to reclaim some shred of glory were quickly swarmed and slain by the bipeds. Most continued to flee, knowing that they were faster than the Humans over open ground, and their only hope of survival and escape was to reach the field and outrun the Marines in a desperate race to their ships.

But the open plain that they had believed to be their salvation proved to be a killing field. What had once been lush, pristine lavender grass had been pulverized into dirty yellow soil pockmarked with craters, stained with the black ichor of dead Vra'Khil, and littered with broken and shattered corpses. And the Marines made it their purpose to add to that macabre redecoration: they pounded the fleeing remnants of the Khat'ahzt with a continuous, unrelenting stream of fire from their heavy automatic projectile weapons, rockets, and the explosives from the sky that the galaxy would come to know as "mortars." The Vra'Khil that fell behind their brethren became easy targets for the Marines and were cut down like panicked shnee-shnee.

After the most terrifying eternity of their long lives, what few Vra'Khil remained at last reached the ships. By some good stroke of fate, the majority retained enough of their wits to all scramble aboard the same vessel; their slain Gorb'ak's flagship. Then came several moments of disparate terror as the Vra'Khil frantically searched for any amongst their number with the knowledge of getting the vessel into orbit, or at the very least, airborne. The terror of the moment intensified tenfold as the Marines targeted the ship with their mortars, and the deadly shells began landing all around and then atop the vessel.

For the first time on that dark standard cycle, fate was on the Vra'Khil's side, for Khov'la the navigator, and member of a different vessel's bridge crew, had survived. After a dangerously abbreviated startup sequence and an all-but-disregarded takeoff checklist, the two Vra'Khil jerked the vessel off the ground and piloted a wobbling course up towards what would be a frightfully sloppy orbit. Then fortune smiled upon them once more: the Humans had either tired of their pursuit and slaughter, or more likely lacked weapons able to engage and destroy the ship once it had left the ground.

An awed, terrified silence had fallen over the War Dome by the time Khov'la finished his tale.

"Of the six hundred Vra'Khil that had comprised the feared Khat'ahzt of Xu'ul, The One Which Knew No Mercy, when we landed upon Serilia," Khov'la continued, "a paltry forty-two of us escaped that horrific place with our lives. I assumed the title of Gorb'ak over the survivors, and have spent many centuries rebuilding my Khat'azht to rival that of the slain Xu'ul.

"Such destruction as occurred on Serilia had never been witnessed upon any Khat'ahzt before, but this was only the first such massacre. Word of terrible slaughter inflicted upon us by these Terran Space Marines quickly spread from Khat'ahzt to Khat'ahzt until it reached Khil itself, and from there across the known galaxy. Some Khat'ahzt, and several other species of marauders, believed the tale to be fiction; a fabrication meant to soften the disgrace of Xu'ul's supposed cowardice and incompetence. They sought out and attacked other Terran Space Marine Corps units to prove their superiority over the pathetic Humans and their beliefs regarding my fallen Gorb'ak. The majority of these foolhardy ventures all ended in the same manner: with the utter annihilation of the attacking force. Those few that managed to achieve victory were swiftly and surely hunted down with overwhelming force by other Marines and wiped out.

"My Khat'ahzt will not share that fate. Not again. No, so long as I remain Gorb'ak over you, my word shall remain law. And my word is this: we shall never attack any element, no matter how small, of the Terran Space Marine Corps. We shall leave the Humans alone. To do otherwise shall lead to nothing but our most assured doom."

Repel Boarders!

DANIEL G. ZEIDLER

HELDRON, COMMANDER OF THE marine detachment aboard the Guardian clipper *Tempest*, watched the main imaging field intently as a solitary Dii armillaridyne sped toward the Rift. The powerful magical energies radiating from the Rift flared brightly as they struck the Dii vessel's shields, but flowed harmlessly around them and trailed off behind the armillaridyne like the tail of a comet. The imaging field began to haze over as a pressure wave radiating from the Rift approached.

"Retract main sails. Secondary sails to thirty degrees," Corren, sitting in the captain's chair a short distance behind Heldron, said and leaned thoughtfully back in his chair as his order was repeated and then carried out. A moment later, the pressure wave swept past the *Tempest*, but with only the secondary sails deployed, the clipper merely shuddered as it passed.

The Rift was located where, billions of years earlier, a massive star had once burned in splendor and fury unrivaled by any star in its half of the galaxy; so violent had been the mighty star's death that it tore a permanent hole in the fabric of the universe. The Rift opened onto an in-between space known by various names—*thru-space*, or *Jump space*, or even *the shadow realm*—that was both nowhere and everywhere at once and through which flowed currents of magical energy that could be as wide as entire star systems. The energies pouring out of the Rift made approaching it in normal space a fatal prospect, and while it was possible to get close to it in thru-space, doing so was extremely risky. Actually flying *into* the matter-shredding energies of the Rift was suicidal, a fact no one seemed to have told the Dii. In recent months, the Dii had flown well over a thousand vessels into the Rift; singly, in pairs, and sometimes even a dozen at a time.

Heldron looked down in front of him, where Casperia was staring intently at the imaging fields and status indicators of her console. Her magical talents made her uniquely suited to tracking Dii armillaridynes against the chaos of the Rift. It was clear the Dii were using the Rift to travel somewhere, and Casperia was determined to figure out how they were doing it. She sensed him looking at her and sent a quick smile in his direction before turning to Corren.

Her smile broadened in response to his unspoken question. "I have a good track on the Dii vessel, Corren. After they enter the Rift, I'll have enough data to figure out how they are doing it."

As the bridge crew let out a cheer, a feeling that something was amiss pulled Heldron's eyes back to the sensor station. To the Founders' original technology, thru-space had appeared empty, but when viewed through magical means, like the imaging field or the aetherprobes, it appeared as a gently flowing haze of luminescence and shadow through which could be seen a faint, ghostly duplicate of normal space. On the imaging field, the Dii armillaridyne continued to accelerate toward the Rift, its crew either unaware of the *Tempest's* presence, or they considered it beneath their notice. The aetherprobes status display beneath the imaging field indicated that there were no other vessels in the vicinity of the Rift. Heldron found he could not shake the feeling that they were no longer alone, no matter what the imaging field and the aetherprobes were showing.

Magic-powered sensors could be deceived if one knew their attunement frequencies, and they could also be circumvented through sabotage; either method required betrayal. Heldron, however, had other means available to him for inspecting the *Tempest's* surroundings. He removed a featureless metal rectangle about the size of his palm from his belt and tapped it with one finger.

Almost immediately, a male voice spoke from the comm-tile. "Master Boarding Sergeant Corrado. What can I do for you, Commander?"

Heldron smiled. When the Founders established the Guardians, they created a system of formal military ranks for it, but after the first hundred years, the Guardians had phased out most of those expressions of rank. Guardians were immortal, and no one wanted to be a private forever, nor did it make much sense for everyone to eventually be promoted to general. One of the ranks the Guardians kept in use was the rank of master boarding sergeant. "How many snipers do you have in the rigging, Master Guns?"

Technically, the clippers had no rigging, as their sails were planes of magical energy projected by the clipper's masts, but after it had become necessary to install armored fighting positions on the ends of the secondary masts, the phrase had stuck. Individuals with the right sorts of magic Talents were often able to spot things in thru-space before the aetherprobes detected anything. "Priya is on Mast One, Geir is on Mast Six, and Maren is on Mast Seven. Expecting some action, sir?"

"Just an uneasy feeling..." Heldron looked at the imaging display and shook his head. "Send snipers up to the tops of the remaining masts and tell them to stay sharp."

"On it, sir. I'd like to also— Just a moment, Commander: Priya is calling in." Corrado was silent for less than a moment. "Movement in the mists! Bearing three-three-zero by zero-two-zero. Range—well, range is two miles and closing, but it's Priya, sir. You know she has a knack for this sort of thing."

Heldron turned to Corren. "Possible contact. Recommend we go to battle stations."

Corren nodded, then ordered, "Shields up. Sound Battle Stations. Run out all cannon." He looked at the imaging display and frowned before turning to Casperia. "Anything showing up via the 'probes?"

Casperia furrowed her brow and adjusted the inputs for the aether-probes. "Nothing." She looked up at Heldron. "Who spotted it?"

"Priya. She has a Talent for finding things."

"And she's hyper-accurate, too." Casperia looked back down at the aetherprobe readouts and shook her head. "At two miles and closing, whatever it is would be well within range...either someone has figured out a way to mask the ships from the aetherprobes or—"

"—Or someone back at the Citadel betrayed us and tampered with the clipper's 'probes before we departed," Heldron said, and waited for either Corren or Casperia to insist there was no way another Guardian would have sabotaged their clipper. He found their quiet agreement slightly trou-bling, but continued, "We could retune the port aetherprobes if we take them offline and overcharge the wards. It will take them out of synch with the other 'probes—will you lose track of the armillaridyne without the port bank?"

"I can do even better than just the port bank—I could retune the dorsal and ventral 'probes, as well," Casperia agreed, then looked over her shoul-der to Corren. "I only need the starboard 'probes as long as we keep that armillaridyne to starboard."

"All right, let's see what's out there."

Casperia placed her hand over the aetherprobe controls and retracted all but the starboard 'probes. She ran the retracted 'probes through the retuning sequence several times to burn through any magical tampering that might have been done to them, then redeployed the probes. Less than thirty seconds later, the image generated by the three banks of 'probes snapped into focus on Casperia's display screen. Her eyes widened, and she twisted around in her chair to make eye contact with Corren.

"Jeger clipper on intercept course!"

The Founders had used various names for the canid aliens who served the Dii such as Cynocephali and Anubii, but to the Guardians, they were the Jeger. The origins of the Jeger were unclear; the Dii had either uplifted them or altered them to hunt down other Dii who had been corrupted by the Darkness. Jeger who followed uncorrupted Dii nearly always ignored humans and human vessels, but the corrupted Jeger whose Dii had succumbed to the Darkness were brutal and sadistic, with a taste for human flesh.

Their standard tactic, and the reason why sniper stations had been added to the masts of Guardian clippers, was for Jeger vessels to make a fast pass by a target vessel while deploying a swarm of Jeger marines wearing vacuum plate and armed with plasma cutters. In thru-space, a clipper's shields stopped destructive energies, but merely slowed projectiles down to a velocity at which they would harmlessly impact the hull; a fact the Jeger marines used to their advantage in order to safely land on the hull of the clipper. Once there, they would begin trying to cut their way into the ship or, at the very least, try to cause as much damage to the exterior of the ship and the masts as possible. The most effective counter to this tactic was to position marine snipers with a Talent for finding things, in this case finding precisely where to aim a capacitor rifle to take out a Jeger berserker, on the clipper's secondary masts.

Heldron slipped into a more formal tone to make his report. "All snipers are in position and reporting ready for action. The rest of the detachment is standing by to repel all boarders, Captain."

"Snipers are free to immediately engage on contact with the enemy." Corren focused his attention on the main imaging display and saw the Dii armillaridyne was only about a minute from entering the Rift's event horizon. He withdrew a comm-tile from its slot in his display panel and directed a trickle of magic into the wards that would connect it to the ship-wide address system. "This is the Captain speaking. We have a Jeger clipper making an attack run on us, but we need to hold to this course until that armillaridyne enters the Rift. It won't be much longer, but things will likely get interesting. All hands assume Combat Posture Four and stand by to repel boarders. Starboard Gun Deck, prepare to engage Jeger clipper."

❧❧❧❧❧ ❦❦❦❦❦

In the sniper position atop Mast One, Priya shut down the firing port energy field and rested the barrel of her capacitor rifle on the stabilizer rail. She felt that calling the weapon a rifle was a misnomer, since it didn't actually have anything like rifling. It would be more accurate to call it a single-shot directed energy emitter cylinder affixed to a stock and trigger assembly and powered arcane capacitors loaded via a rolling block breech, but that would have been exhausting, so capacitor rifle it was. Had they been in normal space, it would have made more sense to use combat magic, but thru-space was inundated with magic—it *was* magic. A Guardian using combat magic in thru-space was almost certain to burn out her nervous system, or worse, her brain. A capacitor rifle with a mundane, low-tech breech solved that problem in a fashion that wouldn't blow up because it absorbed too much ambient magic. The arcane capacitors only absorbed a set amount of magic, and they safely discharged it in a single burst. It took sixty seconds for a capacitor to recharge itself, so with six spare capacitors on her belt, Priya could manage ten shots per minute with her rifle just about indefinitely.

Outside the firing port and off to her left, she could see the bronze-colored hull of the *Tempest* gleaming in the eerie light of the Rift. As the clipper sailed forward, magic coalesced around the leading edges of any protuberances on the *Tempest's* hull, then streamed back along the clipper like contrails made of stardust. The endless murkiness of thru-space was everywhere beyond the ship, like a dim pearlescent mist threaded through with currents of shadow. The closest thing to it, Priya felt, was being out on the water back home on Seuthes on a foggy, two-moon night. Off to her right, she spotted the Jeger clipper, sails fully deployed and racing past too quickly for any of the Tempest's batteries to take a shot, but also too quickly for the Jeger to take a shot, either. The Jeger ship vanished into the mists as quickly as it had appeared, and Priya snugged her capacitor rifle's stock up against her shoulder while looking out into thru-space over its barrel.

At this stage of a battle, the Jeger's ship was only a distraction. If the *Tempest* took the bait and turned to pursue it, then the marines the Jeger dropped when they started their pass would hit the clipper's aft shields and, thanks to the vagaries of shields in thru-space, they would be funneled together onto the stern where they could cause mayhem *en masse*. It was more advantageous to take the incoming Jeger marines on the lateral shields where they would end up being dispersed across the Tempest's 500-foot main hull, or at least the ones who made it past the Guardian marines like Priya.

Capacitor rifles were typically equipped with optics, but Priya preferred a clean rifle. She, as well as two of the other snipers assigned to the *Tempest*, possessed a rare magic Talent that was simply called Scout Talent. A Guardian with Scout Talent could determine the precise direction and distance to anything she was interested in with just the slightest bit of concentration. Priya always knew exactly where to aim her capacitor rifle in order to hit her target, and she had no use for fancy optics. In theory, she didn't even need the rifle's iron sights, but in practice, she found they helped her concentrate.

Jeger vacc-plate had a weak spot where the helmet and gorget met beneath the chin, and a hit there would result in instant death. It was a challenging shot to line up; the shooter and the targeted Jeger had to be at precisely the right angle relative to one another. Under normal circumstances, the Jeger, being intelligent beings, naturally took pains to ensure such opportunities did not arise, but when their boarding parties soared through the mists of thru-space, mistakes happened. Priya focused on the forward sight of her rifle, then reached out with her Talent and found one of those mistakes. She adjusted her aim, took in a slow breath, then, as she slowly released it, squeezed the trigger and felt the familiar knock against her gauntleted palm when the striker hit the capacitor and completed the rifle's circuit.

The bolt of energy vanished into the mists, and Priya worked the rifle's lever forward to drop the breech block. She withdrew the spent capacitor, slid it into its spot on her belt, then drew and loaded a fresh capacitor into the rifle. She took her second shot and was in the process of reloading for her third when the first wave of Jeger marines appeared out of the mists, and the call *"Contact! Contact! Contact!"* sang out over the comm net. Priya finished reloading her rifle and ignored them as she lined up her shot; her targets were in the second and third waves. She fired just as the Jeger in the first wave hit the *Tempest's* port shield and were decelerated with enough force to have killed a human, even one who was a Guardian. The Jeger were a sturdy species and did not normally die easily.

The second wave of Jeger marines appeared a moment later and hit the shields just as the first wave landed on the Tempest's hull and activated the grippers on their vacc plate boots. Plasma axes flared to life, and the Jeger began hacking away at the *Tempest's* outer hull under a steady hail of sniper fire from the other masts. There were more efficient ways to breach the hull of a clipper, but the corrupted Jeger were just as mad as the corrupted Dii they followed. The second wave of Jeger reached the hull just as the third wave came out of the mists; the bodies of the three Priya had killed struck the hull and bounced along it as the *Tempest* continued to sail on. Two of the bodies struck Jeger marines from the first wave, knocking them loose from the hull and sending them tumbling away from the ship to vanish into the mists.

As Priya sought out her next target, she heard the hiss of the comm as it went live. "Mast Five. Count of thirty in the first wave."

She took her shot and grimaced as she reloaded. A full platoon of Jeger in the first wave was bad news; it meant there would likely be four waves, not three, and each wave would be a full platoon. It meant their ship would be severely undercrewed and vulnerable to counter-boarding actions, but it also meant they had no intention of returning home and every intention of making certain the *Tempest* didn't, either. Priya edged closer to the firing port to give herself a better field of view of the clipper's hull and began alternating her shots between the incoming Jeger and the Jeger already on the hull. Even with a full company on the task, it would take the Jeger five minutes to carve their way into the ship, and in theory, the *Tempest's* snipers only needed half that time to clear them off the hull. It was just a matter of maintaining steady, accurate fire.

Two minutes into the battle, the Maneuver Warning Indicator rang over the comm net three times in short succession, and Priya saw light and shadow play across the hull as the *Tempest* changed course. She frowned.

The fourth wave of Jeger had just come out of the mist, but hadn't yet hit the shields; if they did so while the ship was maneuvering, it would be difficult to say where the shields would send them. The only reason the captain would order a change of course with Jeger marines inbound would be if the Jeger clipper had closed to within canon range. There was a bright flash of light behind her, and she darted a look back over her shoulder.

Priya saw the Jeger clipper's sails first, glowing brightly enough for her to see them clearly through the mists off the *Tempest's* starboard side. A bolt of energy from a Jeger canon streaked out of the mist and impacted against the *Tempest's* shields in another flash of light. Then, streaming glowing contrails of magic, the silver, needle-shaped hull of the Jeger clipper came into view. The *Tempest's* gunnery crews fired a full broadside, sending bolts of energy lancing out from the gun deck to impact and explode in coruscating, white-hot ribbons against the Jeger shields.

Something struck the exterior of Priya's fighting position hard enough for her to feel the vibration.

Priya hit the chin switch for her comm. "Mast One, impact! Can I get a visual?"

She saw motion in her peripheral vision and dropped back toward the center of the fighting position as a massive, gauntleted hand lunged toward her through the open firing port. Just outside the port, she saw the visor of a vacc-plate helmet and the Jeger glaring out at her from within it, his alien eyes like multifaceted rubies with a dim glow that stood out against his jet-black fur. She fired her capacitor rifle from the hip and hit the Jeger's visor; the armored visor held, but her shot left it with a deep gouge and a fine web of cracks centered on the Jeger's forehead. The Jeger pulled back out of her field of view as she reloaded her rifle.

"Jeger marine on Mast One! Does anyone have a shot?"

"Mast One, Mast Five. No shot here. He's using your firing position as cover."

"Mast One, Mast Four. No shot here, either."

"Mast One, Mast Two. No shot, but be advised, he just powered up his axe."

"Priya, this is Heldron. You should get out of there before he carves his way into your fighting position. You'll be able to get him when he follows you down the mast access ladder."

"He's fixated on getting me right now, Heldron," Priya replied as she slapped on the firing port shields. The fighting position immediately began to repressurize. "If I leave, he'll switch his focus to the mechanicals, and we'll lose the sails on Mast One. We've got a Jeger clipper in canon range—we lose a sail, we lose our ship. I've got this. I already dinged his helmet; two more shots, tops, and he's a goner."

"You sure you'll have time for a second shot, Priya?"

"Sure. No problem." With the fighting position once again filled with air, the sound of the Jeger chopping away at its exterior became clear. The armor protecting the fighting position was much thinner than that on the main hull. Priya shrugged, even though Heldron couldn't see her. "Worse comes to worse, I'm tethered in. I'll just tackle him off the mast and somebody can reel me in while he goes for a swim."

"That's a last resort, Priya." Heldron's tone was stern, but he didn't tell her *no*. "I'm sending a response team to your location now. Heldron out."

"Much appreciated. Priya out." Priya laid down on the deck of her fighting position and aimed her rifle up at a section of the interior bulkhead that had already begun to glow red hot. Beyond that glowing patch and in a direct line with her rifle was the weak spot in the Jeger's armor. If the Jeger was overcome with bloodlust, then he would position himself to be able to come through any breach he created as quickly as possible, which meant the atmosphere leaking through the initial breach would throw him off balance for a moment. She only needed a moment.

If his bloodlust *hadn't* overcome his caution, however, things would get dicey...

❧❧❧❧❧ ❧❧❧❧❧

"Pressure wave incoming!"

"The Jeger still have the main sails fully deployed—their ship will be torn to shreds."

The comments pulled Heldron's attention away from his comm panel and he looked up at the main imaging screen. The Jeger not only had their main sails fully deployed, they had their secondary sails fully deployed, as well; they had to angle their sails almost parallel with their direction of motion in order to keep from racing ahead of the *Tempest*. Inefficiency and stress on their hull aside, it also meant their sails were at the worst possible angle relative to the oncoming pressure wave. Instead of allowing the energy within the pressure wave to sweep past their clipper, the sails would absorb all of it and burn out every structural ward on the ship. There would be a massive debris cloud, but none of the debris would get past the *Tempest's* shields. It made no sense...unless...

"They're hiding something." Heldron spun his chair around to face Corren. "They are taking in all that magic with their sails and using the halo to blind our aetherprobes."

Casperia, the puzzled expression on her face clearly visible through her helmet's visor, turned to face Corren, as well. "If that's their goal, then they are a little late. The armillaridyne's already crossed into the Rift; we were able to record the entire event."

"Pressure wave impact in ten...nine..."

Corren's eyes went wide. "There's a second ship! Helm, evasive action, hard to port. Sound collision. All hands prepare to repel boarders."

The collision warning sounded just as the pressure wave shredded the Jeger clipper; one moment, it was a ship, the next, it was an expanding cloud of debris. The pressure wave continued on its course, pushing the debris cloud up against the *Tempest's* shields. The main imaging display hazed over, and for a moment, Heldron hoped Corren had been mistaken. Then the needle hull of a second Jeger clipper thrust through the debris, headed straight toward the *Tempest's* heart.

The deck lurched violently as both the Jeger clipper and the pressure wave hit the *Tempest* at the same time. The sounds of the collision thundered loudly enough to be both felt and heard, before giving way to a chorus of alarm tones and warning sirens. Commotion on the opposite side of the bridge drew Heldron's attention, and he saw the Weapons Officer and the Comm Tech easing the injured Assistant Engineer out of his seat and onto the deck. Crew armor wasn't as protective as marine vacc-plate, and some shrapnel from the shattered console had penetrated the heavy fabric covering the Assistant Engineer's upper arm. Channeling magic in thru-space was risky, but Heldron judged they wouldn't have any trouble healing the Assistant Engineer. The bulkhead behind the ruined engineering console, and as well as the deck beneath it, however, were both noticeably bugling inward, suggesting the *Tempest* had taken significant damage from the collision with the Jeger clipper.

Corren reset the bridge alarms and turned to Selig, the Damage Control Officer, for a status report, but Heldron had reports of his own to take. His comm clicked, and he tapped it on and immediately heard a defiant, "Heldron, Priya. Mast One is secure!"

"Good job, Priya! Reinforcements are on the way," Heldron told her, then switched to the command channel. "Section leaders, situation reports." Heldron listened as the reports from the other snipers and the squad leaders came in, then issued instructions. With that accomplished, he turned his attention to Selig's damage report.

"Hull breach, starboard side, aft of Frame 398 on the 01 Level and Decks One and Two. The Jeger ship has penetrated at an oblique angle almost to our centerline; the tip of their clipper's bow has breached the maintenance room just forward of the aft buoyancy cylinder." Selig adjusted a dial and passed a hand over an engraved metal panel on his console. A new image snapped into focus on his display, and he continued his report. "It looks like they were going too fast when they hit us; probably received a boost from that pressure wave. The starboard side of their ram deployed normally, but the port side's jammed in the forward position and it's completely obscuring the port side sally ports. They almost certainly took heavy casualties during the collision."

Corren turned to Heldron. "What are we looking at as far as Jeger boarding parties go, Heldron?"

"Externally, between our snipers and the collision knocking some of the Jeger loose, we are down to about two squads of Jeger left on the hull. It will take another two minutes to clear them off. One Jeger marine was able to create a breach in the Mast One sniper position, but Priya took down the Jeger before he was able to gain access to the ship. Master Boarding Sergeant Corrado is now backing Priya up on Mast One." Heldron paused and pointed to the deck and compartment displays on the bulkhead above the damage control station. "Internally, based on unit makers on their armor, we have what appears to be a reinforced platoon composed of individuals from multiple units that has boarded the *Tempest*. The good news is because they were only able to use their starboard sally ports, their entire force is concentrated on the starboard side of the *Tempest* forward of Frame 398. The bad news is their entire force is concentrated on the starboard side of the *Tempest* forward of Frame 398 *and* they have two fireteams armed with Dii inertia rifles. They've seized control of Gun Compartment Four and are holding there."

A new red light appeared on the Damage Control board, and Selig gave it a puzzled look. "Gun Fifteen just went offline! I'm not sure how it— Gun Thirteen just went offline, as well... How are they doing that?"

"They're carving things up with their axes, just for the sake of destruction." Corren shook his head and turned back to Heldron. "When they run out of things to destroy in the Gun Compartment, they're going to start cutting their way through the bulkheads and the deck. Any thoughts on how we can keep them from doing that?"

"Due to the position of the Jeger ship, all approaches to Gun Compartment Four from the stern of the ship are obstructed. The only clear approaches lead to the compartment's forward hatch, and the Jeger marines know it. They assume that we will launch an assault on the forward hatch. It's what they would do under similar circumstances, especially the corrupted Jeger, so they've set up their defenses accordingly. Trose and his team are going to maintain some aggressive pressure along that approach to keep the Jeger thinking that is exactly what we are preparing to do," Heldron explained. He pointed to the deck display again. "Scouts report that while the port hatch for the aft buoyancy cylinder's head-end maintenance room is possibly jammed shut, the maintenance room itself doesn't appear to be significantly obstructed by the prow of the Jeger's clipper. Joren and his team are on their way there now. "

Corren frowned at the display. "If they can cut through the hatch without alerting the Jeger, Joren and his team will be able to outflank them, then Trose and Joren can whittle down the Jeger's numbers with their crossfire. Seems like a big if, though. Joren could open that door and be facing another platoon of Jeger marines or, worse, when he and his team are fighting the Jeger in Gun Compartment Four, the Jeger remaining on the ship can come out behind them, and then it will be our marines who are trapped in a crossfire."

Heldron shook his head. "The Jeger are holding one compartment instead of trying to spread out throughout the ship like they normally do, and it's a mixed unit. I don't think they have anyone else left to send out. If they do, these are corrupted Jeger, which means they'll charge out of their ship the moment we cut that hatch open— One moment. Joren and his team have reached the hatch; he's ready to make his report."

Corren tapped the side of his helmet. "Go ahead and patch him into the bridge command channel, Heldron. Let's hear what he has to say."

Heldron nodded and linked Joren into the bridge channel. "Go ahead, Joren. What do you see?"

"The first thing that stands out is the bulkhead around the hatch has some slight buckling that extends to the hatch frame, which has been distorted a bit. The hatch is jammed shut from the damage; the only way to get it open will be to cut it open." There was a slight pause. "Looking through the viewport, I can see the nose of the Jeger ship jutting into the room—it's actually touching the aft buoyancy cylinder. The secondary ram covering the bow sally port has been jettisoned, and it's sitting on the deck in the middle of the maintenance room. There's enough room for humans to get past it, but I doubt the Jeger would be able to do so. The maintenance room's starboard hatch and bulkhead have been completely mangled by the prow of the Jeger clipper. There's no way we are getting that hatch open without a heavy plasma cutter or a breaching satchel.

"The Jeger's bow sally port is open, though, and I can see into their ship. It's a pretty grim view; the deck is covered with the bodies of dead Jeger. This," Joren hesitated, then pressed forward, "this might sound crazy, but, given the number of Jeger casualties that I see from here, I say we board the Jeger ship through their bow sally port and then exit through their starboard sally ports and outflank the Jeger that way. You know how these corrupted Jeger are—if there were any left alive over there, they would have started shooting at this hatch the moment they saw me peering through the viewport."

Heldron nodded in agreement. "He makes a good point, Corren. There's a risk, of course, but it's a lower risk than letting a Jeger boarding party having extra time to hack away at the interior of the *Tempest*."

Selig looked over his shoulder at Corren. "Gun Eleven just went offline."

"Some might call that a sign," Corren said. "All right, make it happen. Keep us updated on your progress."

"Will do, Captain. Joren out."

"Heldron, Corrado. Commander, we have an anomaly."

"What sort of anomaly, Master Guns?"

"I'm here on top of Mast One with Priya and, well, I'll let her explain it, Commander."

"Priya here, Heldron. Do you remember that Dii bomb-thing we encountered at that old Dii base? I think it was about twenty years ago."

Heldron blinked in surprise. "Yeah, I remember it. Casperia was the only one who was able to make heads or tails of the Dii wards powering it."

"Right," Priya agreed. "And if she hadn't been able to figure out how to disarm it, then it wouldn't so much have exploded as it would have ignited the local magic field and killed us all with a massive plasma fire, right?"

"I find myself growing increasingly concerned. How does this relate to the anomaly?"

"Well," Priya began nervously, "ever since then, I've been a little anxious about running into one of those things again, so I sort of dialed my Talent in to alerting me if we ever ran into another one. There's another one of those Dii bomb things on that Jeger clipper, Heldron, and it's drawing in a lot of energy. A lot more than that other one was. It looks like it's in the armory for the aft troop compartment."

"Understood. Good job, Priya. We're on it." Heldron signed off and realized his helmet comm was still tied into the bridge command channel. He rotated his chair around to face the center of the bridge. "You heard all that, Corren. It looks like someone really wants— Wait." Heldron looked over to the main imaging screen, then back over to Corren. "It's a fire ship! The Jeger marines are just a distraction—the real threat is the *ship*."

Corren arched an eyebrow at Heldron. "A what?"

"During ancient times on Old Earth when naval vessels were wooden-hulled sailing ships, a tactic of the era was to take an old vessel and load it up with explosives or highly flammable cargo. A skeleton crew would set the fire ship on a collision course with an enemy ship or an enemy fleet, light the ship's fuses, and abandon ship. The goal was for the burning fire ship to become ensnared in the enemy's rigging and then either damage or destroy the enemy's ship."

"Right." Corren looked over at Selig. "How long before the damage control parties cut us free of the Jeger ship?"

"The Chief Engineer says it will take the better part of a day, Captain." Selig motioned toward the main imaging display. "It wouldn't matter, though, not with a breach in our hull that size. We couldn't get far enough from an explosion meant to kill the *Tempest* to escape being killed."

"I can disarm it," Casperia said unexpectedly. Her eyes widened in surprised when everyone turned to her at once. "I disarmed the last one. I'll be able to disarm this one."

"You aren't wearing vacc-plate, Cassie," Corren told her, speaking as much as her husband as her captain.

"I am," Heldron said as he stood up from his chair. "Joren can send a squad to link up with us after he and his team have cut that hatch open."

Corren frowned. "How exactly are you planning on getting there with every other path blocked?"

"If we pull the floor panels in the corridor up," Heldron said as he pointed toward the door leading off the bridge, "there's an access hatch for the buoyancy cylinder. We'll just go up the interior of the buoyancy cylinder and exit out of the head-end access hatch."

Casperia gave him an uncertain look. "You want to go inside the buoyancy cylinder? That's crazy."

"If it were active, yeah, but it isn't even powered up right now. It will be fine," Heldron said, and clapped her on the shoulder. "Piece of cake."

❦

Accessing the interior spaces of a buoyancy cylinder was an activity that was normally limited to those times when a clipper was in drydock and the cylinder had been purged of all magic. Crawling through the cylinder, even when it was inactive, during a boarding action and after the clipper had been heavily damaged wasn't as simple or as risk-free as Heldron had optimistically claimed, but he and Casperia were able to arrive in the maintenance room without incident. Heldron glanced over at the port hatch and saw the metal around the lower hinge point glowing as the marines on the other side of the hatch worked to cut it free. Joren gave him a jaunty wave through the hatch viewport, which Heldron returned before advancing to the entrance to the Jeger ship.

He and Casperia paused on the threshold of the open sally port, and Heldron peered into the interior of the ship over the barrel of his capacitor rifle. A fifteen-foot passageway, broad enough for two armored Jeger to walk down side-by-side, led to the forward troop compartment, which was lit by the dim blue glow panels that the Jeger preferred to use for emergency lighting. Whatever protective systems, magical or mechanical, the Jeger had employed to protect their marines during ramming had clearly failed and armored bodies were piled against the compartment's forward bulkheads. A few of the bodies had spilled into the corridor when the inner hatch opened, but the path into the ship looked otherwise clear.

Heldron turned his head toward Casperia, who had taken up position on the opposite side of the sally port with her capacitor pistol drawn and aimed down the passage. She met his gaze and he saw one corner of her mouth quirk up in a hint of a smile through her visor. "Ready, Cassie?"

"I can feel all the magic that device is pulling into itself from here," Casperia said without answering his question. He heard her take in and release a deep breath. She tried to mask her tension with a cheerful tone. "Ready or not, let's go diffuse that mysterious alien explosive device! Lead on, *Armor Boy*!"

"That's the spirit, although I kinda wish you'd picked a better superhero name for me than *Armor Boy*." Heldron stepped cautiously into the passageway and began making his way toward the troop compartment. "Don't keep me in suspense now—what superhero name did you pick for yourself?"

"Isn't it obvious?" Casperia asked, the tension in her voice increasing slightly as they drew closer to the bodies in the passageway. "I'm *Wisely Let the Guy in Vacc Plate Go First Woman*."

Heldron threaded his way past the bodies in the passageway and paused beside the doorway into the troop compartment. The dark gemstone eyes of a Jeger who'd been killed either when he'd struck the doorframe or when he'd been crushed by his companions stared at him through a shattered helmet visor. He ignored the dead Jeger and stepped into the compartment. "Hey, Cassie?"

"Yeah, Heldron?"

"*Next* time we have to sneak onboard a clipper full of dead Jeger to diffuse a mysterious alien explosive device? *I'm* picking the superhero names."

"Sounds like a good deal to me, *Armor Boy*."

Heldron let out a short chuckle as he advanced quickly across the troop compartment to the open hatch on the far side that led deeper into the clipper. The corridor beyond the hatch was twice the width of the bow sally port passageway and was flanked on either side by hatches leading to additional troop compartments, three to port, three to starboard; each compartment was large enough to hold a platoon of Jeger marines in vacc plate. The force of the collision had been just beyond what the typical Jeger could be subjected to and survive; the Jeger holding Gun Compartment Four, who'd either come through the collision unscathed or who'd been injured and then healed up, were the toughest and meanest Jeger on their clipper. The Jeger who were only slightly tougher and meaner than average might have only been rendered unconscious by the collision rather than killed outright, and after their accelerated self-healing kicked in, they would wake up spoiling for a fight.

Heldron and Casperia advanced steadily down the corridor, pausing by each hatch only long enough to be certain that none of the Jeger bodies within each troop compartment had started showing any signs of life. The airtight door at the far end of the corridor was closed, and Heldron stood protectively by Casperia as she bypassed the arcane circuits controlling the hatch. When the hatch rolled open, the external microphones on Heldron's vacc plate picked up a rush of air coming from inside the ship. Another long, dimly-lit corridor flanked by troop compartments stretched out before them and led to another sealed airtight door.

The troop compartments in this section, unlike those in the forward section, were used for deploying external boarding parties on the clipper's initial pass of its target, and as a result, they were all empty. Heldron felt the emptiness gave the ship even more of a crypt-like feel, eerie and unsettling, even if it did allow them to pick up their pace. They paused by the controls of the second airtight door, and Casperia immediately set to work forcing it open.

Heldron heard her say, "That's odd..." and suddenly the door rolled open to reveal a Jeger in vacc-plate standing beside the control panel on the other side of the door. Heldron's capacitor rifle was only slightly out of line for a shot at the Jeger, but the Jeger's reflexes were faster than Heldron's.

The Jeger lashed out with his plasma axe and cut Heldron's rifle in half. Heldron launched himself forward to tackle the Jeger to the deck, but the Jeger pivoted to one side and slammed Heldron with a left cross that sent him crashing into the bulkhead. The Jeger brought his axe around to attack Heldron, but was knocked off balance when Casperia shot him with her pistol at close range.

The Jeger turned and moved to attack her while she was reloading. Heldron lashed out with a sweeping kick that tripped the Jeger and caused him to stumble down on to his hands and knees. Heldron leaped onto the Jeger's back, drew and activated his utility cutting tool, then plunged it into the Jeger's armored neck in an attempt to sever his right carotid artery. The Jeger's gorget, however, did its job and deflected the energy blade from its intended course just enough for Heldron's blow to miss. Heldron saw the inner glow of the Jeger's ruby-like eye sharpen in anger as it focused on him.

There was a blur of motion as the Jeger marine rose to his feet and threw himself backwards, slamming Heldron into the bulkhead and causing him to lose his grip on the Jeger. Heldron landed on top of the lower half of his rifle when he fell to the deck and quickly activated the melee shield in his left bracer. The Jeger's plasma axe slammed into the shield, throwing off sparks and plasma as the Jeger's frustrated roar erupted over his external speakers. The Jeger ignored Casperia's second shot as he locked eyes with Heldron and leaned forward to put his weight behind the plasma axe, pressing it down against Heldron's melee shield. The arcane circuits powering the shield began to smoke and pop, causing the shield to shimmer as it neared its failing point.

The Jeger pulled back his axe to finish off Heldron with a double-handed blow, but Casperia's third shot knocked him off balance again. When the Jeger turned his head to roar at her, Heldron thrust the lower half of his capacitor rifle up under the Jeger's chin. The rifle's broken barrel made it useless as a ranged weapon, but as a contact weapon, it was more than up to the task. Heldron squeezed the rifle's trigger, and a burst of energy exploded into the Jeger's helmet. The Jeger's lifeless body toppled like a fallen tree and landed on top of Heldron.

"Heldron!" Casperia ran over and helped him roll the body to one side. "Are you injured?"

Heldron groaned quietly and propped himself up on his elbows. "Yeah, thanks. I'm fine. I'm adding *unnecessarily heavy* to my list of reasons that I hate fighting Jeger."

Casperia chuckled and patted him on the shoulder. "I think you already have that on your list."

"Oh, yeah...well, I'll put a little gold star next to it, then. Nice shooting, by the way." Heldron tossed what was left of his capacitor rifle to one side and picked up the Jeger's plasma axe. He stood up, turned it on so he could inspect its balance, and then turned it off.

"We're down to a pistol and an axe. Should we wait here for reinforcements?" Casperia asked as she looked back along the direction they had come. "Or do we press on?"

"We press on. It will be a while yet before any reinforcements can come our way, and there's no telling how long it will be before that bomb goes off." Heldron hefted the axe and gave Casperia a grim smile. "This will do me just fine for any more stray Jeger we might bump into on the way to the aft armory. Once we're there, I can just grab a Dii inertia rifle from one of the weapon racks and hunker down by the door while you diffuse the bomb. Piece of cake."

"Now where have I heard that before?" Casperia shook her head, the fell in behind Heldron as they progressed deeper into the Jeger ship.

The next section of the ship contained several more pairs of troop compartments, each with a pile of dead Jeger slumped against the compartment's forward bulkhead, followed by a series of storage and maintenance compartments near the center of the vessel. The compartments were devoid of Jeger bodies, but they were also devoid of the supplies that should have been within them. The corrupted Dii who had sent these Jeger out, Heldron decided, had not intended for them to return and had been cold enough to have sent them out with empty holds. The rest of their journey down the central corridor was much the same: sporadic lighting, crypt-like silence, empty storerooms, and troop compartments containing tangled piles of dead Jeger. Heldron risked a sigh of relief when they finally stood before the aft troop compartment's airtight door.

The airtight door was unlocked, so Heldron took up position beside its control panel with his appropriated plasma axe powered up, while Casperia with her capacitor pistol took what cover she could a short distance further back along the corridor. When she signaled she was ready, Heldron hit the door control switch with his elbow.

The door snapped open and a tumble of dead Jeger marines in cracked and dented armor fell through the open doorway and collapsed onto the deck. Heldron ignored the pounding of his heart and peered around the doorframe to see the bodies of the compartment's former occupants piled against one another and the forward bulkhead. Beyond the bodies, he saw the open door of the aft armory and the dull red glow of something within the armory outside his field of view. He powered off his plasma axe.

"It looks like the coast is clear—clearish," he told Casperia over the comm. "We're going to have to do a little climbing over the bodies just past the door here to get to the armory."

Casperia stood next him, clearly trying and failing to find a path into the room that wouldn't involve stepping on any of the Jeger bodies. "Only a little climbing? I like how you are trying to keep it positive for me."

"For *you*? I'm trying to keep it positive for *me*," Heldron joked, and cautiously made his way deeper into the room. He pulled himself up onto the pile of armored bodies, then reached down to give Casperia a hand up. He thought he saw movement out of the corner of one eye, but when he turned toward it, he saw only the eyes of the dead staring back at him.

"Why did you do that?" Casperia asked in a tense whisper, her capacitor pistol aimed steadily in the direction Heldron had looked. "Tell me you didn't see movement."

"No. It was nothing." He looked back at her through his visor and shook his head. "Probably just nerves...let's get to that armory."

They scrambled down the other side of the pile of bodies and ran to the armory. The emergency lighting in the compartment had failed, but a cylindrical device as tall as Heldron illuminated the room with the red glow emanating from its cooling fins. Most of the weapon racks in the armory held only plasma axes, but Heldron quickly spotted one that held Dii inertia rifles. He made his way over to it while Casperia approached the device.

"This is the same design as last time, but a lot bigger," Casperia said, while Heldron used his axe to cut one of the rifles free from its place in the rack.

"The glyphs that make up the security wards on the access panels are very distinctive. This bomb was definitely crafted by the same individual who made the last one."

"He seems to have made a better bomb this time. The last one was barely able to get its cooling fins warm, never mind red hot." Heldron told her, trying to keep his tone as casual as he could. The inertia rifle had no power cell, and the power cell charging rack on the back wall of the armor was empty. He used the plasma axe to slice off the power cell housing as close to the barrel of the rifle as he could, hoping he'd be able to figure out a way to power it with his spare capacitors.

"Thankfully not a *better* bomb, just a *bigger* one," Casperia said, then paused. "I don't see any battery packs for those Dii inertia rifles in here, Heldron. Take my pistol. I won't be needing it to diffuse this bomb."

"The battery pack contacts are fused on this rifle, anyway. One of the Dii might be able to channel magic into it to power it up, but the strain would kill any Jeger who tried after a few shots. Everything about this says suicide mission. If they hadn't crashed a ship carrying a big firebomb into us, I might almost feel sorry for them," Heldron said as he put the inertia rifle down on the deck. He went back to Casperia and accepted her pistol. "How long do you think it will take you to diffuse the bomb?"

Casperia gave the nearest cooling fin an unhappy look. "It will be tricky with parts of it glowing red hot...two or three minutes, I think."

A clatter of armored bodies falling to the deck made them both turn sharply toward the doorway. Heldron turned back to Casperia and placed a hand on her shoulder. "Don't worry about the Jeger; I'll take care of them. You focus on diffusing that bomb."

Casperia nodded and slipped the damage control kit she was wearing as a backpack off her back. Heldron moved quickly to the doorway and peered around it into the troop compartment.

A single Jeger rose slowly to his feet, his gem-like eyes glowing brightly and already fixed on Heldron. As the Jeger powered up his plasma axe, Heldron braced himself against the door and lined up the pistol's holographic reticule. The Jeger tipped his head back to roar before starting his charge, and that was when Heldron shot him. He swapped out a fresh capacitor for the expended one and looked back over his shoulder to see how Casperia was doing.

"The inside of this device is a mess, Heldron," Casperia told him as she set an access panel down on the deck beside her. "It looks like when it was powered up half of its arcane circuits burned out. Most of the cells in its energy reservoir are slagged. If it goes off it will still have enough force to kill the *Tempest*, but it's a wonder—"

Heldron looked back over his shoulder when Casperia abruptly stopped talking. "What is it, Cass?"

"This thing was made with Guardian parts!"

"A mistake on the part of whoever made it. We can bring back a piece of the device and finally show the Council proof the Dii have infiltrated our ranks."

"You can have your pick of pieces once I diffuse it."

Motion caught Heldron's eye, and he shifted his aim toward it in time to see two bodies fall to the deck as a Jeger stepped away from the pile. A second Jeger peered over the shoulder of the first, and Heldron realized the lead Jeger's eyes were dark and its arms and legs hung limply from its body. The second Jeger, holding the body of one of his dead comrades before him like a shield, powered up his plasma axe and began advancing.

Heldron fired, hitting the Jeger's visor over its right eye, and leaving a divot in the clear armor that partially obscured the Jeger's vision. The Jeger turned his head slightly to see more clearly past the divot and broke into a run. Heldron swung open the pistol's breech, then without taking his eyes off the charging Jeger, pulled a fresh capacitor from his belt and swapped for the expended one. He returned the expended capacitor to his belt, snapped the pistol shut, and fired a second shot at the Jeger's visor. The Jeger kept charging, as Heldron knew it would, but when he reloaded and fired his pistol for a third shot, he was able to punch through the Jeger's armored visor. The Jeger's body tumbled forward onto the deck and landed barely more than fifteen feet from the armory door.

"Now that I've cleared away some of the parts that melted, I see that I was wrong, Heldron. This is unfortunately both a bigger bomb and a *better* bomb," Casperia said, and when Heldron turned to look at her, he saw the pile of bomb parts on the deck beside her had grown. "It didn't malfunction because the arcane circuits were poorly crafted, it malfunctioned because it was made with Guardian components. The Dii have alloys that aren't even possible to create in our universe, alloys that can handle a great deal more magical energy than anything we can make. When the bomb was triggered, the Guardian components couldn't handle the energy flowing through them, so they burned out or melted like this." Casperia held up what looked to Heldron like nothing but a shiny metal blob.

"So why use Guardian components, then? The Dii either smuggled our parts out of the Citadel, then built the bomb, or, more troublingly, they secretly built the bomb, then smuggled it out of the Citadel. Either way, they would, or should, have access to the Dii supply chain, right?" Heldron ran his eyes across the Jeger piled up on the other side of the troop compartment, searching for movement or the telltale glow of Jeger eyes.

"Not if they're corrupted."

"Right." Heldron focused his gaze on a Jeger body he was certain he had seen twitch slightly. Dii society was complex and not fully understood, but one thing that was certain was corrupted Dii were outcasts and hunted down without remorse. One of the Jeger bodies on the deck abruptly sat up with its back to Heldron. "Hang on. I've got movement."

The Jeger slowly turned its head until it looked at Heldron with an eye that glowed an eerie blue instead of the normal red. Back on his homeworld of Seuthes, humans had been burning the bodies of their dead for centuries in order to prevent corrupted Dii magic in the planet's ambient magic field from somehow reanimating them as feral, vampire-like creatures they called restless dead. Until recently, dead Jeger, on the other hand, had stayed dead, but as the Dii that controlled them became more corrupted, the bodies of corrupted Jeger had also begun reanimating. Fortunately, restless dead Jeger had the same weakness as living Jeger. Heldron shot the reanimated Jeger through its shattered visor, and it toppled back down onto the deck. Heldron's eyes darted across the other bodies, but to his relief, the only eyes he saw remained dark. He switched his comm to the marine command channel.

"Corrado, this is Heldron. What's our status?"

"We've cleared the hull of external boarders, Commander. We have the boarders in Gun Compartment Four pinned down and should have them cleared out soon. Joren just called in to report he was sending a squad your way; they should be there in less than ten minutes. I think we can release most everyone else to help with damage control. Unless you've run into trouble?"

"Casperia is making good progress on the bomb, but I'm staring at a compartment full of dead Jeger on a ship full of dead Jeger, and one of the bodies just reanimated."

The comm was silent while Corrado went offline to vocalize the expletives he felt best suited the situation. "I guess that explains why somebody was willing to send their Jeger on a one-way mission. The only time insane, undead Jeger are a good thing are when they are somebody else's problem.

I'll pass it up to the captain, Commander, and we'll send everyone we can spare your way."

"Appreciate it, Master Boarding Sergeant. Heldron out." Heldron searched for movement or glowing eyes among the dead Jeger, then cast a look back at Casperia. The cooling fins nearest to her had stopped glowing, which he took to be a positive sign. "How's it going, Cassie?"

"This is one of those good news-bad news situations." Casperia paused as she tugged what remained of an arcane reservoir cell free of its housing and placed it next to the other components on the deck beside her. "The bomb is radiating so much B-band arcane energy that it's causing instabilities in the local magic field. It's creating dead spots where my tools don't work; I have to waste time pulling out slagged components so I have room to work. The good news is the bomb is so damaged that it isn't going to go off for probably another fifteen minutes. I'll have it disarmed in another couple of minutes, so we have plenty of time, but it's *really* annoying."

"It's radiating B-band energy? Is that because it's malfunctioning or is it intentional?" Heldron said as he ran his eyes across the Jeger. Arcane energy occurred in three bands, with the B-band being the dominant band of the Dii's home universe as well as the band the Dii drew upon when channeling magic. The dominant band of magic in the human universe was the Y-band, and the Dii were drawn to strong sources of B-band energy in the human universe like desert travelers to an oasis.

"It looks like it's intentional, but that doesn't make any sense," Casperia replied. "I'll be able to figure out more once I'm not worried about anything blowing up on me."

A twitch of motion on the left side of the pile of bodies drew Heldron's attention, and he centered his sight on the Jeger that had moved. A pair of glowing blue eyes stared back at him, and after a moment they were joined by a second pair. On the right side of the pile, three more Jeger with glowing blue eyes rose stiffly to their feet. Heldron aimed for a Jeger with a shattered visor and took it down with a single shot, but as he was reloading, two more restless dead Jeger rose to their feet. There was a clatter of bodies as another reanimated Jeger emerged from deeper within the pile. One of the restless dead remembered how to activate its plasma axe and the others quickly followed suit.

Heldron glanced back at Casperia and saw she was shoulder-deep inside the Dii bomb. He took a deep breath, rose to his feet and stepped out in the troop compartment. Restless dead, whether they were once human or Jeger, were always slow and stiff when they first reanimated, but after a few moments, they were able to move as quickly and as surely as they had in life. He would never be able to stop a swarm by himself with only a capacitor pistol, and they would overrun him and then kill Casperia before she had time to finish deactivating the Dii bomb. Heldron took another calming breath as more reanimated Jeger emerged from the pile. It wouldn't be long before they charged him, and the only way he could stop them would be to channel magic. It was simply a matter of projecting a wall of telekinetic force.

Simple, that is, if he hadn't been standing in a destabilized magic field on a clipper in thru-space. The instability of the local magic field was something Heldron hoped he could use to his advantage; in an unstable field, even a fairly weak wall of force would react violently when it collided with a dead Jeger animated by Dii magic. Channeling magic in thru-space was usually fatal, but if he channeled only enough magic to create a weak wall of force, he'd probably survive. Maybe. Hopefully.

One of the Jeger began shuffling towards him, and Heldron opened himself up to allow the magic to flow into him. He gritted his teeth as his nervous system felt like it was catching fire. His vision went dark around the edges, and he focused on the thought pattern for projecting a wall of force. All of the Jeger had begun walking towards him; one of them managed to break into a trot and raised its plasma axe above its head. Heldron held out both hands in front of himself and concentrated on pushing.

At first, the wall of force was little more than a faint distortion in the air, but within moments, bolts of energy began coruscating across it. The lead Jeger crashed into the wall as much as it crashed into him, and the bolts of energy converged on him, causing him to burst into flames. Heldron dropped to one knee and pushed the wall forward into three more Jeger. The bolts of energy converged on them, then seemed to take on a life of their own as they leaped from the crumbling bodies to Jeger behind them and again to the pile of bodies against the bulkhead. The entire wall of force erupted into a shimmering plane of energy that vaporized the remaining Jeger, glowing so fiercely as it did so that it would have blinded Heldron if he hadn't already collapsed, unconscious and dying, onto the deck.

# # #

Six hours later, Heldron was lying with his eyes closed on a bed in the *Tempest's* medical bay when he heard a knock on the door. He opened his eyes and saw Corren and Casperia standing in the doorway, then waved them into the room. "Hey, guys, c'mon in. How's the *Tempest* doing?"

"She's hanging in there. Luckily, there's enough debris from that first Jeger clipper floating nearby that there is no shortage of material we can use for patching and shoring up," Corren said as he crossed the room. He lightly punched Heldron in the shoulder. "Go easy out there, bro. You had me worried."

"Worried? Over a little magic burn?" Heldron shook his head. "Doc said it's nothing a few months' rest without using magic can't fix."

Corren traded a glance with Casperia and took a slow breath. "I'm afraid we're going to need you sooner than that."

Heldron sat up straighter in his bed and winced. "Oh? What's happened?"

Corren glanced over to the doorway, then nodded to Casperia. She withdrew a small device from her pocket that would prevent anyone from overhearing their conversation and activated it. "I brought back enough of that Dii device to get a rough idea of how it was meant to work and to estimate how much energy it would have released, had it been built using Dii components instead of Guardian components."

"I saw some of the components you pulled out of it, Cassie. I'm guessing if it had worked correctly, it would have generated one big, honkin' explosion, probably big enough to—" Heldron broke off abruptly as his eyes went wide. "The Citadel! They are planning on blowing up the Guardian Citadel, aren't they?"

Casperia shook her head. "The device can be used as a bomb, but that isn't its intended purpose. What we thought were cooling fins are actually meant to generate a sort of pocket dimension around the device that expands as the device charges its arcane reservoir over the course of several months."

"That explains why the ambient magic field in the vicinity of the device had become unstable," Heldron said thoughtfully. "What purpose would the Dii have for something like that?"

"If the device was activated on a planet with a strong, Y-band ambient magic field, then by the time the arcane reservoirs were full, the area affected by the pocket dimension would be at least two miles in diameter. When the device detonated, it would cause a chain reaction that would ignite the planetary ambient magic field in a massive plasma storm. The plasma storm would wipe out every living thing on the planet, and when the ambient field reformed, it would be shifted into the B-band."

"Making the planet more hospitable to the Dii, who have the magic and the knowhow to shape the planet's climate and ecology to whatever suits their needs." Heldron let out a low whistle. "I suppose we can be grateful that these devices go all melty when they are made from Guardian components."

"That isn't all, Heldron," Corren said. "We just got a message from the Citadel calling us back for an emergency Council meeting. The Archivists have recovered more of the Founders' files from the damaged portions of the Core, and it seems two thousand years ago the Founders recovered one of these devices, one made from materials that don't exist in our universe, from the wreckage of a Dii armillaridyne. They brought it back to a secure laboratory on Seuthes to study it further."

"There's one of these things on the planet already? Where?"

Corren shook his head. "The records don't say exactly where it is, but we need to figure it out and find it before the corrupted Dii in our ranks, or any other Dii, for that matter, can recover it."

Just Another Day in the Neighborhood

SHERRI MINES

MARINE SERGEANT REX URSSON and his team were walking down Main Street, his head looking left and right, taking everything in. This...retirement village thing was different.

Even now, three years after the event, the feel of a rundown, seedy theme park remained. The shops on the main street all looked the same: bright and cheery colors starting to fade, the awnings beginning to sag. A sign in one window said, "The Village. Live your Earth dream life. Every day." The landscaping at the end of the road was awash with green grass and trees, but the lawns were ragged, and the trees and bushes looked wild and unkempt. It was clear that minimal maintenance was being performed. The road was lined with carriage lanterns (*carriage lanterns?*). Okay, make that a somewhat *creepy* rundown seedy theme park.

An easy mission, they said. Some extra spending money and a few more bucks in the kitty, they said. Walking through The Village was creepy, and maybe futile, but the survivors needed any and all supplies they could find.

❧❧❧❧❧ ❧❧❧❧❧

Rex was on leave watching netball with Dan'l on Rachel 7 when the message from Lieutenant Astor came in.

Sergeant, you and Corporal Morgan are being volunteered for a mission to the habitats. Don't know all the details: there's money in it for you, and RobinCorp would owe us a favor.

As he was reading, a second message came in.

Remember, our time is valuable. Make him pay for the privilege (Evil grin). Oorah!

YES SIR!

Messages were exchanged, prices were negotiated, and contracts were prepared. RobinCorp was pleased.

I will inform Lieutenant Astor of your cooperation. Maps for this mission will be sent to your apartment. Report to the private spaceport on the south side in five days and take the shuttle to The Village. A clerk will meet you with supplies and a master key to open the neighborhoods and buildings. A Mr. Seymour Brown will be assisting you with your mission: he is from one of the other habitats. Do you have any questions?

Rex had only one question before signing: *Why do you need the Space Marines?*

Crickets.

Sir?

Security and landscapers report strange noises throughout The Village. Snakes and alligators have also been reported living in the Bayou Country neighborhood.

Snakes and alligators? On a habitat?

Rumor has it a resident snuck in the critters to be pets, and they got out when the habitat was evacuated.

Rex glanced over at Dan'l, who gave a faint nod. Why not? These types of missions were what they lived for. Support the Commonwealth, help the populace when needed, and stomp into meat paste anyone who got in their way.

They signed the contract.

❧❧❧❧ ❦❦❦❦

The walk down Main Street seemed to take forever. When the road ended, a large, faded sign directed them to the neighborhoods. Cy liked the lighthouse carving, so they turned left towards Penobscott Bay. Dan'l took the lead to look for oddities or interesting items. In the middle, Cy was driving the vehicle and watching side to side. Rex walked behind them, observing and providing cover.

The meandering road was lined with greenery along the edges and gave the impression of complete privacy. After a few minutes, an elaborate pair of wrought iron gates appeared. A stylized "P.B." in flowing script was encircled by an oval on the left gate. Fishing boats and a lighthouse on the right gate confirmed their destination as Penobscott Bay. When Dan'l reached for the gate, Rex yelled, "Corporal, stop!"

Dan'l turned. "What?" He sounded annoyed.

"The gate is a laser image, and we get zapped if not authorized. Move to the right of the vehicle; I will open the gate, and we walk together as we go in." Rex pulled out the master key. He selected the neighborhood, then Open Gate, and pushed the button. The gates swung open, then faded away. They went through, turned the corner, and stopped. Everything looked real.

Weathered but well-maintained fishing boats floated in the marina. The Harbormaster's building was decorated with the typical fishing nets and cork floats, and offered "Fresh caught lobster, shrimp and oysters" for purchase. Walking down the street, the two-story Cape Cod homes were close together with minimal front yards. A faint breeze carried in a tangy mix of brine and seafood.

Time for some training. "Dan'l, look around and evaluate the buildings. Brown, take the master key and open any doors Dan'l tells you to. Make a quick recon for anything on the urgent list and take notes. Drive forward when I tell you, and we'll load what we can."

Cy blinked, and asked, "What will you do, Sarge?"

"I'm your security, and will cover you." *Grumble, civilians, grumble...*

Every home they entered was empty of survivors (or remains). Most had clothing and looked like the owner would be back later that day. A few had food supplies. One home with a "Doctor" sign in the front yard had very few medical supplies; it was primarily stocked with bandages of various sizes and elastic wraps for sprains. Cy made notes of all of it. When they arrived at the edge of the last block, the surrounding vegetation and faint sound of waves gave the impression the neighborhood was much larger, and the ocean was just around the corner.

The team found a home with two exits that would provide cover for the evening. Paint was peeling from the clapboards in a few places, but gave the impression it had weathered many winter storms, and would be patched and good as new again come spring. The store had yielded a seafood bounty: frozen lobster, crab, and oysters, plus bread and clam chowder in pouches. They dined on the seafood and stashed some bread and chowder in the vehicle as part of their rations. After dinner Dan'l explained the night watch to Cy, while Rex went out for a final reconnaissance as the light slowly faded into evening.

He sat on a bench at the marina at twilight, entranced by the combination of sky and water. Most habitats had levels and ceilings that tried to trick you with sky projections. But this neighborhood was different, and there was no structure above him. Yes, they were still sky projections, but they gave the feeling of being on a real planet with real stars above.

***

Five days later, wearing their "unofficial mission uniform" of deep blue coveralls, Rex and Dan'l took the Habitat circuit shuttle from RobinCorp's spaceport, getting off at The Village administrative area. Two people were standing next to a vehicle: a younger man in brown Village coveralls, and a middle-aged man wearing a badge and holding a clipboard who Rex assumed was the clerk.

"You Ursson and Morgan? Sign here." The badge said his name was Fred.

"Not so fast, Fred. What am I signing for?"

"The vehicle, a master key and some supplies. I need your signature." He held out the clipboard.

"Settle down. We need to look things over first."

The young man in coveralls stepped forward and held out his hand. "I'm Seymour Brown from Habitat 8. Call me Cy. Want me to take a look? It's similar to the vehicles we have on the farm."

"You a mechanic?"

"Not officially, but I work on them a lot at home."

"Go ahead. And thank you."

While Cy inspected the vehicle, Rex and Dan'l checked the supplies in the back. They were given a small amount of food and water, an onboard refrigerator freezer, notebooks and writing implements, and two company-issued pistols designed to incapacitate a person but not damage the habitat.

Cy walked over, wiping his hands on a rag. "It's a typical no-maintenance piece of government crap. I can keep it running for a while. How long will we need it?"

"Best guess three or four weeks."

"I can do that."

Rex signed the forms, returned them to the clerk, loaded their duffels and headed out.

The entrance to The Village was...not normal. Brick walls with barbed wire on top led up to the large wrought iron gates with spiked arches. A massive lock on a large iron chain looped through the gate. Rex wondered if they were keeping people out or keeping them in. One guard asked for their names when they pulled up to the gate, and a second guard checked over the vehicle. Nodding, they opened the large gates and locked them again once the vehicle entered The Village.

***

The team packed up in the morning and made their way to the next neighborhood. This gate appeared to be made from weathered driftwood, sanded and nailed to a large wooden fence. A large sign attached to the driftwood stated, *Welcome to Caribbean Dream*, its bold graphics of a smiling sun, beachgoers, and swaying palm trees starting to fade. *Sun, Swim, and Party!* was in large letters below the images. The sign reminded him of an old Earth postcard his grandfather owned.

Again, they stopped when they walked in, heads turning as if on a swivel. It couldn't be more different from the previous neighborhood. Where the weather in Penobscott Bay was cool and crisp, this was warm, sunny and just a touch humid. The sky, clouds and their surroundings seemed brighter, as if a different sun hung in the sky.

Turning the corner, a large beach and half-empty wave pool beckoned, with the deck chairs, small tables and large umbrellas still open, just waiting to be used again. A tropical restaurant and bar with bamboo walls and a thatched roof stood across from the pool. Signs hanging from the roof offered burgers, fries, tiki drinks and something called boat drinks made with fresh fruit. A hand-scrawled sign attached near the entrance said, "Margaritas: 5 cents."

Large screened-in porches dominated the front of the small, white-painted homes, waiting to catch the breeze. Through the screens, they could see rocking chairs, tables, even a small grill. It was clear the residents had spent a lot of time outside.

Tropical signposts adorned the street corners instead of the traditional street signs.

DOCTOR - 2 BLOCKS with an arrow pointing right

BEACHCOMBER WAY pointing forward

PENOBSCOTT BAY - 12 MILES pointing left

Over the years, residents had added their own signs.

EARTH - 24 LIGHT-YEARS

GLIESE CANTINA - RACHEL 7 SPACEPORT

ANY CATHOUSE - TOO FAR with a sad face

KEY WEST - IN YOUR HEART

IT'S DAYLIGHT SOMEWHERE with a tilted drink starting to spill

This doctor's office contained few medical supplies; the shelves contained treatments for upset stomachs and analgesics, plus a few hangover cures they recognized from shore leave.

Beachcomber Way ended at a parking lot on top of a sand dune. They parked and walked down the path to a light-blue sea that seemed to go on forever, with small waves lapping a beach of white sand mixed with small stones. Eight beachcomber-style shacks sat above the tide line in two groups with picnic tables, fire pits and grills set between them. They decided to spend the night in the shacks. It wasn't protocol, but for some reason, it felt right.

They found very little food available in this neighborhood: mostly canned or frozen pouches of cocktails. They made a picnic from the chowder and other supplies from Penobscott Bay and the back of the vehicle. As they ate, Dan'l made them laugh as he spun a tale of an adventure while on leave. He had a talent for putting people at ease, and most thought he was just a big goofball. They had no idea he was an accomplished tracker and scout, and a valuable member of the Space Marines.

Rex didn't like beaches: the sand got into *everything*. But sitting with the team, listening to the waves and sipping a cold drink in the warm breeze felt mighty good.

Searching the restaurant in the morning turned up some instant coffee packs and frozen breakfast burritos. While the burritos heated, Rex spread the maps out and reviewed the plan. "Our next two neighborhoods are Fairy Tale by the Sea and The Forest. Stay in the same pattern: Dan'l in the front, while I provide rear cover. Brown, you're doing a good job: continue your tasks."

They took every coffee pack, stuffing them wherever they would fit. After all, they were Marines.

❦

The gate at Fairy Tale by the Sea was a large hand-painted mural depicting a small village of Tudor-style cottages nestled in front of a curved white sand beach. A brief hint of the ocean peeked out in front of the beach, and *An Artisan's Dream Come True* was tastefully written in the sand.

Down the road from the gate was a building resembling a stone castle that greeted you with shops selling "Handcrafted Wares and Fyne Food." A quick look inside the shops showed random clusters of tables and display cases. A lone necklace of gold and black stone attached to a woven leather cord had been left behind on a back table. A sign on the front of the bakery proclaimed, "Carnivores and Herbivores Come Hither" and "Pyes Sweet and Savoury." The kitchen was locked, and it took a few tries before Cy found the right building on the master key. A faint smell of spices still lingered in the kitchen pantry, and to their delight, the freezer shelves contained a few trays of hand pies.

While Rex and Cy finished searching the building, Dan'l scouted the road ahead, casually meandering towards The Forest in a loose zig-zag pattern. Just a man in a coverall on a stroll... A few minutes later, he returned to the castle entrance and Rex saw him spread out his hand and hold it at a forty-five-degree angle. "What did you see?"

"There are fresh traces of a human and a dog. Hard to tell in this dirt, maybe a week or so."

Rex nodded. "We're moving out in five minutes: everyone grab the pies and do anything else you need to do. Be alert, but don't panic. Dan'l will let us know when we are getting close." He went inside to do the needful. "This neighborhood will wait."

※※※※ ※※※※

Down the road from Fairy Tale by the Sea was The Forest. The gate was a beauty of polished redwood planks, seemingly tied together with vines. Small blue flowers were growing through the cracks. Cy shone a light on the gate, and the words "The Forest" glowed in the light. Looking closer, the letters had been carved into the boards and inlaid with what looked like a pale semi-translucent quartz. A small sign to the right of the gate stated, *Calm Happens Here*. This gate sparkled as it faded away.

Large trees interspersed with greenery surrounded them. The homes were farther apart here, built in the spaces between the trees in a random pattern. He saw a log cabin, a craftsman-style bungalow and a small dome house, all blending harmoniously into the scenery. Walking paths branched out from the main road, inviting you to take a stroll. Rex could see a picnic table down one of the paths. A light breeze with the smell of pine needles, something green and fresh, and a hint of wood smoke scented the air. A thin layer of fog was visible in the distance, and you could hear an occasional bird chirping and the scrabble of small animals in the background. Instead of an artificial habitat, this area felt *alive*.

Rex smiled. It reminded him of his grandfather's ranch in the TeeGarden system. He and a few Marine buddies bought the property when they retired, with the goal of resting and recreating as much as possible. Rex loved going there on school vacations, running and playing without adult supervision, and just being a kid. He couldn't wait to tell gramps about this latest adventure.

A quarter mile in, Dan'l held up a fist, and the group stopped. Rex stepped to the front. "How far?"

"Tracks point about four houses down."

He nodded. "The corporal and I will take point. Brown, stay in the vehicle and make noise if you see someone. We will move forward slowly." They began walking.

An old woman came out of the house on the left carrying a shotgun. A small furry...thing at her feet growled. "Who are you? What do you want? Go away! Get off my lawn!" She was that unknown older age between fifty and eighty, with dark brown and gray hairs in a long braid down her back.

She wore jeans, a sweater, and an attitude. "I said who are you and what do you want?"

"Ma'am, I am Sergeant Ursson of the Space Marines, and we are here to rescue you and take you somewhere safe."

"A little late for that, sonny!" She raised the shotgun. "How do I know that you're not part of the Corporation that tried to kill everyone? Maybe you want my body for science?"

"What? *No!* I mean we are here to help you, ma'am, not take your body for science." He visibly shuddered at that last statement.

She looked him up and down. "A Space Marine, eh? You're a big one. What are you doing here in the ass end of The Village?"

"Looking for you, ma'am. We are on a rescue mission, looking for supplies and survivors."

"Don't you sass me, young man, show some respect."

"Yes, ma'am. I'm sorry, ma'am."

"*Humph.*"

"Is there anyone else," he hesitated, "alive in the neighborhood?"

"No, just me and Bettie."

"Ma'am, I apologize, but we need to check out the other homes. Can we bring some food back and join you for dinner?"

His politeness seemed to impress her. "Of course, where are my manners. Just the three of you?"

"Yes, ma'am."

Her face scrunched as she was thinking. "Okay, come back at sunset. We will have dinner on the back patio."

They chatted about the old lady while clearing the other homes. *What is she doing here? Why is she by herself? What's up with that dog?*

"Why are you being so nice to her?" Cy asked.

"You catch more flies with honey."

"Huh?"

"I'll explain later."

There were no other people in The Forest: the rest of the neighborhood was empty. Rex noticed the pantries and cupboards were almost bare, guessing the old woman had been taking supplies as needed. "Okay, team, it's time to head back for dinner with our survivor. We'll bring her some pies and a couple of pouches of the chowder."

The old woman's house reminded him of a miniature version of the great lodge Grandpa built. A portico sheltered the entrance with posts of wood and large river stones. The fireplace used the same stones and took center stage in the family room, with comfortable chairs facing the hearth. An oil painting of Rachel 7 highlighting the shipyards and the spaceport hung over the mantel. The interior was paneled in a warm colored wood. He approved.

Cy carried in the box with pies and chowder pouches.

"Oh, you found Hester's pies! Best pies in the solar system. Bettie and I tried, but couldn't get the door unlocked." The old woman smiled. "I bet you're wondering why a Medieval castle sits outside a fancy artist colony."

"The thought had crossed our minds, ma'am."

While the pies and chowder were heating, she told them the story.

Hester was a famous restauranteur who wanted to semi-retire to The Village and open a small bakery. She purchased the building outside of Fairy Tale from RobinCorp and began remodeling the space. Fairy Tale management was not amused: their tony neighborhood was for "true artisans" and (-sniff-) commerce did not belong. They sued to have her removed, claiming her bakery was an eyesore and "a commercial enterprise near Fairy Tale by the Sea is a throwback to medievalism." Hester smiled, brought some pies to the hearing, and offered to modify the contract to give RobinCorp a small percentage of the profits. The company agreed to the change (with an additional clause guaranteeing fifty pies a month sent to upper management, and five pies to the judge).

Fairy Tale had lost. As a final finger wave, she changed the outside of the building to resemble a castle, added shops so the Fairy Tale residents could sell their creations, and changed the theme to a Renaissance Faire.

By the time the story was over, the pies were ready, the chowder was hot, and the old woman had put together a simple side dish of fresh vegetables with a homemade dressing. Everyone helped carry the food through the house to the back patio. Metal raised beds with vegetable plants surrounded the patio fence, and a couple of berry bushes were tucked in the corners. In the middle, Rex saw a card table with a blanket thrown over it, its rips and tears carefully mended. A thermos of hot water, plus a few tea bags in a small bowl, were sitting on the table. Two solar lamps on the table provided light for the food, and a few more lamps throughout the patio were gently flickering. When everyone had a cup of water or tea, she said, "Thank you for joining me. Now pass over them pies."

During dinner, they chatted. She asked them to introduce themselves, and why the Space Marines were here.

"I'm Sergeant Rex Ursson, leader of this..." He waved a hand at the others. "...Team."

"I'm Corporal Lou Morgan. Everyone calls me Dan'l."

"Howdy. I'm Seymour Brown. My nickname is Cy. I'm from Habitat 8, and trying to figure out if I want to join the Space Marines." He grinned. "My uncle is the person who hired you guys; Mom browbeat him until he found this opportunity for me."

They explained their mission to gather and catalogue supplies. She nodded. "There's a few supplies left here, mainly bigger stuff a community might use. Hell, there's a pizza oven on the back corner of Darryl's deck."

Cy's eyes lit up. "A pizza oven? Really?"

Sighing, she said, "Settle down, boy. Yes, it's a pizza oven." *Grumble, wet behind the ears, grumble...*

"Why don't you use it?"

"It burns wood and I don't have any."

Puzzled, Cy looked around, gesturing at the trees. "There's wood all around you."

The old woman shook her head. "Get real, boy. Short? Old? I can't cut down trees, and even if I could, how the hell am I supposed to drag the wood back over to the pizza oven?" *Grumble, get your head out of your stomach, grumble...*

Bettie stayed close to the old woman or walked around the table, keeping an eye on the group. Dan'l tried to feed her a tidbit from his plate, but she put her nose in the air, huffed, and walked away. "I guess she doesn't like people food."

"Oh, she loves people food. She just doesn't trust you."

"You wound me, Madam." Dan'l dramatically put his hand over his heart.

Rex rolled his eyes. "Sorry, ma'am, he's a drama queen."

Laughing, Cy asked, "How long have you lived here, ma'am?"

"Going on ten years now. A few years by myself. Bettie helps by keeping me company. She warns me of trouble and was known to bite a few ankles in her day."

"Why didn't you leave with the others?"

"Well... Bettie and I were under the weather, and I guess we were sicker than we knew. We woke up, and everyone was gone." She bent down, petted Bettie, and changed the subject. They looked at each other, skeptical, but dropped the discussion for now. Over dessert (fresh-picked berries), the old woman asked Rex if he had any coffee.

"I have some instant coffee singles in my pack. Would you like them?"

Her eyes got wide. "If I was younger, I'd throw myself at you for that coffee. Still might, if it would help."

Rex smiled. "It's okay, ma'am, I understand. Coffee is God's way of keeping us from murdering other people."

They helped clean up and prepared to leave. Rex thanked her for her hospitality and let her know they were leaving in the morning to move on to the next neighborhood.

"If you want to watch the roads, I have the keys to a house that looks out over three streets. You can bunk down there for the night and use any supplies that are left. Come on back in a few days—a girl needs her alone time. Tell you what: if you bring some supplies, I will make dinner."

"Thank you, ma'am, we will take you up on your offer."

The house she pointed out provided a good vantage point for watching the neighborhood. They chose the large, sunken living room to bunk down in for the night. After everyone was asleep, Rex left the house, ambled back to the old woman's house and quietly knocked on the door. "Ma'am?"

"What? Do you know what time it is? A girl needs her beauty sleep." *Grumble...*

"Ma'am, can we talk?" he asked softly. "Please."

She stood there looking at him for a while, then came to a decision. "Come on in. Do you drink bourbon?"

He nodded. "I enjoy bourbon, but it's a rare treat."

She pulled down a bottle and two glasses, added some clear ice, and poured a generous serving for each of them.

"This is very good bourbon, ma'am."

A long, slow sigh. "Bob always did have good taste." She looked up. "My husband Bob worked for Allen at the shipyards."

"The shipyards? You knew old man Moranis?"

"Yes. We were friends with Allen and his wife Rachel. Bob was one of the original workers who built the shipyard, then we stayed and made our home on Rachel 7. Remember the big accident?"

"Yes, ma'am, what a cluster f..." He shook his head.

"Bob was seriously injured. Allen gifted us this house, a lifetime pension, and unlimited credit with all the shops in The Village. He said it was the least he could do as a thank you for Bob's friendship and hard work for so many years." She took another sip. "He found peace here. I would wheel him on the paths, and we would sit with trees around us. It helped to ground him in the world. We had five years in this home." Another sigh. "I wish it had been more."

They were silent for a while, just sipping and sharing the quiet. The old woman stirred, set down her glass and saw him out the front door.

"Goodnight, ma'am."

"Goodnight, Rex." Softly, she added, "See you soon."

❧❦

Next stop was The Cocoon. The gate was surprisingly simple: a large white egg painted on the left side of a beige rectangle, and an inscription on the right that said, *The Cocoon. Live Your Virtual Life.*

The neighborhood was just like the sign: beige and bland. No scents, no sounds, no fancy homes or immersive backgrounds. Just row after row of long, low beige apartments, and a light-blue sky projection overhead. Near the gate, the "Food and Delivery" building (beige, of course) had several small delivery robots parked outside waiting to be deployed. They packed up a few supplies to take back to the old woman, and they grabbed some bagged snacks and ready-to-heat meals for themselves.

The apartment buildings were all the same: single story, beige exterior with small clerestory-style windows near the roof providing light to the inhabitants. A line of doors with numbers were the only identifying marks. They chose one at random, opened unit 48-R0, and went in. The apartment had light beige walls and a slightly darker floor. In the small entry hall, he saw an alcove on the right and a door on the left.

The alcove contained a small pre-manufactured kitchen unit from a ship's chandlery, a refrigeration unit, an individual heating unit, and a few storage cupboards. The door opened to another chandlery unit: a small bathroom with a toilet and one-person 'fresher. Rex had seen temporary housing setups with more personality.

Moving all they way in, they spied a giant egg dominating the room, plus a bed and small chest of drawers against the far wall. Walking around the "egg" revealed it to be a chair with a plush, cushy interior. Small electrodes protruded out of the head rest with built-in speakers on each side. A console arm on the side could be lifted up and slid over the edge. The top of the console had large white buttons marked, *Play. Read. Chat. Watch. Food. Housekeeping.*

The cupboards in the kitchen were full. Whoever had lived here was fond of Asian food: they found packs of stir fry, Thai soup, and precooked rice with green onions and soy sauce. They gathered up some packs and moved on.

Every unit they entered looked the same: beige, egg, bed, alcove and door. Occasionally, the walls were painted a slightly different shade of beige. A few units had a larger egg and no bed. That evening, they chose a partially finished unit to sleep in: it had basic facilities, but no egg or bed. Dinner was easy: open the pouch, pull out the utensils and place on top of the heating unit. The pouch lowered into the unit, and came back out steaming in a bowl or a cup. After dinner, you placed your items in the appropriate slot in the cleaning/disposal unit: *Dishes and Utensils, Food Waste, Garbage.*

During dinner, Rex asked Cy why he wanted to join the Space Marines. "Habitat 8 is agricultural. Growing up, it was expected we would get married and join either our family's or the in-law's farm. I want to explore the outside world before I make my decision to stay or permanently leave. Got some talent with machinery and thought the Space Marines might appreciate me." He grinned. "Speaking of my talent, I need some time to look at the vehicle tomorrow. Something is not right in the steering."

Cy and Dan'l worked on the vehicle in the morning, and they got underway a couple of hours later.

The Lotus Eaters gate appeared to be a piece of sheet metal painted in random splatters of color. Copper letters spelled out Lotus Eaters, and below was the phrase, *No Rules. No Consequences.* Pink and white lotus flowers made of metal dotted the top of the gate. They barely made it inside after the gate opened. The devastation and filth were mind-boggling. Everything was burned, destroyed or desecrated. *Why would anyone...? Shudder.* They left after a very abbreviated recon, and returned to their previous shelter in The Cocoon for the evening.

Dan'l had a surprise for them: cocktails he had saved from Caribbean Dream. "Thought this would wash away the taste of The Lotus Eaters." They clinked cans, and toasted never going in there again.

※

When they returned to the old woman's place, they presented her with dried noodles, frozen meat chunks and small containers of freeze-dried garlic, onions, and mixed vegetables. She thought for a moment, then nodded. "Rex and Cy, you will help me in the kitchen. Dan'l, go out back and make yourself useful. Harvest one large cabbage and two onions. If you see a pepper, grab one. Thank you."

"Yes, ma'am!" everyone said in unison, smiling.

Grumble, not your mother, grumble... "Get with it! You don't work, you don't eat!"

Rex washed and chopped the vegetables, and broke the meat into small pieces. Cy heated a large frying pan and added the meat and veggies to the hot pan. The old woman put the noodles on, measured spices into a bowl, and topped them with a bit of the freeze-dried garlic and onions. After a few minutes, she poured the spice bowl into the sautéed meat and veggies, added some noodle water, then stirred in the drained noodles. Dan'l pulled out the dishes and set the table. The completed meal was put in a large serving bowl, and dinner was ready. It was very good, and very filling.

Over dinner, Rex asked about the landscaping. "The trees and plants look real. Do you know how they managed it?"

"The trees and bushes in the front are real for a little over a mile, mostly redwoods, sequoias, and mesquite. Beyond that, it's a background projection of real forest and mountains from elsewhere. Most of the animals are holograms. Rumor has it a few small bobcats are real, specially bred for the habitats to catch rodents. Never seen one, if they exist. I don't know how much it costs to maintain this place, but the fact that I can sit next to a real tree, lean against it and know it's alive is worth more than any money I have."

They helped her clean up, and said they would see her in a few days. "Goodnight, ma'am."

"Dammit, call me Grandma. I *hate* 'ma'am.' And that's an order!"

"Yes, ma'am!" She gave them all the evil eye. "YES, GRANDMA!" they shouted, grinning.

Rex came back again that night, and they chatted over a glass of bourbon. Grandma asked about his name. "Rex...Ursson? It's an unusual name."

A long, heavy sigh. "Our family traces back to the Vikings on old Earth. My grandfather has an old research paper stating aurochs interacted with Vikings during Scandinavia's Iron Age, and decided that the bison was our family's source of strength." She stared at him. "I know, I know, but Gramps was adamant. When he joined the Space Marines, he changed his name to Sigurd Jurgen Ursson. They called him Siggy." Rex reached inside his shirt, pulled out a pendant, and showed it to her. A large, annoyed-looking bison was hanging from a silver chain. On the back, a carved rune was inlaid with a blue stone that seemed to glow. "All Gramps would say is he picked it up during his travels, and that it was carved from a special stone." Rex smiled at the memory. "He wore it as long as I can remember. It was his gift to me when I passed basic training."

"Your name isn't Rex, is it?"

"No, ma'am. My full name is Ragnar Magnus Ursson. My nickname is Rex." He got up to leave. "Good night, ma'am. See you in a few days."

❧❧❧❧❧ ☙☙☙☙☙

The neighborhoods continued on. And on. And on. They became weary of The Village and its many neighborhoods, and wanted this mission to be over and done with.

Looking back, Rex could only remember fragments of the later ones: the bunny slopes and virtual skiing of Alpine Glow, its mirror image, Sun Gods, with virtual golf and putting greens, the giant stadium in Sports City, the colorful shops in the Baghdad Bazaar, the cathedrals and other replicas in Old Europe, and (*smile*) the last day in Bayou Country. His most vivid memories were the dinners with the team and the evenings with Grandma, sharing stories and getting to know one another.

They never found any other survivors, but did find a few corpses: a frozen man in Alpine Glow and a lightly mummified woman in Sun Gods were in the best condition. Others were not so...pleasant, especially the ones in The Lotus Eaters. Cy wrote down their locations, and they kept going.

❦

The next time they returned to The Forest, Cy asked for time to forage. Rex agreed, and Cy came back a couple of hours later with a shirt full of different mushrooms. That night, he cooked a dinner of sautéed mushrooms with rice and freeze-dried vegetables. Everyone approved, and the meal disappeared quickly. Cy explained that his family ate only what they raised or what they traded with the other habitat families. He and his brother grew edible mushrooms indoors to break the monotony, and would occasionally go out into the forest to forage for new species to grow.

When Rex came back that evening, he brought over a bottle of expensive Tawny Port that Dan'l had found. "Will you tell me what really happened here, ma'am?"

She filled two etched glasses with Port and handed one over. For a few moments, she stared into the fire, then into her drink. "Did you see the banner over the sales office? 'The Village. Live your Earth dream life. Every day'. Well, the dream turned into a nightmare."

Quietly, she told him about the pharmaceutical company that paid RobinCorp to run live trials on the residents. How the sales folks grew more and more aggressive, visiting door to door and offering free rent or utilities if they would try the latest colorful pill. She told him about her neighbor Dave bragging about living free for a year just to take some pills, and dropping dead at her feet. There was no pandemic. The Village residents died from the drugs they took.

"My friend Ed worked for the pharma company. He warned me they were coming out to clean up the dead and to collect any survivors for 'additional medical testing.' He told me to hide with Bettie in the crawlspace under the house when they arrived, and that he would enter my death in the computer to keep me safe." She took a deep breath. "Last time I saw Ed, he was in the back of a large truck in chains. The company came through two more times with trucks and guns—Bettie and I hid until they left. RobinCorp still monitors the habitats, and security drives through once a month on a schedule." She snorted. "We spend our days walking the neighborhoods gathering supplies, or working in the garden to get fresh vegetables and herbs." She paused. "It's a quiet life, but it gets lonely. I will miss you when you leave."

Over breakfast, Rex told the team about Grandma's situation and his desire to smuggle her out of The Village. "I cannot order you to do this, not when getting caught means discharge and perhaps prison. It is completely your choice. "

Without hesitation, Cy said, "I'm in. We have to get her out."

Dan'l nodded. "This is wrong; we need to make it right."

They pulled out the maps and hatched a plan. Together, they all walked over and knocked on her door. The old woman was wearing a robe and holding a cup of coffee. *Grumble, too early, not enough coffee, grumble...*

"Ma'am, there are only two more neighborhoods to go. When those are complete, we will be leaving The Village the following morning and returning to Rachel 7. Do you and Bettie want to come with us?"

There was no hesitation. "Yes."

"Okay, we are taking you out of here with us. Pack a couple of bags of personal items and a small bit of food. Do you have something to transport Bettie?"

"Yes, a carrier I use to take her between here and Rachel 7."

"Excellent. We will pick you up in three days. Be ready."

❦❦❦❦❦ ❦❦❦❦❦

They drove into The Forest for the last time on the third morning, and handed Grandma a pair of artistically dirty coveralls with a matching cap. She put on the coveralls, coiled her braids on the top of her head and pinned on the cap. The cargo area in the back had been rearranged to make space for them. Sergeant Ursson carefully helped her inside and got her comfortable. Corporal Morgan picked up Bettie and set the dog next to her. Cy Brown arranged the bags to help conceal them, reloaded the medical supplies next to the doors, and covered the cargo area with a blanket. They drove sedately through the Village until they reached Bayou Country, and parked close to the restaurant.

"Ma'am, please stay down and be quiet. You do *not* want to see this."

The team entered the walk-in refrigerator and retrieved the now thawed corpse from Alpine Glow, carrying it gently over to the edge of the swamp. Using food packs as bait, they threw the contents into the water and watched for bubbles. Two large alligators rose to the surface and swam towards the disturbance. Dan'l and Cy picked up the corpse, and Rex ordered, "On three. One, two, three." The corpse rose into the air and landed in front of the alligators. The startled animals grabbed the corpse, ripping and tearing, then fighting over the pieces.

After cleaning up, the team got back into the vehicle and drove until they were a couple of blocks from the gates. "Okay, everybody, it's show time."

Cy hit the accelerator, and they careened towards the gate, honking the horn.

"Open the gate! Open the gate!"

The gate creaked open. "What's going on?"

"We saw a guy walking on the bank in Bayou Country, and a giant alligator grabbed him and pulled him into the water!"

"Did you kill it?"

"No! It's an alligator, dude! A big one!"

Sigh. "I thought you were Space Marines. You guys go ahead and give your report to the boss. We will send in a retrieval unit and take care of it."

They drove through the gate, hearing the guards muttering about useless contractors. Once out of sight of The Village, they stopped on the side of the road, helped Grandma out and settled her in the back seat. "Bettie, you stay put until we get to the shuttle parking lot." She wagged her tail and laid down.

At the Administration building, they dropped off the report and the medical supplies. The clerk accepting the supplies asked, "Who's that in the back seat?"

"We're giving one of the workers a ride to the shuttle."

"Oh. Okay. Here's your signed receipt. Thank you and have a nice day."

When they parked the vehicle, Dan'l stuck a "K-9 in Training" sign on the dog carrier. Grandma placed Bettie in the carrier, gave her a treat and told her to lay down and stay quiet until she opened the door. The group sat in the waiting room until the shuttle arrived and traveled quietly to Rachel 7. No one gave them a second glance. They were like most of the workers: tired, grubby and a little whiffy. Rex took everyone to his apartment and sent a message to Lieutenant Astor.

Mission complete. Will send a copy of my report to you and RobinCorp within two hours.

Good work, team. We will video convo in the morning at ten sharp.
Yes, sir. Good night.

After a quick bite to eat, Dan'l took Cy over to his apartment for the evening. Rex sent his report, and got Grandma and Bettie settled in the guest bedroom. Everyone managed to get a good night's rest.

The next morning, Rex and Dan'l fired up the video screen and reported in to the Lieutenant. Cy, Grandma and Bettie were in the guest bedroom, with the door cracked open so they could hear the call.

"Good job tea,m. RobinCorp was happy with your work, although they did have one complaint: something about an alligator?"

"Yes, sir. We saw a large alligator eat a person. I guess they expected us to kill it."

Astor laughed. "Oh, no, they did not pay you enough to kill alligators! Again, good job and you two are officially on leave again. They found another problem with the cooling system, and we expect to be grounded for a minimum of three to four months."

Sigh. "Yes, sir. Thank you, sir."

⚘⚘⚘⚘ ⚘⚘⚘⚘

One of the advantages of being a Space Marine is the interesting people you meet during your travels.

Dan'l asked one of these "friends" to discreetly look into Grandma's situation. Turns out Ed never reported her dead, just off-habitat. Her account was still open with a decent balance, and quarterly payments were still being deposited. She wasn't rich, but she had enough to settle down and travel if she wanted to. After a lot of discussion (and a few beers), they decided to contact another friend who specialized in discreetly transporting cargo from one place to another. A plan was formed: Grandma would deadhead during the trip out to the Neon system while he did some business. She would then buy a liner seat to return and officially arrive on Rachel 7. Rex gave her a key and told her to use the apartment if he was away.

Three months later, Grandma (and Bettie) returned. They stayed in the apartment, and Dan'l's friend monitored until it was clear that no one was paying attention. She bought a place on Rachel 7 as a home base and decided to travel around the galaxy for a while. During their next get-together, Cy announced he would be traveling with her for part of the trip. He shrugged. "I don't think the Space Marines are for me. And besides, I've never traveled farther than Rachel 7. It's a big galaxy, and I want to see some of it." Cy Brown ended up settling down near The Belt and became semi-famous for repairing machinery no one else could fix.

They all kept in touch and would visit every year or so. Grandma spent a lot of time with Rex when he was home on leave. Once, she brought him a bottle of very old bourbon from Earth and presented it with a smile.

"Buffalo Trace? Funny lady."

They opened the bourbon, toasted, and gossiped as old friends do. Rex had one more question for Grandma. "I know Mr. Moranis named the planet Rachel for his wife, but what was the 7?"

She got a mischievous grin on her face, motioned him closer, and whispered in his ear. He pulled back, eyes wide. "Really?"

She smiled and nodded. His bellow of laughter made the lamps shake.

A Minor Action

JIM ROBB

ALL OF SHARN'S COMRADES agreed the creatures that called themselves "humans" were repulsive, but there was much disagreement over their most repugnant aspect. Some believed it was their total lack of exoskeleton, their flesh exposed like a forcibly molted victim in a horror video. Others thought it was the face, the thin membrane of hide covering it constantly shifting, as if undermined by parasites tugging at it in a vain attempt to tear it apart and escape its confines.

For Sharn, though, it was those eyes, small, dark and evil, sunk into the head, seemingly in constant motion to compensate for the lack of peripheral vision their placement imposed.

It was the eyes, because one day a few years ago, a pair of those eyes stopped moving and fixed their stare upon Pair Leader Sharn.

Sharn was trapped by those eyes. She couldn't look away from them. They released a terror that had previously lurked unknown and dormant in her subconscious, a terror that seized control of her body and stripped her of her will. She was unable to move, unable to act in her own defense, unable even to cry out as the human soldier aimed its rifle at her and fired.

At that moment, the human soldier itself was shot, disrupting its aim, but the large-caliber bullet smashed into Sharn's right foreleg.

The impact knocked her down. At first, she didn't realize what had happened; she couldn't stand up and didn't know why. In a moment, though, her frustration was replaced by a growing agony that emanated from her leg and spread in waves over her entire body.

"Your soldiering days are over," the medic said, pressing an injector into Sharn above the shattered remnants of her leg.

Sharn could have accepted a discharge from the military with full pension. Because her invalidation was due to a wound sustained in combat, she would have received a promotion to team leader and the more generous pension it carried, effective the day of her release from the military. Sharn didn't want it. In her mind, her behavior had been shameful, bringing disrepute not only on her, but on her military unit and her entire race. She was determined both to erase her dishonor and avenge herself on humankind for the loss of her limb.

Instead of looking to the rehabilitation centre for a new leg, she went to the battalion armorer. He made her the leg she wanted, one with no hinges to bind, servo motors to burn out, cables to break or batteries to run down. It was a simple, solid, straightforward steel appliance built to hold up to the rigors of combat. The armorer couldn't resist building in one fancy feature, as he called it, but he assured her it wouldn't fail her if she ever needed it.

Sharn's determination to avenge the loss of her limb, amplified by the secret shame she felt, didn't just carry her through the recuperative phase. It drove her to achieve the required physical standard required for reinstatement in her unit despite her seeming handicap. Perhaps just as importantly, her performance earned her the respect of those who would manage her career and assess her effectiveness in combat.

She knew fear many times after returning to active duty, but never again did she allow it to rule her. This, coupled with her relentless quest for expiation and vengeance and her many successes in its pursuit, won her recognition and rapid advancement, first a promotion to team leader and then a commission from the ranks.

⚜

Keeping his back against the wall, the rook edged up to the corner and paused for a moment to listen. Hearing nothing, he pivoted to peer down the corridor while still using the wall for cover, throwing his carbine to his shoulder as he did so.

A Vroll was right in front of him, not three metres away.

His mind recoiled at the sight of the creature, but his training steadied him. Without conscious thought, he fired twice. Both shots struck the Vroll in the thorax and penetrated its exoskeleton. As it staggered back, the Vroll made a chirping sound and looked down, its huge protruding hemispherical eyes swivelling to bring the wounds into view, before it fell over sideways and laid still, except for one of its four legs, which twitched spasmodically.

Then it wavered, flickered, and disappeared.

Sergeant David Milne appeared at the other end of the corridor. He was a hundred kilos of solid muscle, with a weather-beaten face and short, prematurely graying hair that made him look much older than his twenty-eight years.

"Not bad, rook," he said as he approached, stopping where the holographic image of the Vroll had been. "That was your best run yet."

"Thanks, Sarge," the rook said.

"Don't call me Sarge."

"But everybody else in the section calls you...that."

"You ain't everybody else; you're the rook. You haven't earned the right to call me that, and 'til you do, 'Sarge' rhymes with 'charge.' Now let's look at what..."

"Sergeant Milne!"

Milne couldn't see who it was and didn't recognize the voice, but he knew the voice of command when he heard it.

"Here, sir," he called out. "Corridor seven."

A moment later, Colonel Palmer appeared around the corner. Milne was surprised; the rook was shocked. Palmer was second-in-command of the entire solar system, which boasted two habitable and two semi-habitable planets. Milne and the rook popped to attention.

"As you were," Palmer said.

Milne and the rook relaxed only slightly, to a position of "at ease."

"Your section is being rotated home on leave, Sergeant," Palmer said. "There's transport outside to take you to the field. Your personal kit and special equipment are going with you, because it's fifty-fifty whether you'll be coming back here."

"The rook, too, sir? He just got here last week."

"The rook...for crap's sake, now you've got *me* calling him that. Yes, him, too."

Milne turned his head toward the rook. "Your lucky day, rook," he said. Then he turned back to Colonel Palmer. "What ship are we on, sir?"

"It's a civilian transport, the *SV Phillip Island*. The captain is Rodney Graham. He can be something of a stuffed shirt, but it's only a few days to the portal, and a few more after the jump."

"I don't mind Captain Graham, sir. I've known him for a long time. We even went to the same school for a while, back Earthside. He's really an okay guy. He only talks and dresses like a stuffed shirt."

"One more thing," Palmer said. "Make sure none of your people say anything about being rotated home. It might cause grumbling, especially among the rest of the work party. Help them load the ship, and then just stay aboard."

※⟫⟫⟫ ⟪⟪⟪⟪

Now a group officer, Sharn had called in a favor to be assigned as the leader of the operation. To her, it seemed like the perfect opportunity to run up the score even further.

The target was an enemy freighter, crewed by civilians with no battle experience, and armed, if at all, with old-fashioned civilian firearms intended for hunting game. Group Officer Sharn knew the creatures would fight to the death rather than surrender, but even so, she decided it was an excellent chance to give a group of raw recruits fresh from basic training their first taste of battle.

The enemy crew would consist of the captain, three or four watch officers and an engineer, so she brought three teams of six soldiers each for her boarding party—a three-to-one advantage, just like the doctrine manual called for. She decided to board the enemy ship, as well, which the doctrine manual frowned upon, but she wanted to exercise close supervision over her green soldiers' first action against a real foe.

Privately, though, Sharn agreed with her superiors that this would be not so much a combat operation as a live-fire training exercise, but with self-propelled pop-up targets to provide added interest and excitement.

The attack started off well enough. When their ship flowed out of hyperspace, they saw the intelligence assessment was correct—the enemy ship was right where she was supposed to be, on the course she was supposed to be following. She was faster than expected, as fast as their ship, but that hadn't mattered. With two perfect shots, the gunner knocked out her communications before she could send out a mayday, and disabled her thrusters so she couldn't flee.

⁕⁕⁕

"What the heck was that?" Sergeant Milne looked up from his meal. "It better not screw up my leave. Rook, find the captain and ask him what's going on."

Milne was sure something that would vibrate the deck plates of a ship the size of the *Phillip Island* had to mean trouble. She wasn't a true interstellar space vessel, since she depended on jump portals to travel between systems instead of sacrificing cargo capacity to carry the required equipment aboard, but she was still a sizeable chunk of steel.

The rook had almost reached the set of hatches leading forward from the mess when he was nearly bowled over by Captain Graham coming the other way. Milne took one look at the skipper and knew there was trouble. Normally a stickler for dress, Graham hadn't stopped to put on the neatly-pressed uniform he always wore on duty. He was wearing instead casual trousers and the sleeveless jumper of his favourite sports team, white with wide blue horizontal stripes.

The *Phillip Island* was a merchant ship and Graham was a civilian, but he was still the captain, so Milne rose to his feet. "What's going on?"

"We've taken fire," Graham said, his Australian news-reader accent making him sound far calmer than he looked. "It knocked out our thrusters and comms."

"How many ships?"

"Just one. She appeared to be one of ours, and I thought she was merely trying to beat us to the jump portal, but as soon as I matched her speed she opened fire."

"She probably *was* one of ours, and the Vroll took her." Milne glanced out the small round-cornered windows on either side of the hull. "Can I see her from here?"

"No, she's almost directly behind us," Graham said. "I can show you what she looks like, though." After tapping a few times on his wrist computer, he pointed to the screen mounted on the bulkhead beside the hatch leading forward.

Milne studied the screen for a moment before he spoke. "Can you fix whatever they shot up?"

"Comms, not until we reach the jump portal. Thrusters, yes, but she'll catch us first." Graham saw the puzzled look on Milne's face. "We're slowing down due to gravitational pull from this system's sun."

"How long?"

Graham looked at his computer screen. "About thirty-eight minutes."

"She could have blown us to hell, but she didn't. Are you carrying something the Vroll need, or that we can't get anywhere else?"

Graham shook his head.

"And they didn't just shoot holes through the hull to kill us and leave the ship more or less intact," Milne said. "They really hate working in EVA suits, and they'd lose out on the honor of killing us in combat, not to mention ruining the meat course of their victory feast."

"But one simply doesn't hang about in space hoping for a ship to happen by," Graham said. "And why did we not pick them up on radar until she was so close? The ship must be interstellar-capable and came out of hyperspace behind us..." Realization dawned. "They must intend to board us, capture my ship, and use it against us like that one. We can't let that happen."

"That's how I read it." Milne raised his wrist computer. "Section, warning order," he said, and waited for the display to flash green. "The ship is about to be boarded by Vroll. We're going to take them out. Usual fire teams. Usual kit, but the new pistols instead of carbines. Jill, you get to play outside with limpet mines. Zero hour in thirty-five minutes. Orders in the mess in ten. Jill, bring my kit with you. Acknowledge."

Milne looked first at his computer display, which had turned yellow, and then at the rook. "Well?" he said. "Do you acknowledge?"

The rook looked startled. "Uh, acknowledged," he said. Milne's display flashed green.

"Haven't you got something you should be doing right now?" he asked after a moment.

The rook said something vaguely resembling, "Oh, crap!" as he fled.

"If that ship out there launched from wherever to intercept us," Milne said, half to himself, "the Vroll must have known we were coming. Someone planetside must be feeding them intel—someone high up, too, if they knew which portal we were heading for."

"Then you are most certainly going to come as a nasty surprise to both the Vroll and the traitor, aren't you?"

"What do you mean?"

"You were added to our consist literally at the last minute," Graham said. "We barely had enough time to take extra rations aboard so we could feed you. You're not even included on the final manifest we submitted just before liftoff."

"And even if they had somebody watching the field, they wouldn't have picked up on us staying aboard when the loading detail left. Palmer, you clever bastard!"

"What?"

"I've been wondering why Colonel Palmer came personally to tell us we were being rotated home, 'cause colonels don't normally give orders directly to sergeants. He must have suspected a traitor, so he put me and my section on your ship with all our weapons and equipment. We take down the Vroll, and they'll think they were set up and take out the traitor for him."

Milne turned to his watch and summoned a holographic keyboard. "Hang on a second," he said.

Graham watched while Milne, working from a template, laid out a schedule starting half an hour in the future and working backward, continuing the conversation as he worked.

"I figure the Vroll won't use our airlock to board us—they'd have to fight the length of the ship to get to the bridge. They'll make an opening of their own, probably right here, and they'll come in on our left side so they won't have to deal with a change in artificial gravity when they board us."

The captain winced and nodded his understanding. He worked his computer for a moment, and a new image appeared in the lower right corner of the screen. "You're quite right," he said, pointing to it. "They're edging to port already."

"Before my section gets here, there's something else we should talk about, 'cause if my section can't take them down, it'll be up to you and your crew. Like you said, we can't let the Vroll have this ship. Jill can give you a couple of demo charges, show you how to use them."

"Blow up the ship, you mean? With us still on board?"

"That's right. They look like a cross between a preying mantis and a crab, but they aren't insects or crustaceans. They're something else, a real horror show, and they like their meat alive and screaming."

Graham turned white and sat down heavily. Then he took a deep breath. "We won't need demolition charges; my engineer is quite good at her job.

I'll post her in the engine room, have her rig a dead man's switch, that sort of thing. Whilst she's waiting on the outcome, she can work at repairing the thrusters.

"That said," Graham continued, "if it's all the same to you, I'd rather take an active role in this fight than cower in my cabin, and I'm quite sure my crew feels the same way. We won't panic at the sight of a Vroll—we've all seen worse, traded with worse, even worked alongside worse on occasion. Might we be of some use to you?"

"Yeah, you sure would. Regs say I can't ask you, but we could really use you."

"Is there anything else you need right now?"

Milne shook his head.

"Then *I* have a question," Graham said. "I received my engineering degree at the same convocation when you received your master's—in English literature. Why do you insist on speaking like a character in a lesser grade of comic book?"

Milne sat back in his chair. "In battle, the losing side is that which first loses heart. If my acting the part of the meanest son of a bitch in the valley can give my soldiers even the slightest bit more heart, then as their leader, I owe them that. Now I guess it's become a habit."

Graham nodded. "In that case, perhaps I should change into something more suitable. After all, I have an image to maintain, as well. My crew and I will be here in time to receive your orders." Without waiting for a reply, he turned and trotted out the forward door.

Milne raised his left wrist again. "Supplemental warning order. Bring four more sets of combat gear to the mess."

Graham returned a few minutes later, wearing a clean, crisply-starched uniform shirt and trousers, peaked cap, and impeccably polished shoes. Next to arrive was Master Corporal Jill Walters, carrying body armour, a helmet, and a belt with a holstered weapon. Her otherwise good looks were marred by a burn mark below her left ear and a scar that ran from her upper lip to her right cheekbone, giving her a perpetual sneer. Her fire team partner, a brash young private named Mick Jordan, was on her heels.

"My kit is at the airlock. This is yours," Jill said to Milne as she laid the equipment on the table. "Your pistol is loaded, safety on."

"What sort of weapon is that?" Captain Graham asked. "I've never seen its like."

Milne drew the weapon from its holster.

"Jill likes state-of-the-art stuff, so she just loves these things. They're brand new. They fire sound waves in a tight beam, something like Vroll weapons but with different tuning. Their rifles will put a hole in a hull plate if they hit it in the same place often enough. This'll make a real mess of anything flesh and blood, including exo, but it'll barely scratch your hull."

"Exo?" Captain Graham interrupted.

"Exoskeleton. The army runs on syllable-saving time. Anyway, you have to watch where you aim, because the sound waves will ricochet off solid objects. We can use that, though. Corporal Olenga will give you and your officers a quickie course after orders."

Graham looked up to see the rest of Milne's section, who had arrived two at a time, and his own four crew members. "I am declaring an emergency and placing us under the orders of Sergeant Milne for its duration," he said to the latter.

Milne stood up. "Section, and crew of the *Phillip Island*: orders."

Once alongside, the crew of Sharn's armed transport locked onto the enemy ship with magnetic grapples, extended their boarding tube, and burned an entranceway through her hull into the midships compartment where their enemies fed. Once they locked the boarding tube in place, one of Sharn's soldiers, a volunteer, ran its length and boarded the enemy ship alone.

This, too, was right out of the book, and it was purely precautionary. Had the enemy elected to defend the compartment, they would have killed the soldier, but Sharn would have retaliated by retracting the boarding tube, leaving a gaping hole in the side of the enemy ship that would have sucked into space anything that wasn't properly secured.

Death in vacuum is neither pleasant nor pretty, so Group Officer Sharn was not at all surprised that the enemy crew chose not to defend the compartment. After receiving the all-clear from the volunteer, Sharn and her soldiers swarmed aboard unopposed.

Jill made her move when the Vroll locked their boarding tube into place. She leaped across the space between the two ships, keeping the boarding tube between her and the gun turret on the side of the enemy ship. Swiftly and silently, she moved around to the top of the hull and then along its length from stern to bow, affixing strange-looking devices as she went, occasionally referring to her helmet display to help place them.

Based on analyses of previous boarding actions, the Vroll doctrine manual predicted their enemy would defend the two most critical areas of their ship: the bridge, in the bow of the ship, and the engine room, in the stern. Sure enough, the hatch leading forward was closed and its handle dogged. Sharn left one team to try and force the hatch open. Whether they succeeded or not, they would wait until Sharn and the remaining two teams determined the strength and disposition of the force defending the engine room before taking further action.

Starting aft, Sharn and the other two teams first cleared the stalls that served as their enemy's sleeping quarters, and still not having made contact with the enemy, continued aft into the first cargo hold. Leaving two soldiers there, Sharn continued through the second cargo hold without opposition. Finally, at the back of the third and rearmost hold, they found what they expected: a handful of humans defending the hatch leading to the engine room.

When the Vroll came into view, Captain Graham and his three officers, aided by Mick Jordan, brought them under fire. The team had three jobs. The obvious one was to protect the engine room. At the same time, they were protecting the airlock, located at the rear of the third hold, so Jill could get back into the ship. Their third task was to draw as many Vroll as they could into the third hold.

※※ ———

Sharn's first sign the operation wasn't going according to plan came as soon as they started taking fire. Instead of the expected firearms, their foes were using weapons she had never encountered before, frighteningly deadly sonic pistols that tore through exoskeleton and shredded the flesh beneath. They weren't as powerful as the sonic rifles Sharn's force wielded, but this seeming inferiority gave them an especially chilling capability, one which made them doubly effective in the present environment. If a shot hit a solid object like the ship's hull, the deck plates or the side of a cargo container, it would bounce off instead of causing damage at the point of impact, but the reflected shot was almost as damaging to flesh and blood as a direct hit.

Before she knew it, two of Sharn's soldiers were dead and two more were on the deck with incapacitating wounds.

※※ ———

With all of her devices in place, Jill returned to a point above the enemy ship's boarding tube.

"Charges set, over," she said.

"Fire now, over."

Jill flipped open the lid of a small box attached to her belt, exposing a knob. "Firing now, wait," she said as she gave the knob a half turn before pressing it and holding it down with the palm of her hand.

The shaped-charge devices exploded, producing incredibly fast-moving jets of metal particles that sliced through the outer and inner hulls of the enemy ship. Jill had placed them above every compartment. The bridge got two charges and the engine room three, just to make sure.

Jill surveyed the results, looking first forward and then aft. A series of perfectly round holes now punctuated the upper hull surface, each issuing a cloud of objects carried by the escaping air.

"All charges fired, wait," Jill said.

Now Jill turned her attention to the boarding tube, but that part of her tasking was taking care of itself. The enemy ship had clearly lost power, because the magnetic anchors holding the ships together had fallen away. Now the enemy ship's nose was drifting slowly upward, putting a twisting strain on the tube. Jill saw a small tear appear a few inches from the *Phillip Island's* hull, and almost immediately thereafter, the tube ripped completely apart. The torn end retracted, and the now-open space between the ships was soon home to an assortment of dinnerware, a dart board, a couple of throw cushions, and anything else in the *Phillip Island's* mess that wasn't bolted down. This included the half-dozen Vroll that had been working on the hatch leading forward to the bridge. The hapless creatures writhed about, screaming silently.

"Boarding tube taken out, over," Jill said.

"Roger, return to ship, over."

"Wilco, out."

The Vrolls' fate was something Jill had no desire to watch, anyway. She turned away and headed toward the stern of the enemy ship. When she was as close to the *Phillip Island* as she could get, she leaped across the ever-growing space between the ships. She landed awkwardly but safely on the bottom of the *Phillip Island's* hull and made for the airlock on the far side. Her fire team partner—next to the rook, the most junior member of the section—was in there, and she didn't want him going up against the Vroll without her.

❦❦❦❦❦ ❦❦❦❦❦

Everything went wrong so quickly, Sharn had trouble keeping up...

A frantic call over the radio reporting multiple hull breaches in their ship, followed by a scream and then silence...

A few seconds later, the enemy ship's decompression alarm blaring its warning...

The radio again, transmitting inarticulate cries of terror from the team tasked with forcing open the airlock leading to the bridge...

Clanging sounds as the pair of hatches leading forward from the forward cargo hold slammed shut automatically to seal off the aft portion of the ship from the now-airless midship section...

Shouts of alarm, screams of pain, human victory cries from the forward cargo hold as an unsuspected enemy force emerged from hiding and gunned down the fire team Sharn had stationed there...

❦❦❦❦❦ ❦❦❦❦❦

When the hatches slammed shut, Sergeant Milne and the rook, along with the other two fire teams, burst out of cargo containers at the front of the first hold. With the element of surprise in their favor, they quickly dispatched the pair of Vroll they found there. Then they moved into the second hold, looking for the remainder of the Vroll force.

Milne's plan had worked to perfection, leaving the Vroll to face the ultimate nightmare scenario for a boarding party. Surrounded, outnumbered after taking heavy losses, facing an unexpected force of elite foes armed with new and frighteningly effective weapons, and trapped on an alien vessel, there could be no victory, no rescue, and no escape.

Milne knew enough of the foe to realize this would not lessen their resolve, merely change their objective. As was the way of their warrior caste, they would seek to sell their lives as dearly as they could.

Still, it was no longer a battle. Now it was a hunt.

Trapped, enemies to front and rear, nowhere to run, no retreat, no escape...

Defeat, destruction, death...

Dammit, Sharn, get a hold of yourself!

She looked around at the remaining members of her boarding party. They understood the situation as well as she did, but they showed a level of steadiness and resolve that made her proud of them. She took a deep breath and gave her final order.

"Spread out," she said. "Take as many of them with you as you can."

Ten minutes later, Group Officer Sharn hadn't taken down a single enemy. At least she was still in the fight, though, somehow having evaded the two enemy forces that had closed in from forward and aft by slipping back and forth among the huge metal containers that held the ship's cargo.

She noted that while some of the enemy combatants were of the ship's crew, others—more than half—were part of a military unit she had fought against before, highly capable fighters who had no business being on a small cargo ship like this one. There had been nothing wrong with the plan of operation, she decided; rather, they had been lured into a trap. The only possible conclusion was that their spy had betrayed them instead of its own kind. From a savage corner of her brain came the hope that the spy would pay for this treachery with its life, slowly and painfully.

She heard shooting coming from the rear of the second cargo hold and followed the sounds, moving slowly and cautiously. The enemy force, operating in pairs, seemed somehow to be everywhere at once.

By the time she got to the scene of the fighting, it was all over. Grain trickled from a cargo container with much of its side blasted away by sonic rifle fire. Two of her soldiers laid on the deck among the spilled grain. At least the pair had managed to strike back, for one of the elite human soldiers laid between them, killed cleanly and efficiently by a single shot to the chest.

A sonic rifle laid on the deck nearby. If it was operable, it would be an improvement over Sharn's pistol, a conventional firearm intended more as a symbol of her rank and authority than a combat weapon. Sharn holstered her pistol, picked up the rifle, and examined it. Its barrel was bent, but this didn't make it useless. If she fired it in this condition, it would explode, creating a shock wave that would have much the same effect as a grenade.

This gave her an idea. From the doctrine manual, she knew the enemy force would hold a post-combat ceremony where they would celebrate victory by eating the flesh of their felled opponents. If she could avoid death until the battle was over, she could catch every member of the enemy force together and destroy them all.

She heard the sounds of humans approaching from both forward and aft. Holding the rifle against her thorax, she dove into the ruptured cargo container and buried herself in the grain.

Clearly the battle had already ended, for the small group of enemy soldiers and ship's crew had come to clean up the aftermath. From her hiding place, she watched as two soldiers put their fallen comrade in a large plastic bag and carried him off on an improvised stretcher. They came back twice more and carried off the bodies of Sharn's soldiers, not bothering with plastic bags. Obviously, she reasoned, they were going to butcher her soldiers' corpses immediately.

Meanwhile, two of the ship's crewmembers picked up the spilled grain and cleaned up the blood and other remains, using a machine so effective it could have been designed for the job. When they left, the only signs that a deadly fight had occurred here were the damaged grain container, a faint chemical smell, and three damp patches on the deck plates.

Sharn remained in hiding for what seemed to her a long time before she made her move. Emerging from the grain container, she worked her way forward. Not trusting the damaged rifle's safety mechanism, she held it well out in front of her by the butt and barrel so as not to accidentally engage the trigger.

She was approaching the huge doors at the front of the second cargo hold when the new plan fell apart, as well.

***

"Last one," Milne said as he cycled the airlock. "C'mon, rook. Let's head to the mess and we can all have a drink to Karl." Karl himself was in the galley's freezer, wrapped in plastic.

The rook was still the rook. He hadn't so much as fired his pistol—Milne was just too good and too fast. In fact, the rook suspected his most useful role in the whole engagement was providing overwatch when Milne reloaded. He felt he'd learned a lot, though, and was looking forward to getting back on the simulator. He especially wanted to try the technique Milne used, a fast shot to the thorax followed by a more deliberate shot to the head.

They saw it near the front of hold two, a Vroll carrying a rifle with a bent barrel, trying to skitter into hiding between two rows of cargo containers. It ran with a peculiar rocking gait and made a clicking sound as it did; one of its legs was prosthetic. The medallion strapped to its thorax marked it as an officer.

"I thought their platoon leaders never went into small-unit actions like this," the rook said. "That's what they taught us in basic, anyway."

"Maybe they changed their doctrine and forgot to send us the memo," Milne said. "Anyway, we've got it cornered. This one's all yours, rook. Make me proud."

The rook drew his pistol and moved to the side of the corridor away from the space where the Vroll had taken refuge while Milne edged along the near side.

"You got a plan?" Milne asked. "Stay out of its line of sight and go for ricochets," the rook said. "That rifle it's carrying might still work." "Makes sense to me. Go for it."

∾∾∍∍∍∍∍ ⊰⊰⊰⊰⊰⊱

Sharn knew the human soldiers had spotted her, so she backed quickly into a corridor between two rows of cargo containers, not worrying about the sound of her prosthetic leg against the deck plates.

She wondered what these two were doing aft until she remembered them as the ones with the stretcher. She realized they had been carrying their enemies' bodies, not forward to the galley, but back to the airlock to dump them into space, just like her soldiers would have done if the fight had gone their way.

Clearly, humans didn't eat the bodies of their enemies, after all. Even the doctrine manual had failed her today.

She turned to make her escape and was shocked to discover she had trapped herself in a dead-end corridor. She was going to have to fight her way out. Leaning the rifle against a container, she took a step back and reached for her pistol.

It was gone.

Before she could move forward to recover the rifle, she heard the shot from a sonic pistol as it sang past. It bounced off the container to her left and struck the near container between her and the rifle. Instinctively, she froze, and then cursed herself. The next ricochet, she realized, would strike right where she was now. She leaped backward as the enemy bounced two more shots off the far container. The second shot hit the near container exactly where she had been standing, and the third struck it another step closer to her.

Sharn saw her chance. She scuttled forward and reached for the rifle just as the enemy took a fourth shot.

The fourth shot was aimed where the first had been.

The impact slammed her against the side of the container, jarring the rifle, and it slid to the deck with its butt in the corridor. Sharn staggered sideways, screaming in pain. A fifth shot ricocheted off the far container and struck her, as well, knocking her to the deck. She landed on her unwounded side, and was thankful for this small mercy. She knew if she had landed on her twice-wounded side, the pain might have rendered her unconscious. This way, she still had a chance, however small, at least to avenge her own death. It wouldn't be the result she had sought, but now it was the best she could hope for.

While she waited for her adversaries to show themselves, she adjusted her position so her legs were pointing at the spot where she expected them to appear.

❦❦❦❦❦ ❦❦❦❦❦

The rook moved to where Milne was standing. "I'm pretty sure I got it," he said, changing to a fresh power pack as he spoke.

"Well, let's take a look, but be careful," Milne said, moving around to stand on the rook's left. "On three," he mouthed. Then he held up his left hand and extended first one finger, then two.

A second later, they leaped into the opening, the rook to the near side and Milne to the other.

The Vroll, badly wounded and in obvious pain but still alive, was lying on its side. When it saw its attackers, it pointed its legs at the rook.

"Look out!" Milne shouted, but it was too late.

The Vroll's prosthetic limb emitted a roar and a belch of flame. The rook was lifted off his feet, to land on his back on the other side of the corridor.

Milne leaped at the Vroll. Seizing the prosthetic leg with both hands, he twisted it while kicking and stomping the point where it was attached to the Vroll, again and again, until he was able to rip the device free and throw it down the corridor. Then he went to check on the rook.

Judging by the hole in the rook's chest, he'd been hit by a large-caliber round. Milne rolled him over on his side and saw a huge bloodstain soaking through the back of the rook's body armour. There was nothing Milne could do for him.

"I wonder why it doesn't hurt?" the rook said.

"I don't know, kid."

The rook lifted his head. "I...I guess I didn't kill it...after all, did I?"

Milne shook his head.

"I guess I'm going to be...the rook...forever." He coughed once and his head fell back to the deck.

"No way," Milne said as he grabbed the rook by the shoulders and dragged him back across the corridor. Using the pistol the rook still clutched in his right hand, Milne took aim at the Vroll.

As Sharn watched the enemy soldier die, her training led her to review the operation. She had failed to capture the enemy ship, she and her entire platoon were lost, and their own ship had almost certainly been destroyed with the loss of a dozen more lives.

Her entire force had been wiped out at a cost to the enemy, so far as she knew, of only two of their number killed in action. Still, her soldiers were raw recruits in their first battle, whereas the soldiers they had killed were members of an elite unit, highly-trained and battle-hardened veterans who would be hard to replace.

Sharn's final thought, as she watched the enemy soldier squeeze the trigger, was of the clutch of eggs she had laid before setting off on this mission. She took comfort in the knowledge that in seven years, after their final molting, there would be a hundred children to replace her, a hundred new soldiers who would avenge her death and erase this final stain on her honor.

Milne pried the rook's hand from the pistol and removed the battery pack before sliding the weapon into its holster. Then he hoisted the rook into a fireman's carry and set off forward.

When Milne reached the mess, he paused out of habit to take a look around. Jill Walters and three others were sitting in easy chairs, each staring at the low table between them and waiting for one of the others to say something. Captain Graham and three of his crew were sitting at a table at the front of the mess, studying a schematic displayed on the screen but saying very little. Milne decided whatever they were looking at wasn't important; if it was, Graham's third officer, a massively-built Scotsman, would have been with them. Instead, he was seated on a couch at the back of the mess, with Corporal Martine Levesque sitting close beside him. As he watched, Martine buried her face against his shoulder.

It's always like this after the adrenaline level falls off, Milne thought. *Soon, maybe even tonight, the dreams will start. Dreams about what you did to the Vroll, about what you saw them do to your buddies, about all those things happening to you. Dreams that make you wake up screaming. Dreams you want to wake up from and can't.*

And what's with Martine and that Scottish thug?

Milne realized he might have lost yet another soldier in this action. Female soldiers could always get a release from military service if they agreed to bear children, children who would grow to be young men and women, in their turn to be fed into the war for survival between humans and the Vroll.

Captain Graham turned away from the screen and saw Milne and his burden. He immediately rose to his feet. In a moment, everyone else followed suit.

Time to put on the mask again. Time to be the tough-as-nails sergeant they need me to be.

"There was one more," Milne said. He walked to the nearest table and dumped the rook onto it. As the body fell back, Milne caught the rook's head and lowered it gently to the table. He looked for a moment at the face staring up at him before reaching down and closing the rook's eyes.

Tough, yes, but still human.

Jill walked up to stand beside Milne, reached out to take his hand, realized what she was doing, and let her arm drop to her side. The rest of the section followed her and stood around the table. The big Scotsman followed Martine, but stopped a few paces away.

"Aw, crap," Mick said. "It got the rook."

Milne looked up and shook his head. "This is Private Macklin. Private Eugene Macklin. He ain't a rookie anymore."

Veterans

M.C.A. HOGARTH

"LOOK, MS. ROBERTS, WE'RE done here, and I'd really, really like it if you stopped trying to 'help' me."

"Hector—"

He gritted his teeth. "I don't need my head analyzed. I need a freaking *job*. If you can help me find a *job*, that would be the help I *need*."

The italicizing hadn't worked, apparently, because she awarded him one of her tender looks, the kind just dripping with condescension. Maybe they'd taught her that in some special class in her Social Work program, "Showing Pity to the Dumb Grunts 101."

"Hector, you've gone through a lot. And you still haven't really talked to anyone—" By "anyone," she meant *her*. "—About...the accident."

"It wasn't an accident," he said, acerbic. "The slimes were *trying* to blow off bits of me." She hesitated, and he forced himself to go on. "I appreciate your visit, but I need rest. I get tired, you know, rehabilitating."

It was a lie, but one she had been conditioned to cave to, so she leaped to her feet. "I'll be back next week to check on you."

"Do yourself a favor and stay home," he said as he herded her to the door, ignoring her mute pity. Shutting the door on her felt better than hours of therapy. He stayed by the door until he heard the click of her heels receding on the concrete sidewalk, then sighed and rubbed his temple with his remaining hand. She meant well, but what in hell's business did they have sending her by to help him "transition into civilian life"? When she didn't know the first thing about the life he was transitioning out of?

Hector pushed himself off the door and went down the hall to the bedroom to let Hexa out. The mutt bounced to him and stopped, waiting for a pat on the head. He scratched her behind the ears and smiled as she wagged her fringed tail. "She's gone," he said. "You can go do your business."

The dog smiled, all gape-jaws and lolling tongue, then trotted toward the back door. Maybe that wasn't a bad idea. A beer outside with the laptop while he checked on any leads. And a girl who didn't give him stupid looks. Hexa's most floppy-eared, slobbery smile was still more honest than that social worker's.

She also wasn't a barker, so when he heard the growl, he almost thought it was something else: a truck going down the street? His razor, switched on by ghosts? An earthquake (in Georgia)?

No, Hexa was growling. Barking now. Alarmed, Hector went for the door, putting his back to the wall and looking out. He didn't see anything armed or even human, so he strode out. "Hey, pup, what's doing?"

The dog was dancing with excitement in a semicircle around a glob on the grass. For a moment, he thought something had yarfed there, but it was a glimmery white, so maybe it was someone's wet laundry, fallen over the fence?

He bent over Hexa's tense body and went for the weapon that was no longer on his body with the arm that was no longer there. "Jesus—!"

The slime didn't rise from the grass, didn't fire one of its burning pulses at him. Didn't do anything, in fact, except change color, a ripple of purple and blue mottles that flashed up its flaccid hood like LEDs firing in sequence.

Hector stared. He'd seen that pattern before on slimes. He couldn't believe he was seeing it now.

Again, the flash, weak.

"Stay," Hector said, though he wasn't sure who he was talking to, the slime or his dog. When Hexa kept barking, he said, "Quiet! Sit! Stay!" and this time he jumped back on the porch and pounded into the house. Cellphone, cellphone...crap, this had been easier when the HUD had done the translating for him, but here at home he had to rely on some garbage hack-job someone put together for fun. He grabbed for the phone, realized he was still using the wrong arm, and swore before swiping it and the earpiece. Fixing the latter in place, he thumbed through the apps until he found the translator, then brought it back out and aimed the camera at the alien.

HERE TO TALK

"Jesus," Hector said again, and a pattern flashed on what he could see of the slime's body.

PLEASE REPEAT? [accuracy: 70%, please aim camera at entire hood]

Shaking himself, Hector said, "What are you doing here? How the hell did you get here!"

WE FELL [untranslatable: possibly figurative]

"Explain," Hector said, fingers twitching. He could feel his heart racing. The slimes were weeks away from here by jump-ship. The fighting had been on the colonies, not on Earth. This thing shouldn't be here.

CAME TO DIE

Hector stared at the screen. "What?"

CAME TO DIE IN PEACE

"What the hell!" Hector said. "You want to die in peace, so you come to the homeworld of your worst enemy?"

NOT WORST ENEMY

He stared at the limp creature, then at the translation. He tapped it, and it popped up an accuracy rating: ninety percent. Ninety was about as good as the translations got with the slimes.

"If we're not, who is?" he asked.

WE ARE

The thing shifted, and Hexa yipped. Hector reached for her collar and dropped the phone. Cursing, he grabbed her and pulled her to his side, then picked up the phone again. "Say again?" he asked.

CAME TO DIE IN PEACE

"Is that why you're not floating?" he asked warily. When it lifted one of its tentacles, he twitched back so hard Hexa started growling.

AM SUPERFLUOUS [accuracy: 50%; possible synonyms: "unnecessary," "injured"]

Hector frowned at the phone, then at the creature. All his training was encouraging him to step on it, crush it, kill it...but he'd never heard of the slimes reaching Earth. This was way above his paygrade. But if it was about to die... "How long have you got?"

[untranslatable: color pattern indicates confusion]

"How long before your injury kills you?" Hector tried.

[untranslatable: no reference]

"Hell," Hector muttered.

YES

Startled, he looked up at the slime. It was still flashing colors.

WE ARE COMPROMISED [accuracy: 60%; possible synonyms: "injured," "retired," "dead"] AND DID NOT DESIRE TO BE REMOVED SO WE FLED

A pause as the colors faded from the slick integument, then a final flourish of shimmering orange and pearl.

CAME TO DIE IN PEACE

"You're saying...that if you're injured, they kill you," Hector said slowly.

THE SUPERFLUOUS ARE SUPERFLUOUS

"How does one become superfluous?" Hector asked.

WHEN WE CAN NO LONGER KILL

He sank to the grass across from the creature. He wanted to believe the picture he was putting together in his head was some fantasy fueled by his own frustrations with his separation from the service. For twelve years, these aliens had been attacking their colonies, floating down from their ships like candy-colored jellyfish. What few negotiations had been attempted had never gone anywhere. To feel anything other than the necessity of their extermination was traitorous.

"You're trying to tell me when slime soldiers are injured, other slimes kill them?"

NO

"Then what—" he began and stopped as the colors continued flowing over the thing's deflated hood.

WHEN SOLDIERS ARE SUPERFLUOUS [untranslatable: unknown] KILL US

Hector said, "I... I don't understand that word. Who kills you?"

A flicker of light. Agitated, maybe?

[untranslatable: unknown] WHO TELL US TO KILL

"Someone who tells you to kill," Hector said. "Your own race? Some alien one? What do they look like? Have we met them?"

THEY ARE US—He drew in a breath to speak, but it wasn't done—YOU HAVE NEVER MET THEM

"So who the hell was negotiating with us all those times?" he asked.

WE WERE IT IS WHY WE LEARNED TO LISTEN TO YOUR AURAL SOUNDS

WE HOPED TO END THIS BUT THEY TELL US TO KILL

WHEN WE ARE SUPERFLUOUS THEY KILL US

As Hector stared at the slime, a muted palette washed over its wrinkled hood.

IT IS EASY TO DIE

WE ARE DYING NOW

THANK YOU FOR PEACE

"No, wait!" Hector exclaimed. "What's wrong? Can you be fixed?"

THERE IS A HOLE AND WE LEAK

IT IS THE WAY

"A hole? That's it? How bad?" Hector said, leaning over. "Why can't you just have it, I don't know...sewn up? Stapled? Put a dressing on it, for God's sake!"

WE DO NOT KNOW THESE WORDS

THERE IS A HOLE AND WHEN WE LEAK WE DIE

"Show me," he growled.

The slime rippled, then slowly straightened one of its panels until he could see the tear. It was rare to see any kind of injury on a slime: if you hit them, they tended to explode. The problem was getting close enough to hit them when their natural weapons were so deadly from a distance, especially when they seemed to know how to hide from long-range weapons fire. Hector frowned. "Shrapnel, maybe? Slicing wound?"

WE DO NOT KNOW

WE ARE DYING NOW

"Shut up," he muttered. "This thing's barely the length of my pinky. That'll kill you?"

WHEN WE LEAK WE DIE

"Stay here," he said, and got to his feet. "Hexa, come!"

The dog followed him to the bathroom. As he took down the first aid kit, he wondered what he was doing. Giving comfort to the enemy? Would that get you shot if the enemy had information you really, really needed to get to the brass before it died? He hoped so. He didn't want to become "superfluous." Losing an arm was bad enough.

Outside, he crouched alongside the slime. "If I help you, will you tell other people what you just told me?"

IS THIS IMPORTANT?

"Yes," he said, wishing he could stare at it and the translation at the same time. "It really is. Maybe...maybe we can stop fighting if we know why the negotiations keep failing. And who it is that's killing you for not fighting us."

WE ARE DYING

BUT WE WILL TALK IF WE CAN

"Good," Hector said. "Can I touch you?"

YES

He stared at the alien, fighting the instinct to let it die. There had been at least three or four autopsies that had proven that the creatures weren't caustic to the touch...not on the hood, anyway. The tentacles and fringed weapon arms beneath them were the problems. But he'd never touched a slime. Slimes were for killing, not touching.

Hector got out a pack of bandaids and reached out with his remaining hand. Touched his fingers to the slime's skin. He expected it to be cold and slimy. It wasn't...it was warm and textured, regular little bumps he could just feel, like gooseflesh. "Don't be scared," he said. "If this works, you'll be fine. If it doesn't, you'll die like you planned. Maybe not in peace, but by choice."

The little ripple of pearl white that played over its surface didn't trigger a translation. Maybe the camera hadn't caught it. Hector bent close and went to work, pinching the tear closed and beginning to tape it over with bandaids. He guessed there was some proper way to do this: sutures or surgical clips or, God knew, cauterization. But the only thing he thought had a chance of holding this thing together without making new holes was adhesive, and the bandaids seemed less violent than duct tape.

As he worked, some of the fluid leaked onto his fingers, made them slippery. He'd had slime goo on him before. This was the first time he was trying to put it back in the suckers instead of shooting it out. It was a strange feeling.

When he was done, he leaned back. "There. How's that?"

Mottled purple, dark.

WE ARE UNCERTAIN BUT WE DO NOT LEAK [uncertainty indicated]

"Good," Hector said. "Stay here. I have some phone calls to make." He hesitated. "This may take a while."

IF WE LIVE WE LIVE IF WE DIE WE DIE

"Yeah," Hector said. "I know it."

The conversations went about how Hector expected. He took photos and sent them along, described his talk with the alien, got told he was making things up, was informed that he had poor taste in jokes, et cetera, et cetera, blah blah. He finally got a hold of someone willing to listen to him, though whether that would result in anyone showing up at his door to examine the evidence, he had no idea.

So he got the beer and a rawhide bone for Hexa and went outside. The slime was still there, looking utterly surreal with the six tan bandaids on its side. When he approached, it rippled a sheen of colors, the same as when he first saw it: the parley sign. He sat with his back to the fence and aimed the camera at it.

DO THEY COME?

"Hell if I know," Hector said, tossing Hexa the rawhide. She snapped it from the air and settled down to gnaw. He popped the cap on his beer. "How'd you know how to get here, anyway?"

WE ALL KNOW

The cold that ran down his spine made him hesitate in the middle of lifting the bottle to his lips. "The hell, you say. If you know, why haven't you killed us all?"

WE KNOW BUT [untranslatable] DO NOT KNOW

WE DO NOT TELL THEM

He stared at it.

WE WILL KILL BECAUSE WE DO NOT WANT TO DIE BUT WE WILL NOT HELP [untranslatable]

"And if there was another way?" Hector asked, low.

The thing shivered, as if trying to move its deflated body.

WE CANNOT IMAGINE ANOTHER WAY

"Maybe like your untranslatables can't imagine actually healing you instead of killing you when you're injured," Hector said. "Saves them the effort of actually looking after you when you're down." He had a sudden imagine of himself walking amid a swarm of limp and fallen slimes, taping them together while they flashed their blue and green colors. Hell with job placement. Alien-whisperer sounded a lot more interesting...and might do a lot more good. What if stopping the war was possible?

What if he could help end it?

TO LIVE IN PEACE WOULD BE MORE DESIRABLE THAN TO DIE IN PEACE

"Yeah," Hector said. "Tell me what I need to know about the untranslatables and the soldiers.

"Tell me everything."

Other
Anthologies from
Raconteur Press

Ghosts of Malta

Knights of Malta

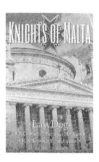

Saints of Malta

Space Cowboys

Space Cowboys 2: Electric Rodeo

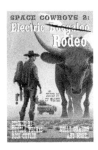

Postcards From Mars

Printed in Great Britain
by Amazon

23323162R00128